It's Simon Kaye again—the tough private eye who can find trouble without looking for it. On his way home from an evening of chess with his friend Father McGuire, he is kidnapped and beaten up by hired thugs, and has no idea why. Thereafter, he is threatened with more violence so often that even the philosophical Kaye begins to get annoyed. However, life has its compensations. Such as the ever-eager women who gather around him. Veronica Dean engages him as bodyguard but Veronica is about as much in need of a bodyguard as a man-eating tiger would be. What's *really* at stake is a buried hoard of gold bullion . . .

THE VERONICA DEAN CASE

Hillary Waugh

ATLANTIC LARGE PRINT
Chivers Press, Bath, England.
Curley Publishing, Inc.,
South Yarmouth, Mass., USA.

Library of Congress Cataloging in Publication Data

Waugh, Hillary.
   The Veronica Dean case / Hillary Waugh.
      p.   cm.—(Atlantic large print)
   ISBN 0–7927–0050–3 (lg. print)
   1. Large type books.   I Title.
   [PS3573.A9V4 1989]
   813′.54–dc20

F
WAU
CI

89–34905
CIP

British Library Cataloguing in Publication Data

Waugh, Hillary
   The Veronica Dean case.
   I. Title
   813′.54 [F]

   ISBN 0–7451–9611–X
   ISBN 0–7451–9623–3 pbk

This Large Print edition is published by Chivers Press, England, and
Curley Publishing, Inc, U.S.A. 1989

Published in the British Commonwealth by arrangement with Victor
Gollancz Ltd and in the U.S.A. and Canada with the author

U.K. Hardback ISBN 0 7451 9611 X
U.K. Softback ISBN 0 7451 9623 3
U.S.A. Softback ISBN 0 7927 0050 3

Copyright © Hillary Waugh 1984

Photoset, printed and bound in Great Britain by
REDWOOD BURN LIMITED, Trowbridge, Wiltshire

THE VERONICA DEAN CASE

CHAPTER ONE

It was one of those silken evenings in late August when the moon is mellow, the breeze is a caress, and the insects sing, but don't bite. It was a night for love and romance, for tender words and deep kisses. It was a night to make even a man of thirty yearn for his lost youth.

That's the way it was outside.

Inside, where I was, a hot floorlamp shone on a green and white chessboard and I had my head in its glare while I pondered the pieces.

The night was a Monday and Monday nights are when Father Jack McGuire and I play chess together in his booklined study. The books all deal with religion in one or another of its various forms, none of which I have any truck with. 'Look out for yourself,' is my motto because God, if there is such a thing, works to His own purposes and doesn't shape the world to our taste. Tasteful shaping is a do-it-yourself operation.

Jack takes the opposite view, of course. That's why he's a priest and is called 'Father', gives out wine and wafers, listens to confessions, conducts services, and enjoys the perks of priesthood. He can have the job, and welcome. You'd give it to him too if you had a parish in his neighborhood. They called it the slums when we were growing up there, and it's been going downhill ever since. I'm a private detective and when I grumble about my lot, all I have to do is see what he's up against and it's better for my morale than a tray of vodka martinis.

We played three games and I won two. In the course of them we sipped wine, kidded each other, nibbled the crackers and cheese Mrs Honeywell, his housekeeper, had supplied, and wiped the sweat off our brows. I also broke down and had a couple of the cigarettes I don't smoke, except in stressful situations, but that was during the game I lost.

When the big grandfather clock in Jack's hallway struck midnight, we'd finished our games and he was talking about the lifelong dream that had made it on to his agenda—a trip to Rome. By Rome, he means the Pope and St Peter's. I said there was more to Rome than that, but when I told him about the Forum and the Colosseum, he only nodded. The catacombs grabbed him a little.

He saw me out the door and we inhaled scented air together on the steps. He said, 'Where's your car?' and I said I hadn't brought it, I'd walked over.

'From your condominium?'

'It's no big deal—two and a half, three miles.'

'Simon Kaye, Nature Boy.'

'I had to miss Friday night's karate session. I was on assignment.'

'And your conscience tells you to make up the exercise?'

'Right, and to start now, because it's late and I need sleep.'

I bade him farewell and got moving, for the walk would be long. Most of it is through city streets, but there's an early stretch along the edge of Monmouth Park, a large, Edenesque canyon in the residential part of town, supposedly free of all sin except copulation. It's the summer hangout for the boys and girls who don't have a bed or a car.

I walked on the park side of Monmouth Street, across from the two-family flats with their sidewalks and streetlights. It was quiet there, wooded and pleasant. The park would be empty now, all the young lovers gone home.

Except that the park wasn't quite empty. Close by, dark shadows moved. They weren't trees, they were men coming out from behind trees. They were coming for me. I counted three, front, side and rear—shadowy creatures, but they moved quickly and there was the rustle of grass.

The one in front held what appeared to be a .38. You couldn't mistake the weapon the one on the side carried. It was a sawed-off shotgun. I couldn't see what the one in the rear had, but I could feel it. He came up close and a hard, steel muzzle bruised my liver. Into my ear, he growled, in first-class B-movie lingo, 'Don't move if you know what's good for you.'

The guy in front was the man in charge. He wore a wide-brimmed Al Capone fedora pulled low on a low forehead but, even in the shadows, it didn't hide his apelike features. It was a face to remember. It was a face *I'd* remember.

'Keep those hands up and your mouth shut,' he ordered in more movie dialogue. The words were funny, but his tone wasn't. I complied.

'Turn around.'

I did that too. It gave me a look at the mug who'd been poking me—with a hot little Saturday night special. He had a bent nose and a wispy mustache. I wouldn't forget him either. The guy with the shotgun was farther back, cradling it in the crook of his elbow, his eyes on the lookout for cops. Him, I couldn't see so well. He was bulky, wore glasses, dark clothes, and a visored golfing cap. That was the best make I could do on him at the moment.

I stood still and looked off down the road while a rough hand emptied my pockets and explored for hidden weapons. The loot included my wallet, gun, switchblade, private detective's license, handkerchief and small change.

Ape-face with the Al Capone hat inventoried the haul with a pocket flash, and it wasn't enough. He and bent-nose went over me again, looking for places they'd missed, but they'd already cleaned me out of all but my fillings. Ape-face didn't like it and muttered what sounded like foreign expletives. Bent-nose stepped back and held his gun on me. 'Want me to make him talk?'

Ape-face signalled something I couldn't see and bent-nose eased up. They turned me around, ape-face packed my belongings into his pockets and they marched me, parade fashion, to a large limousine around the next corner. Inside were folded jumpseats and a laprobe. They planted me face down on the floor, threw the laprobe over me, boarded the limo and took off, the guy with the golf-cap driving. Ape-face and bent-nose rode in back, holding me down with their feet.

Through it all, outside of the orders, they hadn't spoken to me, and what they communicated to each other, I didn't get.

The car went right at the next corner and I knew where we were. I followed our route for a few more blocks, but then they jazzed up the trail, varying speed and making turns. You can't tell much from the floor of a car, and after a couple of zig-zags I was lost. Right then, though, I didn't figure it mattered. These were no junkie muggers out to make a

5

score. I was in with the pros and this jaunt in the limo had the smell of the traditional ride. I could see my body being found in the trunk of a stolen car with bullet holes through my skull. 'Gangland killing', the cops would say and wonder whose body it was and why. I was wondering why myself.

Since there was nothing else to do, I lay still and listened. Maybe I'd hear their voices, hear their plans, pick up their inflections, get something so I'd know whom to hunt, if I got out of this.

They didn't talk, however, and I was left with no clue. They had my credentials and knew who I was, so it didn't look as if they'd picked up the wrong guy and I wondered whom I'd antagonized lately. There were a number of people. I'm good at antagonism. But who was there with this much muscle and this much grudge? I try not to step on the really big toes in town.

So my listening only got me the sound of the air-conditioner. The car glided through the streets in ominous silence. It didn't speed, it stopped at all the lights. With the windows up and the climate control on, not much from the inside got out, not much from the outside got in. I did catch, at one light, the chump-chump of a sump pump. Then the smell of doughnuts got sucked through the vents. I thought of diners I had known and excavations that wouldn't stay dry.

We went for miles, making occasional turns, but we never left the city for we were still hitting red lights. The only thing that hadn't been taken from me was my wristwatch and I timed us by the luminous dial. The minutes dragged slower than they seemed, but it was still a long ride. I counted twenty minutes already and the time was quarter of one.

At ten minutes to, I heard the chump-chump of a sump pump and I started sniffing. Yes, there it was again, the smell of doughnuts. They were circling to confuse me. It wasn't a ride after all, they were going to let me live.

And I was going to make them wish they hadn't.

Just before one o'clock, the limo turned and crunched along a gravel drive for 45 seconds, then backed and filled and stopped. I was kicked sharply and the kicker told me to keep my head down or he'd crack my skull. The laprobe was pulled off and I was handed a black hood with drawstrings. 'Put this on and don't try to see out.'

I didn't get a chance to do more than obey before he pulled up the drawstrings under my chin and tied them. The bag was porous and a little light seeped through, but not enough to show me anything. The guy—it was ape-face—knew what he was doing.

Doors opened, ape-face gave me a boot in

the rear and told me to get a move on. I stumbled out and the other two grabbed my arms. They marched me over grass and stones for thirteen paces until I fell on some steps. Bent-nose cursed me and the other man—it had to be golf-cap—cursed him. 'He's blind, you damned fool. Whaddaya think?'

Hands under my shoulders pulled me upright. There was another step, then a door. I was pushed through into a room with a lot of furniture. I bumped into all of it.

They steadied me between the pieces in a clearing near the middle. More lights went on and there was a clatter as my belongings were dumped onto a table. Muttered comments attended their minute examination and I could feel ape-face come close. 'Where's the rest?' he said in my face.

I couldn't see through the bag, but I could feel the heat of him. I could almost feel his spittle.

I didn't answer and got slugged for my pains. 'Ya hear me?' he said, his voice rising.

The blow showered the inside of my head with stars. That was something else I owed him. I didn't want to owe him too much and I wanted to stay conscious so I talked for the first time. 'Rest of what?'

He elbowed me in the gut and doubled me over. 'Where'd ya put it, punk?'

It took me a couple of seconds to get my breath. I gave it one more try. 'Put what?'

From behind, bent-nose whacked my skull with an impatient gun butt. 'Answer the man. You heard him. Answer him.'

That crunch put me down and I found myself on the floor with my senses reeling, groaning instead of answering. He kicked me in the side and he knew where to put his toe. I managed not to scream, but it took a lot of effort. I tried to roll over and grab his leg—anybody's leg, but I was sluggish now. My fingers brushed a trouser, but that was all. I did get to my knees, though, and I pulled at the drawstrings of the bag with one hand and swung the other in a wide arc, hoping to land a punch on anyone who came near.

What that got me was a smack in the head with the butt of the sawed-off shotgun. It felt like Hank Aaron hitting one out of the park, and, while I was still conscious, I was no longer mobile.

Through the haze I was aware of ape-face's voice. 'Take him to the back room while I get on the phone. Strip and search him, and I mean *search*. We're gonna get what we want whether he talks or not.'

The other two dragged me off. Since I couldn't walk, each took a leg and hauled me feet first down a hall. I had enough sense to try to undo the drawstrings and get the bag off my head. If I could only see, I might have a chance.

The hall wasn't long enough. They got me into the back room in time to see what I was doing.

'Cute kid!'

Bent-nose kicked me in the side of the head and then stood on my hand, grinding the markings of his sole into my flesh. Golf-cap went to get his shotgun and swung it against my skull like a driver.

I heard the stock split, then all of my lights went out.

CHAPTER TWO

I awoke to darkness, to hate and rage and pain and frustration. The black bag was still in place and I lay where I'd fallen for I could feel the sticky stain of blood against my face. There was no sound and no presence. A sixth sense told me the room was empty. Slowly, I flexed the fingers of my right hand. Its throbbing reminded me that bent-nose had tried to crush it. The fingers moved. They were swollen and stiff, but they worked. The hand was only damaged, not broken. But he'd meant to break it. He'd meant to hurt me as much as he could. And someday I was going to hurt him back. And ape-face. And that sadist who'd broken his shotgun against my cranium. My head was aching now with a

10

low, pulsing beat. It robbed me of initiative, of energy, of caring—even for my own survival.

I made myself fight against it. I told myself I had to get out of this place, and the hell with how I felt. Giving up to pain was a luxury I couldn't afford until later. First I had to get the goddam bag off my head. Except that I found my hands had been tied behind my back. I moved them experimentally and the back they rubbed against was bare. My whole body was bare. Bent-nose and golf-cap had been told to strip search me. For what it was worth to them, they had.

I lay there trying to focus on a way out of the dilemma. It would have been easier if my head didn't feel like the exhaust phase of a rocket booster, but hate was pumping adrenalin into my blood and that compensated. But vengeance could wait. Survival came first. I was naked, blindfolded, hands bound. The first order of business was to get untied.

I worked my wrists against the ropes for fifteen minutes, by which time the skin was raw. When you can't break the bonds and you can't untie them, what's left? You stretch and loosen them, pull the knots tighter, work the rest freer. It was a slow process, but I was making progress.

Then company came. The door opened and

11

I heard the clump-clump and click-click of two pairs of shoes. I rolled over to hide my hands and lay still. Ape-face's voice said, 'There he is. Okay?'

The answer was a sniff of disdain and the clump-clump, click-click went away again.

I got back to my work and wrestled with my bindings for another fifteen minutes, but it was hopeless. I could not get them loose enough and I couldn't locate anything in the bare, rugless room to cut them with.

Footsteps approached again and I reassumed my womblike position, feigning coma. This time, my visitors came wordlessly and in silence. No clump and click, no 'There he is.' Nobody even said, 'He's unconscious.'

Two pairs of arms yanked me to my feet and trundled me out of there. I had a feeling it was bent-nose and golf-cap, but they didn't kick or beat me so I had no way of being sure.

*   *   *

I was hustled through a hall, a room, a doorway, into the outside night air, and back on to the floor of the limousine, where I was covered with the same-smelling laprobe, with other things, including shoes, being heaped on top. Various of the enemy got in with me, doors slammed, and off we went on another ride.

12

We drove for twenty minutes, I under the same old laprobe, with the same old feet holding me down. I listened and sniffed and sought for clues, but this time there were none. The same old sump pump and smell of doughnuts weren't on the itinerary. I didn't know where the hell we were going this trip.

When, at last, the car stopped, I had no idea of the time. With my hands bound, I couldn't see my watch. Doors opened and I was dragged out on to some grass. Things were thrown out after me. Clothing dropped on to my body, a shoe hit my head.

I rolled over and got to my knees. It wasn't easy the way my hands were tied, and I didn't know what trouble I was inviting, but I have a stubborn streak in me and I wasn't going to lie and take it. I had to show some kind of fight.

Nobody punished me for my rashness. All that happened was, ape-face said, close enough for me to smell his breath, 'You're lucky, you bastard. If you want to stay lucky, forget any of this ever happened.' His hand gripped my chin through the bag. 'Remember that, Buster. It never happened.'

He let me go, grass rustled and sounds faded. Doors slammed, the purring engine roused and the limousine took off.

I got to my feet and followed the sound, treading through grass till I found the road and the kerbing alongside. The kerb was

13

rough and I sat and rubbed my bindings against its edge until they wore through and I could free my hands.

When my fingers got enough circulation back into them, I undid the drawstrings and removed the bag from my head to see where I was. I'd been dumped where I'd been kidnapped—the same spot on the edge of Monmouth Park. Strewn around on the grass were my clothes, shoes, socks, and a paper bag which contained the rest of my things, including wallet, switchblade and gun, even all the money that had been in my wallet. They were giving me a message. They were saying, 'Sorry, our mistake.'

They'd be sorry, all right. When I got through with them, they'd be damned sorry.

★   ★   ★

I dressed slowly. My head ached and my body was sore. It was three o'clock in the morning, the houses were black, the woods were silent, nothing moved. It was an empty, dead world.

I walked home and it took forever. I wanted to think, but my head hurt too much. I even had to hold the railing to climb the steps to my condo storm porch.

When I made it into the upstairs bathroom, I got myself a ration of aspirin, gulped the tablets down with water and paced the floor until the pain eased enough so that I could undress and go to bed. I went to sleep thinking vengeance and how the hell I was going to get it. Tracking them down wouldn't be easy. They hadn't given me much to work with. That was all right. That only whetted my appetite.

CHAPTER THREE

The phone woke me at quarter past seven, which didn't put me in a good mood. This was the morning I was going to sleep in and heal.

'Yeah?'

'Where the hell were you last night?' It was Jack.

'Playing chess with you, you dummy.'

'After that. I tried to call you at half past one. What did you have, a late date?'

'You could call it that.'

'I pity the girl who marries you. Are you like this every morning?'

'No girl's going to marry me, and I'm only surly when I get waked up. What the hell are you calling for at this hour?'

'Your late date must've given you a hard time if you aren't even up yet.'

'Yeah,' I grumbled. 'Sorry about that. As a matter of fact, it wasn't a date. I got hijacked.'

'Hijacked? You're kidding.'

I said I wasn't kidding, I'd really been kidnapped, and given a good going over as well.

It made a believer out of him and he became suddenly solicitous. He wanted to know all the details.

Normally, I don't bother with long stories, but his uncommon curiosity, plus my aches and pains, made me feel like a little sympathy, so I gave him the rundown.

He listened in silence and then he said, 'I'll be damned.'

'I'm not making it up, you know.'

'They brought you back? They plunked you back down where they picked you up? They obviously made a mistake.'

'They sure as hell did. Which reminds me. Do you know of a place in town where a sump pump would be running near a doughnut shop or an all night bakery?'

'Not offhand. Why?'

'Their hideout is less than a ten minute drive from the two of them.'

'Yeah? Well, what of it?'

'If I can find that spot, I can find *them*.'

'Hey, now listen!' Jack carried on like a mother hen. 'You don't want to go looking for trouble. They told you to forget it.'

'I'm not looking for it, I'm going to be dishing it out.'

16

'What you ought to do is report it to the police. Tell them what happened. They'd be interested.'

'I've got nothing to tell them. And if I had, what do you think they'd do about it? Even if I rounded these guys up and brought them in, what do you think the cops would do—could do? This is a personal matter.'

Jack carried on like two mother hens. 'Look, figure you're lucky. You got out of the night with only a few bumps and bruises. It could've been worse. If you'd been the guy they thought you were, you could've been killed. It's lucky for you they found out their mistake. You ought to thank God you're still alive and let it go at that. Chalk it up to experience.'

'That clerical collar you're wearing must be turning you soft. You never used to talk like that.'

'I just got smart over the years. Smarter than you. Think about it. You've got a business to run. If you spend your time trying to track down—'

'Don't worry. I'll take care of my business. Chasing them will be a hobby.'

'What if they don't like being chased?'

'I don't expect them to like it. What're you bringing that up for?'

'Just a warning.'

'I don't know what you're so hot to keep me out of trouble for. Fifteen years ago, it

17

was I trying to keep you out. You had some of the wildest schemes—'

'We grow up in time. Some of us grow up.'

'Look, stop worrying. I'm a big boy. I look up and down before I cross the street. I bite wooden nickels. What were you calling me about last night?'

'It's of no consequence. Forget it.'

'Gladly. What're you calling me for now?'

There was a moment of hesitation. Then he said, 'Well, when I couldn't reach you last night, I thought I'd check and make sure you got home all right.'

I held the phone away and looked at it. Into it, I said, 'The hell you say.'

'You might have fallen in the bathtub and knocked yourself out.'

I burst out laughing. 'I'm touched,' I said. 'I'm going to remember you in my will.'

'And if you'll take my advice—'

'I know, I'll turn the other cheek. Forget it. Jesus and I don't see eye to eye on some things.'

'Too many things. All right, be pig-headed if you want, but, one thing. Anything you find out about those kidnappers, let me know. I wouldn't want you getting involved with them without someone else knowing what you're doing.'

'Yeah, sure,' I said and hung up. He was acting strange for this hour of a Tuesday morning.

CHAPTER FOUR

I made it to the office in time for the finish of Eileen's coffee break. Eileen is my secretary, a twenty-three year old whizz with a typewriter, stenopad, file cabinet and the rest of what a secretary is all about. She's also a raven-haired green-eyed temptress with a figure that would melt the polar ice cap and, in all honesty, I suspect her body brings in more business than my brains.

I gave her a cheery hello and otherwise tried to distract her from my condition by querying her about a client named Wilby and pouring myself coffee from her Silex.

She's not easy to distract. She briefed me on Wilby and said, 'What happened to you?'

'Me?'

'Your head. You've been hurt.'

I sipped coffee, felt my head and feigned surprise. 'Oh, that's right, I did get a nasty bump last night. I'd forgotten about it.'

'You look as if you got hit by a truck.'

'Actually, it was a *small* truck—a very small truck.'

'Have you been X-rayed?'

I shook my head. 'It was an *extremely* small truck.'

Eileen's given up trying to get me to take care of myself. 'I'm glad your skull is so thick,' she said. 'It's a great asset in your profession.'

I smiled, sipped coffee, and popped a couple of aspirins into my mouth when she wasn't looking. Then I retired to my office and didn't come out again, even for lunch. I considered myself recovered, but I didn't feel like active assignments just yet.

Thus I was on hand at half past three that afternoon when Eileen came in with the evening paper in her hand and her nose in the air. 'There's someone to see you,' she announced, as if she were holding a dead cat by the tail.

'Female?' It was a rhetorical question if you know Eileen. Her manner said, 'young and attractive female,' the kind she doesn't like to have come around. It's her motherly instinct. She wants to save me from temptation.

'The name is Veronica Dean,' she answered with the right touch of acid.

'A client?'

'I wouldn't know. She won't talk to anybody but you.'

'She sounds interesting.'

'I wouldn't trust her. She's up to no good.'

'Is that an unprejudiced evaluation?'

Eileen gave me her Devil-doll smile. 'I don't have any unprejudiced evaluations where women are concerned. I thought you knew that.'

I slipped into my jacket and adjusted my

tie. 'Well, show her in and if I yell for help, come running.'

'Just so long as she's not the one who yells.'

The woman Eileen showed in was everything her coming attractions had promised. She was a young, trim, make-believe blonde with shoulder-length waves and a buxom figure. She wore a thin, low-cut rayon print and had alluring, seductive features with a too-knowing look in her large, dark eyes.

Eileen noted my approval and made a face behind the woman's back, deliberately leaving the door ajar when she retreated. She wasn't going to miss any cries for help.

I said, 'Miss Dean, or Mrs Dean?'

'It's Miss Dean.' The hand she extended was warm and inviting, but her expression was clouded and she was gnawing her lower lip.

I helped her into the customer's chair and she perched on the edge, her blonde hair shining like a halo. The purse she clutched was gray suede. It went with the dress and matched her shoes. She wore the look of the well-off—comfortable, but not rich.

I resumed my seat and adopted the proper pose, forearms on desk, my face expressing the appropriate degree of interest. 'And what can I do for you, Miss Dean?'

'Are you—have you done—bodyguard work?'

'Yes, we do that.'

She sighed and visibly relaxed. 'Good. I think that's what I want.'

'For what times and for how long?'

'I think for one night, or for just a little while. It's just—tonight.' A query came into her eyes and she leaned forward. 'You would be free tonight?'

'Yes. That could be arranged.'

Miss Dean sat back as if some hurdle had been leaped. 'I don't like to bother you,' she said, 'but I would feel much better if you were with me.' Her eyes were assessing me now, judging not how much help just any man would be, but how much I would be. It was a quick evaluation, but a personal one, a reaching out for me with her eyes.

'Perhaps,' I said with my encouraging smile, 'you'd like to tell me what you want a bodyguard for?'

'Yes, of course.' She rummaged in her purse and handed me a folded sheet of yellow foolscap. 'This was in my mailbox today.'

Printed on it with a felt pen in bold letters were the words, 'Have dough ready by ten tonight.'

I looked at the back of the paper, turned it upside down, and held it to the light, but nothing could be discerned. The letters could have been made by anyone, except that they suggested a male hand. 'What dough?' I asked, handing the paper back.

Miss Dean sighed. 'Twenty-five thousand dollars. I have it. It's all wrapped and ready.'

'I think you'd better tell me the whole story.'

It had to do with her sister, she said, lowering her gaze. 'My parents—our parents, died seven years ago, when I was twenty-one. Samantha was fifteen. We were left quite a bit of money, both of us. Hers was in trust, of course. I was her guardian.' Miss Dean shrugged. 'I wasn't very good at playing mother. Samantha wasn't very good at playing daughter. She never had been. She's a headstrong girl.' Miss Dean raised her eyes to mine. 'At least she was. I've had her in finishing school and she's been spending her summers in girls' camps as a counsellor and leader. She'll be all right. But there was a time when she wasn't.'

Miss Dean was speaking earnestly. She wanted me to understand. I nodded. That didn't mean I understood, because I didn't, but it was to keep her going. I wanted her to know she was telling her story to the right pair of ears.

'When Samantha was seventeen,' Veronica Dean went on, 'she got in with a bad crowd.' Miss Dean opened her purse for a cigarette. 'I don't know how,' she continued, 'and I don't know who.'

I reached for the table Ronson next to my Charles Addams ashtray, but she preferred a disposable butane lighter tucked in with her cigarettes.

All of this took time, but Miss Dean wasn't in a hurry. It was more mportant that I should have a full understanding.

'I'm afraid,' she went on, not meeting my gaze, 'that she involved herself in a pretty bad scene.' Her eye was on the tip of her cigarette now, and she leaned forward, exhibiting some very attractive cleavage.

There was a pause while she waited for me to comment, but I didn't know whether I was to remark upon her cleavage or her story, so I put my elbows on my desk, leaned my chin on my knuckles and concentrated, with her, on the tip of her cigarette.

When there was enough ash, she rolled it off in the Charles Addams ashtray and broke the hovering silence. 'There was a bank heist,' she went on. 'I think there were several.' Miss Dean looked up to register my degree of shock.

I gave her a bland, heard-it-all-before nod, and she got on with it. 'Samantha wasn't directly connected. She drove one of the cars. But she was involved. And eventually there was—armed violence. A bank guard was killed.'

'And?'

'Three of the gang were eventually caught and went to trial. Samantha's name, thank God, was never brought into it. The three went to jail.' Miss Dean exhaled sadly. 'That was five years ago.'

I hurried her along. 'And as of today?'

'Now one of the men is out of jail.'

'And he's trying to blackmail you?'

Miss Dean nodded.

'What's he been doing? You know which one he is?'

She shook her head and drew on her cigarette nervously. 'Not by name, I didn't know any of them by name. I didn't want to know them. And Samantha wouldn't talk about it. She wouldn't tell me anything. I didn't want to hear anything.'

'What's happened then?'

Veronica Dean mashed out the cigarette and immediately lighted another. 'Samantha's in school. I told you. But nobody knows where. I've been careful about that. Once I rescued her from that gang, I made sure she kept away from them from then on.'

That worked, she assured me, exhaling smoke and putting away her butane lighter. All was well with Samantha.

'What about you?' I said. 'How're things with you?'

'As for me, I'm a—I try to get work as a publicist.' That remark was followed by an apologetic smile. 'I suppose, since I've been left a fair inheritance, that doing publicity for groups and organizations is more of an avocation than a career. But I do get to move

25

around a lot.' She heaved a heavy sigh. 'For that reason, I didn't think about myself.' There was another sigh. 'I made sure that Samantha couldn't be traced. I didn't make so sure that I couldn't be.'

'And the gang tracked you here?'

'Yes, or at least one of them did.'

'Or that's what you think. What happened?'

Miss Dean studied the tip of her cigarette. 'A few weeks ago,' she said to it, 'I don't remember when, now, I got a phone call.' Her eyes met mine. 'I didn't recognize the voice. The man—it was a man—asked if I were Veronica Dean. I said I was and who was this? He didn't answer, he only said, "How's Samantha? Where is she now?"' Veronica's brow creased. 'I didn't answer him. I hung up.'

I pulled over a pad and made a note.

'He called again,' she said, 'as I knew he would. And again, and again. He kept asking about Samantha and I stopped hanging up because he mentioned a certain bank hold-up—the one where the guard had been killed, and he asked me what I knew about it. That was when I started getting scared.'

I jotted down a couple more notes. 'And now he wants money for keeping his mouth shut?'

Miss Dean nodded and put out the second cigarette. 'It came to that after a while. He wants twenty-five thousand dollars.' She put a hand on the purse which held the note. 'As you see, he wants it tonight.'

'And you intend to pay him?'

A corner of her mouth tightened. 'I don't have any choice.'

'You have a number of choices.'

'If I do,' she answered, straightening, 'I don't intend to take them.'

'That's up to you.' I leaned on my elbows over the pad. 'And what is it you want from me?'

Miss Dean patted the purse again. 'As the note says, he's going to call me tonight to tell me how to deliver the money. It's not that I don't trust him, but I'd like someone— you—to go with me. I don't want to go alone.'

'Perfectly understandable.'

She opened the purse again and took out a wallet. On the edge of my desk she laid three hundred-dollar bills. Her eyes met mine hopefully. 'Would this be enough to pay for your time and effort, and protection? I don't know how long it'll be. I don't know what he'll want us to do. Would this be enough?'

I said yes, it would be enough.

Miss Dean eased herself back in the chair. She was relaxed now. Another hurdle had been leaped. 'The note says ten tonight. Maybe if you came at quarter of—?'

'This is all by voice?' I asked. 'How does

27

this man identify himself? How do you know he's what he claims to be?'

She sat straighter. 'He knows about Samantha. I mean, he knows that she was involved in that bank robbery.'

'Or so he says. How do you know he's one of the gang?'

'He must be, because he knows—'

'It might be hearsay, Miss Dean. He might be a friend of a friend who was told that such and such a girl was involved, but her name never got mentioned. That's meaningless, Miss Dean. I can announce that your mother and father were implicated in the Kennedy assassination. Would you pay me twenty-five thousand dollars to keep still?'

She shook her head. 'You don't understand. My parents weren't involved with Kennedy's assassination, but Samantha *was* involved in the bank hold-up.'

'That's according to your own personal knowledge. My point is that, unless it's a member of the gang itself, someone who can give details of Samantha's involvement, and can back it up with evidence, the authorities will laugh in his face. Anybody can say anything, true or untrue, but the authorities are only going to take action if there's evidence to substantiate the rumor. What evidence does this unknown phone-caller have that links Samantha with the bank holdup?'

'Why,' she stumbled, 'I don't know.' She was shaken, but she wanted to believe. 'If he really is a member of the gang—'

'If he really is a member and not a phony, there might be some reason for believing he could turn your sister in, that's true.'

Miss Dean chewed her lip. 'I've seen him,' she said. 'I think I've seen him. Is that proof?'

'Seen him? Where?'

'Lurking around the neighborhood.' She hitched forward anxiously. 'It happened after the phone calls started. I wouldn't see him often, but there would be this man—in the shadows, in the alleys—and I could tell it was because of me—that he was keeping an eye on me.'

'And you recognized him?'

She nodded. 'He was—I hadn't seen him since the trial—but he was one of *them*.'

'He give any sign of recognizing you?'

'No. Whenever I saw him, he looked the other way—went the other way.'

'You're convinced it's his voice on the telephone?'

'Yes.'

'It's been five years since the trial.'

'I know,' she agreed, 'but all the same, that's something I wouldn't forget.'

I picked up my pen again. 'Describe him to me.'

That bothered her. Hesitation and

uncertainty took over. She'd been bold enough in asserting the voice went with the man. Now she wasn't sure what the man looked like. 'Dark,' she finally said. 'Dark and swarthy looking.'

'That said little. 'How tall?'

'Short,' she decided.

'What kind of build? Any particular outstanding features about him?'

All she could produce was the claim that he was of slight build, short, slender and dark. It wasn't much but that's the kind of description you can expect from civilians. If she saw him, though, she'd know him.

So much for that. Now she wanted to pay me three hundred dollars to accompany her to the rendezvous he would name later this evening, and stand by while she turned the money over to him.

I said to her, 'After I go with you and you deliver the money to this man, then what?'

'We come home again.'

'I mean, what do you think that twenty-five thousand dollars is going to buy you?'

'Peace of mind.'

'For how long?'

She resisted the temptation to go for another cigarette. 'How long? What do you mean?'

'How long do you think the twenty-five thousand dollars will keep him quiet? How long before he'll be back for another twenty-five?'

'Oh,' she said, as if that were a matter of no consequence. 'I'll be gone by then. The next time he tries to find me, I won't be there. I'm going to cover my tracks hereafter.'

I smiled and rose, picking up the three hundred-dollar bills. 'All right, Miss Dean, if you'll come this way, my secretary will take your address and give you a receipt for this money. The note says ten o'clock. I suggest that I arrive at your apartment at nine.'

'I'm so relieved,' she told me and clung to my arm going into the outer office.

CHAPTER FIVE

'She's gotten to you,' Eileen said sourly when I returned from seeing Miss Beautiful to the elevator. 'All men are suckers.' She returned her receipt book to its drawer and closed it with her thigh.

'Oh, I'm not totally bewitched,' I told her, and indicated the three century notes still lying on her desk. 'She's a paying customer and it's good business to butter up well-to-do clients.'

The three hundred dollars pushed the wolf farther from the door, but they didn't lift Eileen's spirits. 'Who do you have to kill?' she asked, her eyes as green as the money.

31

'Nobody important.'

Eileen made a face. 'I didn't trust her when she came in and I don't trust her going out, no matter what she pays you. And it's not just because she's another woman.' She stuffed the money into an envelope as if it might bite her, sealed the flap and stamped it down with her fist. 'What do you do for all this money?'

'I don't have to do anything,' I said, pouring myself some of her coffee. 'She's paying me to walk into a trap.'

Eileen's eyes darted, not to my face, but to the parts of my head that had been damaged last night. Eileen doesn't think I'm as tough as I think I am. 'What kind of a trap?'

'I have no idea. But I'll be finding out.'

Eileen marked the envelope with a skull and crossbones. 'If you don't get out of the trap, this money wouldn't buy you a decent burial. Have you thought of that?'

'Yes. It's my motive for not getting caught.'

Eileen watched me musingly while I sipped my coffee. 'I wonder what it's like to be big and brave!' She shook her head with regret. 'Men are such suckers. Veronica Dean doesn't give a damn about you, you know. She's trying to lure you, but she doesn't give a damn.'

I put a finger on Eileen's chin. 'Thanks for the intuition. It's bad for my ego, but there's a kernel of truth there. I think as you

32

think—that Miss Dean regards me as expendable.'

I shouldn't have said that. It made her shiver. But she knew better than to try to dissuade me. 'When do you start?' she asked.

'Nine o'clock tonight. Actually, I'll be reconnoitering from before eight.'

She gave my bumps and bruises one last look and shook her head. 'It's a good thing you don't have a wife. She'd be gray by now.'

I finished my coffee and rinsed the cup at the water cooler. The trouble with Eileen is she cares about me. She's been my secretary since I opened the office and has gotten herself involved. I told her to go type a letter and went back to my desk.

The evening paper was where she'd left it and I unfolded it to see what the world was up to. First off, on the front page, were big headlines about two murders in the Monmouth Park area last night. Our town isn't crime-free by any means, but twin murders, cheek by jowl, is a dish the media can't help but go on about. Throw in the possibility there's a connection and the press gets excited as hell.

The bigger murder, complete with picture of the victim, was Arnold Saydecker, wealthy collector and recluse whose large, second-story apartment overlooked the park. He was, according to the papers, forty-six years old, unmarried, of uncertain background, and he lived alone, except for a manservant. He had been shot to death in his study and had been found when the manservant returned from an evening out. Reports had him in his dressing gown, lying on his back on the carpet with three bullet holes in his chest.

There were open drawers and messed up papers, as if he'd been killed by an intruder, but his large, elegant apartment had been little disturbed. Various valuables remained in place and the motive for the murder was unknown.

The other victim had been stabbed to death on the edge of Monmouth Park and had been found in a grassy patch, close to the road, less than a block from Saydecker's apartment. All that was found on him was a revolver from which three bullets had been fired. He was a tall, muscled man in his mid-thirties with dark hair. Since he carried no papers his identity was unknown but, because his gun was the same caliber as that used to kill Saydecker, police believed he might have been Saydecker's assailant. A ballistics check would be made.

Details on the second murder were that policemen, en route to the Saydecker killing, heard a moan and, investigating, found the man, bleeding from his wounds, semiconscious. He died before the ambulance reached him and Father McGuire, from St

Benedict's Church, administered the last rites.

When I got to that part of the story, wheels clicked. So that's what the sonuvabitch was pulling! I threw the paper aside and dialed Jack's number. He needed to be talked to.

Needless to say, he wasn't home. He never is. Mrs Honeywell told me it was a Knights of Columbus meeting that was occupying him at the moment and she promised he'd call me back.

He did, in fact, and it was sooner than I expected. He caught me just before Eileen and I closed up shop for the day.

'Hi, Simon,' he said, all bright and chipper. Things had obviously gone well at the meeting. 'What's up?'

I said, drily, 'I hear you gave last rites to a suspected killer last night.'

'Oh,' he replied. 'You read the paper?'

'Let me see if I can put the pieces together. The cops didn't know who the guy was. The cops didn't know who stabbed him to death. And after you administered the last rites and talked to the cops, you telephoned me. How'm I doing so far?'

'A thousand percent. What're you bucking for, gold-star detective?'

'Let me take it a little further. The reason you phoned was because I'd walked that route going home and you thought I just might have seen or heard something. Am I warm?'

35

'You're a red-hot psychic. What's this all about?'

'I'm practicing detecting. Now one more try. When you didn't reach me last night, you called me this morning. And you learned I'd been kidnapped and roughed up and was pretty goddam sore and planning revenge. But you'd seen the dead hood and the gun he carried and you decided he belonged to the gang that grabbed me and you decided, on that basis, that they were a bunch of tough guys and you were afraid if I went after them, I'd get hurt.'

'Well, now—'

'You thought I was a little sissy and had to be protected.'

'Nobody said you're a sissy. You're not. What you really are is a damned fool.'

'And you decided to save me from myself. Let bygones be bygones. Forgive and forget.'

'Simon, I'm not kidding you. The cops don't have an ID on the guy, but they're pretty sure he's got a record. The guys who grabbed you thought they were grabbing him. It's some kind of a gang battle and if you try to join it, you might get caught in the crossfire.'

'I might do a little firing of my own.'

'All I'm trying to tell you is I don't want to be saying last rites over you.'

'You can't. I don't go to your church.'

'Why don't you get smart in your old

age—so that you'll have an old age?'

That was as far as we could go without trekking over the same old ground. I assured him I wouldn't play with the big boys without oiling my gun. He assured me I had a skull you couldn't crack with a jackhammer.

I said, 'The cops connect your guy with the Saydecker killing?'

He said, 'Only because he carried a gun with three bullets missing and was found by cops who were working on the Saydecker case.'

'But they don't have any motive?'

'Only burglary, except that my guy didn't have anything on him but his gun.'

'What he stole from Saydecker might have been stolen from him. Who knows what he carried besides a gun? Do the cops think the gun was a plant?'

'A plant?'

'I'm just wondering. Maybe the guy was a derelict and Saydecker's killer stabbed him and left the murder gun in his pocket.'

'I don't know,' Jack said. 'The cops didn't tell me much—only that a man had been murdered in his apartment and the investigating police had found this man a block away.'

'But you think my kidnappers meant to kidnap him?'

'I'm just guessing about that.'

'It's kind of interesting guessing.'

37

'Don't tell me the same thought wouldn't occur to you.'

'I thought my kidnappers just liked beating people up.'

Jack decided I was hopeless. He said, 'Do me a favor. Make out a will and leave everything to St Benedict's Church.'

I told him he shouldn't get upset because I wanted a little vengeance. God liked a little vengeance himself, now and then. Besides, I didn't know who the kidnappers were or where they were. So what could I do about it?

After I hung up, I said goodnight to Eileen and went out to my car. But I didn't go directly home. I checked on the first three bakeries in the yellow pages to see if any of them were located near a sump pump.

CHAPTER SIX

Veronica Dean's abode was a third floor apartment with a backyard view of fences, clothes lines, garbage pails, alley cats and garages, with a fire escape to get down to them by. The building, on the whole, didn't look as good as the girl. What she wore to my office was two cuts above her home. Not that the quarters were shabby, only ordinary.

I spent an hour checking out the neighborhood, recording license numbers of parked cars, noting the looks and locations of people on the streets, exploring the alleys and back lots, getting all those odds and ends out of the way before ringing Miss Dean's bell promptly at nine.

When I got out of the elevator, she was waiting in her doorway, dressed as she'd been that afternoon, her hair well brushed, her face made up, its expression sober. I got a whiff of Chanel Number Five as I stepped past her into the living room.

'I haven't heard from him yet,' she told me, closing the door and following.

'I haven't seen any sign of him myself,' I said.

'Sign of him?'

'Someone playing this kind of game would very likely make his phone call from this neighborhood so that he could watch you when you leave for the rendezvous. There's an outdoor phone three blocks away. It might be worth staking out.'

Veronica sat on the couch, clasping her hands in her lap. 'Stake it out? What for?'

'To pick him up if he makes the call from there.'

She was dense. 'But I'm hiring you to go with me to make the delivery.'

I perched on the edge of a facing chair. 'I don't mean *I'd* stake out the phone, Miss Dean. I'd stay with you, of course. But I could put a man on that booth to pick up the blackmailer if that's the phone he tries to use. It'd cost you a little more, of course—'

'But I don't want him picked up,' she insisted. 'Don't you see? That's the point!'

'It would be a gamble, of course. But it might save you twenty-five thousand dollars.'

She removed a cigarette from the box beside her and tapped it nervously. 'But I don't want to save the twenty-five thousand dollars. I want to be rid of the man. If I don't pay him, Samantha will go to jail.'

'There's no guarantee she won't go to jail even if you do pay him.' I lighted her cigarette.

'It's the peace of mind,' she answered, puffing. 'I told you that this afternoon. I want to pay the man and be rid of him. I don't want to try to catch him. I want to do what he says, pay him what he asks, and be free.'

'That's up to you, of course.' I got up. 'While we wait, I want to look around.'

'Oh,' she answered uncertainly. 'Is there anything in particular you want to see?'

'No, it's only habit. I have to know where everything is—exits, entrances, the rest of it. There's a fire escape to your back window. Do you keep your window locked?'

'No. It's summer. I keep it open.'

'Bad thinking.' I pushed aside the curtains of the living room windows. They looked down on the asphalt driveway between buildings. The room itself contained, besides

40

the couch and coffee table, two chairs, end tables, lamps, phone, a color TV on a stand, vases of dried marsh reeds and berries. The rug was fluffy under the coffee table, but otherwise worn and frayed. 'Furnished apartment?' I asked.

'Well, yes.'

'How long have you lived here?'

'A few months. The PR job I was hired for didn't work out. I'll be moving on shortly.' She said, encouragingly, 'That's why I'm not worried about the blackmailer coming back for more. He won't know how to find me.'

'How did he find you this time?'

'I don't know.'

'It didn't take him long, did it? What makes you so sure he won't find you again?'

She doused the cigarette and followed me into the dining room. 'What are you asking all these questions for? What difference does it make?'

The room was small, cramped by a table and four chairs. Windows were on the left, a counter on the right, with a walk space beside it into a tidy kitchenette. There were cupboards under the counter on the dining room side, sink and drainboard on the other. The kitchenette contained refrigerator, more counter space, cupboards, and an exit door.

'The difference it makes,' I said, 'is that if he finds you again, he'll be after more money. If a blackmailer stumbles on to a victim who pays, he's going to use that victim as a continuing source of income. Thats what blackmailing's all about.'

She followed me into the back bedroom, growing testy. 'Look,' she snapped, 'I'm hiring you to protect me when I give this man a package. I'm not paying you to tell me not to do it. Do you understand that?'

Her money called the shots. I didn't argue, I looked around. The bedroom contained a closet and dresser on the left, the dresser bearing a portrait photo of a young, brunette edition of Veronica Dean.

'The sister?'

'That's Samantha. And she's worth protecting.'

The main feature of the room was double windows at the back, giving access to the fire escape. Both windows were open, their curtains stirring. On the fire escape was a tray of herb pots.

A foot from the windows was the bed, a double; table, lamp and extension phone beside it, its headboard against the adjacent wall. Behind the wall, off a tiny hall, was the bath and, beyond that, a closet-sized maid or guest room with a connecting door to the kitchenette.

When I had completed my sortie, I put my hand on the extension. 'When this guy calls,' I told Veronica, 'you take it in the living room and I'll listen in here. Does he know you're not going to be alone?'

She shook her head. 'You saw the note.'

I left a light in the bedroom and we returned to the front room. 'You've talked to him on the phone,' I reminded her. 'He give you any instructions?'

She helped herself to another cigarette and mouthed it nervously. 'He didn't say anything about how I was to deliver the money. He only told me to get it.'

'Any idea why he left a note today instead of calling?'

She accepted my light and sank on to the couch. 'No.'

'How have you got the money?'

'It's wrapped and sealed. Don't worry, I have it.'

'What kind of bills?'

She got angry. She dragged hard on the cigarette and exhaled deep blue smoke. 'What do you want to know for? What business is it of yours? I'm not going to tell you anything more, except that I've got it. You're too damned nosy. You can't stop asking questions.'

'It's a habit of mine.'

'Well, I've told you all you need to know. What we're supposed to do is sit and wait for the phone to ring. That's what the note says, doesn't it? All I want you to do is obey orders. That's what I'm going to do.'

'Obey orders? What if he orders you to

come alone?'

She hesitated. 'I don't know.'

'You haven't planned this out,' I said, getting snappy myself. 'It's a mistake not to do your homework. The reason I asked if he knew you intend to bring me with you is to find out whether you're going to obey his orders or not.'

'Well, I—I do want—need protection.'

'Which is why he'll probably insist that you come alone.'

Veronica took another drag on the cigarette and rolled off its ash in the glass tray on the coffee table. She didn't look at me. 'What should I do?'

'When the phone rings,' I told her, 'you wait till I get to the bedroom extension and call you. Then you pick it up and answer. Since the blackmailer doesn't know about me, I won't say anything. I'll just listen. Meanwhile, keep him on the line as long as you can.' I paused and studied the blonde girl. She seemed to be nervous, and she was avoiding my gaze, but there was a hell of a lot more to her than appeared on the surface. She might have had a kid sister who got into bad scenes, but I'd bet her retainer she had a past of her own. This was no innocent virgin trembling before me and I knew a lot more than peace of mind lay behind her eagerness to pay off a blackmailer with nothing of even token value in exchange. But, as she kept telling me, that was her business and for what I was being paid, I wasn't going to manufacture problems for myself.

'By the way,' I said. 'Does he have a way of identifying himself?'

Miss Dean shook her head. 'Only by his voice. I recognize his voice.'

'And you never met these bank robbers?'

'No.'

'All right. When this guy calls, keep him on the line as long as you can. Ask him questions. Insist that whatever directions he gives you be repeated as many times as you can make him. Tell him you have to write it all down. Stall. You get the idea?'

She frowned. 'But what for?'

'I'm going to want to familiarize myself with his voice. I want to learn as much about him as I can.'

'There you go again,' she yelped, jumping up and pacing the room. 'I tell you and tell you, I don't want you to try to catch this man, I don't want you to interfere in any way with this operation.' She came to a halt in front of me. 'I want to do everything he says.'

'Except,' I reminded her, 'you want me to ride shotgun for you. And if I do, I'm not just going along for the ride. You want protection and I'm going to give you protection. But that means you're going to do things my way, not yours, do you understand?'

The girl backed off, biting her lip. 'I don't

want to get him upset.'

'Good, then don't get me upset. I'm telling you what I want you to do. Sit down and listen and absorb it.'

She obeyed, resuming her seat, taking puffs on her cigarette and chewing her lip. The lip-chewing was becoming a little much.

'You have a car?' I asked.

'Yes.'

'Where do you keep it?'

'It's in the first garage out back. It's a red Pinto wagon.'

'That's what we'll use. As soon as you hang up after he calls, I'll go down the fire escape and get into the back of your Pinto. You get your things and pick up the car as if you're alone. Obey the directions and don't talk to me except to answer questions. As much as possible, I want you to be alone and feel alone. Do you understand?'

She nodded and ventured a smile. 'It's—I thought all it would be would be you holding my hand. Now it sounds like cloak and dagger.'

'It's not cloak and dagger. It's really hand-holding. You won't want it to be anything else.'

CHAPTER SEVEN

The phone didn't ring until half past ten. Veronica Dean spent the time looking at, but not watching her color TV. I spent it prowling the apartment and thumbing through the couple of magazines she had. (There wasn't a book in the place.) I also acquainted myself with the picture of Veronica's sister, Samantha. Her hair was dark, the real colour of Veronica's, and there were certain resemblances of feature. There was the same generous mouth, bright eyes and small nose. Samantha's face, however, had a happy smile, an expression foreign to Veronica. But then, Samantha's picture had been taken circa age eighteen and girls that age have more to smile about.

Except that Samantha, according to Veronica, had been through a sex and drug stage and partaken in at least one bank hold-up in which a guard had been slain. Well, Samantha's eyes might be smiling, but they didn't look innocent.

At the jangle of the phone, Veronica jumped as if a fire alarm bell had gone off in her ear. The call was half an hour late and she'd been getting the jitters. Six cigarette butts had been added to the coffee table ashtray in that intervening half hour. She swung and reached for the phone so fast I had to speak sharply to remind her to wait. She swallowed and nodded and I betook myself to the bedroom and called, 'All right,' when I had a hand on the extension.

I lifted it slowly and the two sounds were like one. Then Veronica's voice said, 'Hello?'

What answered was a mumbled attempt at disguise. 'You got the dough?'

'Uh, yes.'

'Listen, then. Drive out Railroad Avenue to the corner of Braxton Street. Wait in the phone booth there for my next call.'

There wasn't much to be derived from the voice. It was guttural and the words hard to distinguish. However, all the disguises in the world can't alter voice prints and I was holding my pocket tape recorder as close to the receiver as my ear to get every syllable down on the record.

'Yes, yes,' Veronica answered. 'Railroad Avenue and Braxton Street. Is that right?'

'You heard me.'

'Yes. Let me write that down.' Then she said, 'You'll call me at that number?'

'That's what I said.'

'When?'

'In less than an hour.'

'You mean before—uh—eleven-thirty?'

'That's what I told you.'

'Uh, should I bring the money?'

'What do *you* think?'

'Should I come alone?'

'Yeah.'

'Uh—let me see—'

She was trying to hold him on the line as I'd told her to, but she didn't succeed. The line went dead.

I put down my receiver and pocketed the recorder. When I rejoined her, Veronica was standing with her hand resting on the cradled instrument, staring at nothing.

'You all right?'

She came to and nodded. 'Railroad Avenue and Braxton Street.' She showed me the phone pad. 'I wrote it down.'

'Get your things and lock the window after me. I'll meet you at the car.'

She followed me to the bedroom and closed the window when I started down the fire escape. There was a floodlamp lighting the drive and a curtained glow in a couple of neighboring windows. Otherwise, all was darkness.

The free swinging bottom segment of the ladder creaked when it arced to the ground under my weight. It was the only sound. It creaked again, swinging back when I dismounted, and its free end climbed slowly past my shoulder as I looked around. I was alone in the yard, and not readily visible.

The garages were a row of six across a rutty stretch of dirt, back by the ratty fencing. The doors on the stalls were ill-fitting for the

49

structure was losing its plumb, but the hasps still fitted the swivel eyes, and most of them bore locks. Veronica's didn't and the door opened with a squeak. Inside was her red Pinto wagon and I got into the cramped back seat.

Five minutes later, Veronica opened the Pinto door and got behind the wheel. Before putting the key in the ignition, she said, 'Do you know where Railroad Avenue is?'

I told her I did, and when she pulled out of the alley gave her directions.

It was a fifteen minute ride and we spent it in silence except for my guidance. I watched our route and kept track of what went on, but kept my head low.

There was, as the caller had said, a phone booth on the corner of Railroad and Braxton. It was beside a bridge and Veronica could pull off the road on to the surrounding dirt area and park three feet from the door. From there, we would hear it ring.

She went through three cigarettes in rapid order, swore at herself for smoking, and asked if I believed in lung cancer. I said she might as well ask if I believed in chicken soup and that it was best if we didn't talk.

'I mean, do you believe what the surgeon general says, that you can get lung cancer from smoking?'

'I think some people can.'

'What's it like being a private detective?
50

How'd you get into that kind of business?'

'We aren't supposed to talk, Miss Dean.'

'"Miss Dean"? That sounds funny. You should call me Veronica.'

'We aren't supposed to talk, Veronica.'

'And I'll call you Simon. Just how did you get into the detective business, Simon?' She turned in the seat. 'I really want to know.'

I sighed. Some people are hard to educate. 'Your blackmailer friend told you to come alone. You asked him if you should, and he said yes. Don't you think you should at least pretend you're alone?'

'Oh, stop it, Simon. You sound like my great-aunt. How's he going to know? He's going to be on the other end of the telephone.'

'If I were the blackmailer, I'd be watching this car right now.'

'That's nonsense. There's no one anywhere around.'

'And if I were watching this car right now, it wouldn't be from any place you could see.'

'Oh, now, this is ridiculous. What would he want to watch this car for?'

'To see if you are obedient.'

'Oh, come on, Simon. Obedient? All he wants is my twenty-five thousand dollars.'

'He also wants not to be caught. Twenty-five thousand dollars isn't usually as easy to come by as you're making it for him. He expects to have to work harder for it than

51

he actually does. Most victims aren't going to be quick and pliable like you.'

'Pliable?' She didn't like that. 'I'm not just giving in to him. I hired you to come along, and he doesn't know that.'

'If he's watching this car, he ought to know it by now.'

Veronica lighted another cigarette and swore. After about three puffs, she said, being less obvious about it, 'If I don't look your way and keep my voice low, like this, that would fool him, wouldn't it?'

'If you behaved as if I weren't here, that would fool him more.'

'Why don't you talk to me?'

'Because I'm waiting for that phone to ring.'

She cursed and, not to my surprise, used some unladylike language. As I say, she was a girl who wore innocence as a guise, but it didn't become her. I was reminded of the smiling eyes in that portrait photo of her sister and the hint of something else underneath. It was here too. What is it they say, 'Birds of a feather'? Or is it, 'Blood's thicker than water?'

Silence followed and Veronica smoked more cigarettes. I quit a long time ago, but now and then break down. Usually it's times like this when I decide to indulge, but tonight I had no urge. Maybe it was due to imminence—the expectation of the call.

Maybe it was having company. (Lonely stake-outs lower my resistance.) Maybe it was watching Veronica smoke enough for both of us.

The phone didn't ring. Eleven thirty passed, then eleven forty-five. It was nearing twelve.

Veronica searched for another cigarette, cast a crumpled pack out the window, and ripped open a new one. She was swearing like a sailor. 'Do you have a light?' She turned and leaned over the seat.

I lighted her and sat straighter. Nobody was watching. There was going to be no call. Sometimes blackmailers do that, send you out on a dummy run and monitor your behavior. If they're satisfied, they'll give you a second set of orders which is for real. Of course, they only do that if they're cool, cautious, and in no hurry. That's big time. Small time is always snatch and run. That's by way of saying this looked like a bigger-time operation than just some kid convict fresh out of jail putting the arm on the relative of a fellow accomplice.

And twenty-five thousand dollars? A punk would ask for five. A punk wouldn't even know if the relative would be good for twenty-five. There were a lot of unknowns in this equation to which Veronica Dean seemed deliberately oblivious. She looked willing to pay money to anybody for anything.

53

On the other hand, Veronica had her own little games. One of them was advertising that she wasn't alone. I put my lighter away and she smiled. 'I hope my language didn't offend you.'

I shook my head and suggested we go back. 'That phone's not going to ring.'

'I suppose.' She faced front, studied the empty booth and deserted lot while she took deep drags on her cigarette. When she'd had enough, she let the butt dangle from her lips, twisted the ignition key and started the engine. 'I want you to come back to the apartment with me,' she said around her filter tip. 'He might call again.'

'I'm sure he will,' I said.

'Sure?'

'You've got twenty-five thousand dollars he wants. He hasn't got it yet.'

CHAPTER EIGHT

It was half-past twelve when we re-entered the apartment and Veronica turned on all the lights, even the kitchenette, bedroom and bath lights, everything except the bulb in the midget guest bedroom. The dining room windows were open, but she unlocked and threw open the bedroom ones as well to get some circulation. There was no air-conditioning and nothing but a floor fan by the bedtable to make life bearable.

'How long before he calls again?' she asked, coming up to me with a fresh cigarette in her hand.

'I'm not an oracle,' I said, lighting her, 'but my guess is one o'clock.'

'What if we don't hear by then?'

'We wait.'

'You're sure he'll call?'

'I'm sure.'

'What if it's not until very late?'

'Don't worry about it. When he calls, I'll be here. I won't let you go meet him alone.'

Veronica sighed. I couldn't tell whether it was from relief or resignation. 'Meanwhile, we wait?'

We were in the dining room near her bedroom door. 'Well,' she said brightly, going to the cupboards under the counter, 'we might as well live it up.'

That's where she had her bar, the glasses, ice bucket, and liquor bottles: Scotch, rye, vodka and some wine. She plunked a pair of glasses on the countertop and mashed her cigarette. 'What would you like?'

Her smile was glittery, like spangles and sequins. It was showy, but promised nothing. It was a superficial gleam and didn't reveal whether what it hid was fear, unease, or uncertainty. Veronica Dean was a hard one to figure.

I shook my head at her liquor cabinet. 'Coffee,' I said, 'if you've got it.'

She ignored that and set rye and Scotch bottles beside the glasses. 'Don't destroy me, Simon. You absolutely can't be a teetotaler.'

That was as shiny as her smile. 'I don't mind a drink,' I said. 'Right now, I prefer coffee.'

She put her hands on her hips. 'Because you're on a job?'

'That's one reason.'

'What's another reason?'

'You don't have a chaperone.'

That made her laugh. It delighted her. 'You mean you're afraid—you want me to believe that if you have a drink, you'll lose control and ravage me on the dining table?'

The table was a clumsy piece of furniture. I said, 'No, not on the table.'

Now her laughter tinkled. 'Thank you for sparing me that. I'm sure the table can be put to better use.' Now that hurdle was past, she held up the two bottles. 'Which would you like?'

'Coffee,' I repeated.

Veronica was finding me cumbersome. She set the bottles down. 'Really, what is this "duty above all" bit? That's ancient history. It doesn't impress anybody any more. All you have to do is watch me pay a man twenty-five thousand dollars. How much ability is that going to take?'

'I don't know yet.'

She flounced. 'What if the man doesn't call? What if he doesn't call until three o'clock?'

'I'll be here.'

'What if I want to wash my hair ? What if I want to go to bed?'

'I'll be by the phone in the living room.'

Veronica wasn't getting what she wanted, whatever that was. She contemplated the bottles on the countertop and said, 'What the hell, who wants to drink alone?' Now, when she faced me, she was wearing a Mary Pickford smile "All right, coffee." She went around the counter to the kitchenette and put the kettle on the stove. She leaned on the counter and was soberer. 'What do you think's going to happen?'

'I think you'll get another phone call giving you another message. I think this one will be for real, giving you the proper directions.'

'What if he doesn't call again?'

'It would mean he doesn't trust you and wants you to sweat.'

'Sweat? What for?'

'So that next time you'll obey his orders without reservation.'

She leaned on her elbows. 'All right, if we're going to spend time together, entertain me. Tell me what it's like to be a detective. What's the most fascinating case you've had of late?'

'Recovering a ton of gold bullion from a sunken Spanish galleon.'

Her eyes widened at the thought, but she didn't believe me. 'I think you're pulling my leg.'

'If you say so.'

'You have a beautiful secretary. Are you in love with her?'

'You're very inquisitive all of a sudden.'

'We've got time to kill. We might as well talk. I'd like to know something about the men I employ.'

I said, 'Your water's boiling.'

She made instant coffee, a cup for each of us, and we had it in the living room. There followed more questions: how did I become a detective? What kind of cases did I get? Did I have to do illegal things?

My cases, I said, were confidential—not to be discussed.

She tried pouting. 'You can tell me where you were born, can't you? You can tell me about your childhood. That's not privileged information, is it?'

'What I can tell you about detectives is that we don't dispense information, we collect it. How about telling me where you were born and about your childhood?'

She didn't like that and nudged a toe with a toe. 'My past is very uninteresting.'

That was as believable as her telling me she was paying the blackmailer for peace of mind.

'Let's try something else,' I offered. 'Tell me about the recent past—what you've been doing this month.'

The pout was turning sulky. 'Come on, Simon. Good Christ, if I wanted to talk about myself, I'd hire a priest, not a detective.'

That put an end to the inquiry on both sides for the duration of the coffee break. She turned on the television and watched that without comment until one o'clock. Through it all, the phone remained deathly still. Veronica began muttering during the commercials and turned to me. 'What do you think? Why hasn't he called back?'

'I can't tell you. If he knows I'm here, he might be waiting for me to leave.'

That made her shiver. She lighted another cigarette. The pack I'd watched her open was half gone. 'I don't want you to leave me. I don't want you to go until morning.'

'I'll be right here.'

She smoked the cigarette and watched more television. It was one fifteen when she put it out. 'I'm going to get ready for bed now,' she told me, rising, '—take a bath.'

'Go ahead. Lock your bedroom windows first. I'll stay here on the couch.'

'Lock the bedroom windows? What for?'

'It wouldn't be hard for someone—the blackmailer, say—to come up the fire escape and get into your bedroom.'

'What would he want to do that for?'

'He's arranged a situation whereby you've got twenty-five thousand dollars in cash here in your apartment. Maybe he wants to make his second call in person.'

'Well, it's too damned hot to keep the windows closed.'

'And it's too damned risky for you to be alone in there with the windows open.'

'Well, if it's going to be that important to you, you can guard the windows and I'll undress in the bathroom.'

I didn't want her getting any wrong ideas. 'It would be easier if you just shut—'

'You think I need protection even in my own apartment, then give me protection. You've been trying to run this whole thing ever since you got here. You keep trying to stop me from giving him the money.'

The hell with arguing. I'd had a long day. We did it her way. I sat on the bed in the dark, watching out the windows with my back against the headboard while, behind it, on the other side of the wall, there was the sound of bathwater running, of splashing and, after about twenty minutes, of the tub being drained.

Ultimately she came in to me and stood beside the bed. She was wearing a low-cut, embroidered, form-fitting, knee-length nightgown that could have served as a cocktail dress except that you could see through it. The seeing through didn't seem to

60

bother her. 'Let's have a nightcap.'

'No thanks.'

'God damn it,' she flared, 'I've been through hell today and I need a drink, and I'm damned well not going to drink alone. I'm paying you, and I want your company. He's not going to call again. All you have to do is sleep. You can damned well drink with me.'

I shrugged and got off the bed, following as she stalked to the kitchenette to empty ice cubes into the bucket. She plunked that on the counter, came around to where I was and brushed back her hair with a hand and a toss of her head. 'All right, what do you want?'

My eyes wandered momentarily to the embroidery over her bosom and she smiled. Her lips parted and there was the hint of teeth. 'Rye on the rocks,' I said, and smiled back, giving her a glint of my own teeth.

She picked up one of the squat glasses and poured me enough rye to kill a horse. 'Here,' she said. 'Help yourself to the ice.' She trickled herself a dainty Scotch and laced it with a pint of water, leaning over the counter to reach the faucet. She added a small ice cube and turned around, almost into me. 'Chug-a-lug,' she smiled, clinking glasses. She sipped and turned out the lights so that all we had to see with was the glow from the windows across the alley. It was enough. It was plenty.

I tasted the rye and it was good, if unknown. She watched the result as if it contained a mickey. It didn't and she took my hand. 'Why don't we go into the living room and sit down? It's going to be a long night. We can get quietly drunk together.'

I didn't know whether the game was to get me drunk or to get me into her bed and I didn't understand the motivation for either. Give her time, though, and the message would come through. Perhaps even the reason might come through. The reason would be worth waiting for. Right now it was the dark at the end of the tunnel.

I detached my hand and took another drink of the glass of rye. 'I'm all right here, and I don't want to get drunk, either alone or together.'

She didn't press. She took a sip from her own glass. Her eyes were large and waiting and watching. There was enough electricity in the air to light Las Vegas.

I slid a shoulder strap off her shoulder. She didn't move. I slid it halfway down her arm and the embroidered top crept down her breast. When she still didn't move, I pulled the strap down to her elbow. The embroidery fell away and everything came into view.

She could have been a statue.

'What are you after?' I said.

'What do you think?'

That was more lure. She was still playing

games. I set down my glass, drew the embroidery back over her breast, and slipped the strap back over her shoulder. I said, 'I thought you were hiring a bodyguard, not a male prostitute.'

She swung her hand at my face with everything she had, and it promised to be a lot. I caught her wrist and half her watered Scotch slopped down the front of her nightgown. She threw the rest of it in my face, ice cube and all, and called me a lot of names in the sailor language she'd sprung on me before.

I wiped myself free of the excess water and pushed her away. I picked up my rye and had a couple of quaffs, enough to kill half a horse. Sometimes I *do* drink on the job.

'Look at me,' she said, staring at her soaking nightgown. She slapped her glass on the counter, went around to the kitchenette side, stripped her nightgown down to her waist and started wiping her breasts and body with a dishtowel. 'I'm a mess.'

I leaned on the counter and watched her. 'What's the real story?'

She looked at me. 'What?'

'Why am I here? What's the real reason?'

'I'm in trouble,' she answered, toweling between her breasts. 'What the hell do you think I came to you for?'

'You're in trouble? Yes, I think you are. And since you hired me, I'll tell you what

63

you're going to do about it. You're going to go into your bedroom and close and lock your windows and go to sleep. Do you hear me?'

'And what are you going to do?'

'I'm going to sleep on the couch by the phone.'

Veronica threw her towel at the sink. 'I'm not going to lock my windows!'

'You're cute,' I said. 'You throw nice tantrums. Sometimes they're very convincing.' I looked at my watch. 'At two,' I said, 'I'm going to have a relief take over for me. He'll guard you till morning and you can play games with him.'

'Hey, no!' She caught me at the phone. 'No, I'll behave. I don't want anybody else. I'll lock the windows and you can sleep here on the couch. Don't call anybody else. I won't feel safe with anybody else.'

My instincts told me not to believe a word she said and to get the hell out of there. But her appeal to my emotions, or whatever she appealed to, outweighed my instincts.

She retired to the back bedroom and I slept on the couch.

CHAPTER NINE

The phone never rang, there was no other disturbance, and I slept soundly until six a.m.

I got up with one motion, looked around at my undisturbed belongings, jacket and tie over the chair, shoes under the coffee table, and padded through in stocking feet to Veronica's bedroom. She had removed the wet nightgown and was sleeping nude, the sheet up to her waist, her back to me, her head buried in the pillow, her position womblike.

Facing her, the fire escape windows stood wide open. She was supposed to keep them locked. Never trust a woman.

I went back, dressed, and took my car past another bakery in a hunt for sump pumps on the way to my condo and a shower. It had been an interesting night but I didn't know what to make ot it.

When I let myself into my condo and looked around, though, I began to get some answers.

You have to be observant—meaning you have to have cops' eyes—to pick up such things. The condo looked as it always did. The carpeting in the foyer was in no more need of vacuuming that it ever was after fifteen days. In the kitchen, no more dishes lay in the sink than I'd left there. The decor of the living room, as viewed from the entrance steps, was no different from before.

It was only in the bedroom that I picked up the clues. In the top bureau drawer, some of the socks which I keep on the right were on the left, and a folded handkerchief was out of its pile.

I checked the next drawer. The paper strip across the front of one of my laundered shirts was broken, and it hadn't been when I put on a clean shirt the preceding morning.

I closed the drawers and began looking around in earnest. Someone had been in my place in my absence.

So that was why Veronica Dean wanted me to spend the night? That was why she paid me three hundred dollars? But what did I have that was worth that much? Not the TV, not the typewriter. They were in place.

I checked out the whole condo—living room, dining room, kitchen, bath, master bedroom, guest bedroom, and upstairs bath. I even went through the garage.

The signs of the search were so slight you'd almost believe there hadn't been one. You'd almost believe you'd torn the strip on the laundered shirt and forgotten about it, or that you had carelessly dumped socks in the wrong part of the drawer.

But it wasn't so. There were drops of water in the kitchen and downstairs bathroom sinks. The bathroom sink I haven't used in a month, the kitchen one hadn't been used in twenty-four hours. No way would they be wet. The bathroom had been used all right and the condo had been scavenged.

I went through everything with my camera

eye, but nothing had been taken. Not only were no valuables gone, no unvaluables had been removed either. My file cabinet—they'd gone through that, but no papers were missing, only disarranged. What was interesting was that everything had been left as near to normal as possible. It reminded me of two nights ago, when I had been searched and nothing taken, and I'd been returned as near to normal as possible.

Somebody thought I had something. Somebody had meticulously searched my apartment in my absence. And how had that someone got a key? Well, it wasn't all that hard. The kidnappers had stripped me of all my possessions. Give them five minutes with my keys and they could get into everything I owned.

And what about Veronica Dean? What about that blackmail story she paid me three hundred dollars to buy? Did she really have twenty-five thousand dollars in cash in her bag when we went off on that wild goose chase? Or was she only keeping me out of my condo for the night?

I showered and got into clean clothes and prepared a leisurely breakfast: eggs Benedict (I had time to fuss, but I did fake the Hollandaise), cereal with sliced peaches, cream and sugar (I don't have a weight problem yet),. and Irish coffee (not customary, but you have to do something when you find you've been burgled).

I went to the office early, looked around for things out of place (but found none), did a few chores and had the decks cleared by the time Eileen arrived at five minutes of nine. She said I was a busy little beaver and she wasn't accustomed to finding the door unlocked. I said, 'Look through your files, will you? See if anything's missing, if anything's been disturbed. You know what's there and I don't.'

Eileen, removing her typewriter cover like a mother unswaddling a baby, paused. 'You think someone's been in here?'

'My condo was very thoroughly searched last night. I'm wondering if the office was as well.'

She opened the file drawers and right away said. 'Yes, someone's been here.' She removed the most recent folders. 'These have been taken out and put back in again. They aren't quite the way I left them.'

'Bright girl. You're observant.'

'You've taught me.'

I moved over beside her. 'Check the latest files. Try to remember what's in them. See if there's anything missing.'

She opened them on the desk and I watched while she turned the contents, sheet by sheet. 'No, Simon. I'm sure there's nothing missing. But somebody's looked through them. I wouldn't have noticed if you

68

hadn't said anything, but they've been tampered with.'

'It figures,' I said. 'They wouldn't know where I might be keeping whatever it is they're after.'

'You don't know what they're after?'

'No, but they'd be checking out recent clients—see if some particular person had come to me, might have hired me for something or given me something.'

'The last person who hired you was that Dean woman. Do you think that's what they wanted to know?'

'It could be. Miss Dean is a mystery.'

'Did she—you and she—make that payment?'

I shook my head. 'The blackmailer gave her instructions, but he never tried for the money.'

'Do you think they searched the office to find out about her, or used her to find out about somebody else?'

I patted her hip. 'You ask very good questions, my dear. I'm about to go talk to the young lady and find out.'

CHAPTER TEN

I buzzed Veronica Dean from the lobby and she came on the intercom. 'Oh, it's you?

What do you want?'

It wasn't a friendly approach from someone who'd tried to seduce me the night before. I told her I wanted to see her.

'Well, I'm—really, I don't need you now. You've done your duty.'

I said, 'Sister, are you going to let me in, or do I break in? I said I want to see you, and I mean, Right Now.'

That silenced her for a moment. Then she tried to be flip. 'My, you certainly are macho this morning. You weren't that eager last night.'

'Just buzz the buzzer,' I said. 'We'll talk when I get up there.'

She hung up and I thought she was going to try to stop me, but the buzzer sounded and I got through into the lobby.

When I got to her floor, she wasn't waiting in the doorway as she had the evening before. I had to ring twice and wait. My temper was short and I didn't go for the dallying. Then the locks turned and she unlatched the door, looking around it to see if I'd taken the place by storm. It was hard to tell whether she was frightened or just nervous. Maybe bewildered is the word, for she seemed to have no idea why I was there.

I pushed in and my face must have looked like Mt St Helens in eruption for she drew back and now she did look scared. What she had on was a blue satin robe, cinched with a

70

sash at the waist.

'What's the matter?' she said, clutching the door-knob. 'What's gone wrong?'

'That's what I want you to tell me,' I said, pulling the door from her grasp and slamming it shut. 'Suppose you give me that story again, about why you wanted me to protect you.'

She backed off but she was fighting me. 'What the hell's got into you? What's happened?'

I caught her by the wrist. 'Just the story. No questions. Just tell me the story.' When she hesitated, I jerked her up close. She was tough, and hard to scare, but now she started to tremble.

'But what do you want me to tell?' Her eyes were wide and fixed on mine. She'd tried to play it as a game and it hadn't worked. It was dawning on her that I was serious.

'What'd you come to me for yesterday afternoon? Who sent you to me?'

'Sent me?' She gave three sharp hysterical bursts of laughter. 'You're out of your mind.'

'How'd you find me?'

'In—in the phone book—the Yellow Pages.'

'Simon Kaye! Why not Gregory Abbot?'

'Huh?'

'There's a private detective in town named Abbot. He's listed first in the Yellow Pages. How'd you get down to Simon Kaye?'

71

'I didn't get "down," I opened the book and yours was the first name I saw. Honest.' She tried to twist in my grip. 'Please, you're hurting me.'

I ignored that. 'And what did you need a detective for?'

She blinked. 'I don't understand. Don't you know why I hired you?'

'No, I don't. That's what you're going to tell me.'

Tears started. 'Please let go.' Her face was white. It wasn't all an act.

I pushed her on to the couch and she huddled, cradling her wrist and rocking. What was interesting was that she took it. There was no screaming or fainting or outrage. She was used to the tough guy act. It was part of her life. 'Okay, let's hear it.'

'I have this sister,' she said, weeping, her head bowed. 'She got into trouble a long time ago. I sent her—'

'How long ago?'

'Five years. Back when she was seventeen. I tried to raise her right. I've kept her in school. She's all right now. She's reformed. But they don't forget. One of the guys who was in things with her just got out of jail—'

'What jail?'

'I don't know. It all happened out west somewhere. I was in the east.'

'How'd he find you?'

'I don't know.'

'Go on with it.'

She told the rest of it the way she had before. He made threatening phone calls, he demanded twenty-five thousand dollars or he'd involve her sister in the bank crimes.

'And you were going to pay him twenty-five thousand dollars, just like that?'

She looked up at me beseechingly. 'I've got to protect my sister.'

'That's no protection at all, and you know it.'

'What do you want from me?'

'I want to know whom you work for—who's paying you.'

'Paying me to do what?'

'Keep me here last night while my apartment and office were searched.'

'Your apartment and office were searched?'

I caught her arm and yanked her to her feet. 'That's right, searched. And you know why. What is it that people think I've got? What am I supposed to be hiding?'

'Please, you're hurting me.'

'I haven't even started. What am I supposed to be hiding?'

She gasped with the pain but shook her head. 'I don't know what you're supposed to be hiding. I don't know what you're talking about.'

It was all coincidence. That's what she was saying.

I couldn't prove it wasn't coincidence. But

the pieces dovetailed so well it was hard to believe the events hadn't been manufactured. 'That packet of money,' I said. 'That twenty-five thousand dollars. Where is it?'

Her voice came up in little cries. 'You can't touch that. I'm not going to show you. You'll take it.'

'Show me your purse.' I shoved her in the direction of the bedromm. 'Let's see what's inside that packet.'

She balked. 'You can't have that money. You'll steal it.'

'If I wanted to steal it, I'd have taken it last night.' I marched her to the bedroom. If she actually had the dough, her story would stand up. If she didn't, it would be a new ballgame and I'd give her a bad time for as long as it took to get the truth.

She stumbled ahead of me, fighting my grip, muttering curses. She didn't like it that women aren't as strong as men. At the door, she stared inside, jumped back and screamed. It sounded like an air-raid warning.

I pushed her aside to see what she'd seen. Outside the open windows, crouching on the fire escape, was a small man with an apelike face. Two nights ago that face had been shielded by a broad-brimmed fedora, but it was a face I didn't have to see well to remember. He was the leader of the gang that had kidnapped me.

He saw me as I saw him, and he was off.

I vaulted the bed to get to the window, but he was scrambling down the fire escape like the mouse down the clock. Then it was through the window and on to the fire escape after him, but he leaped the last ten feet and was around the corner and out the drive before I reached the second floor level. But the jump had slowed him. He was dragging a leg.

I took the same ten foot jump, like a damned fool, but I thought I could catch him. I rounded the corner, though, and he was gone. I slowed and took my gun out. There are rules against shooting people, including fleeing criminals, but self-defense is something else again and it was time I showed some brains. If he'd pulled a gun of his own and waited for me in the driveway, he'd have had a close-up target.

So I hugged a wall and went quickly because if he poked a gun muzzle around a corner up front, I didn't have any place to hide. However, when I reached the sidewalk, he was nowhere in sight. Either he'd skirted the building or ducked into a doorway.

I reholstered my gun. The sidewalk was empty of pedestrians, but there was passing traffic. It was a residential neighborhood and there was nothing much around, a few parked cars, trees by the kerb, a couple of little girls with doll carriages by the mailbox at the corner.

I tried the vestibules of Veronica's building and the one next door, but they were empty. I started up the alley again toward the back, and I don't know what for. It turned out not to be a good idea.

Before I was half-way there, a car came out of the yard and there wasn't room for both of us. The guy behind the wheel was ape-face. He recognized me and stepped on the gas.

I ran for the street like a triple crown winner and it was a damned good thing I didn't have a leg dragging. As it was, I took a headlong dive on to the pavement and the bumper of the car nicked my shoe as the car roared into the street, ran over the opposite kerb overshooting its turn, and side-swiped a parked car making a getaway. If some unlucky motorist had been coming along just then, he'd have been totaled. But ape-face was shot with luck. He straightened his wheels and took off, battered, but free.

I didn't get all of his license number either. It was two letters and the numbers 235.

CHAPTER ELEVEN

I rested on the sidewalk for a minute. I could have used six, but an old woman with a shopping cart was approaching and I was afraid she'd call an ambulance.

I climbed to my feet, brushed myself off and smiled at her. She sniffed the air for alcohol fumes and looked the other way.

It was back to Veronica's vestibule where I rang her bell and prepared to eat some crow. Ape-face's appearance on her fire escape put a complicating complexion on things. Just when I thought the answers were getting simple, they got murky. Just when I tied Veronica to the kidnappers, she turned out to be one of the victims.

She let me in, though I wouldn't have blamed her if she'd told me to stay away. This time she was waiting for me in the doorway, her robe neatly sashed, her face solemn and pale.

As for my face, the less said, the better. I had scrape marks on my chin from my sidewalk swan dive, I was mad at not getting the whole license plate number, I was scared because I'd almost been killed, and I was guilty because I hadn't believed Veronica needed protection. She needed it more than she knew.

'You didn't catch him?'

I said no and swore.

She sighed and closed the door behind us. 'You're bleeding. Your jacket's a mess. Are you all right?'

'I'm all right. I'm always all right.'

'Coffee? You'd like a cup of coffee?'

I said I'd have some coffee and locked her

bedroom windows while she poured. Her purse was on the bureau and I opened it, but there was no money packet inside. I don't know if it had been there when I dove out the window or not, but I didn't ask. If it was real money, she wasn't going to let me see it. If it was phony, she wasn't going to tell me.

The coffee was in two cups on the kitchen table. I took the chair at one end and she put the decanter back on the stove. 'That guy,' I said. 'You ever see him before?'

She nodded and got milk from the refrigerator, a pitcher from the cupboard. 'He's the one I told you about, the one I've seen lurking.'

'Can you identify him as one of the bank robbers your sister knew?'

Veronica produced a sugar bowl, filled the pitcher and put the milk back. 'I never saw those people. I don't know anything about them.' She sat down and looked at me. 'I can't be sure he's not just a burglar.'

'He's more than a burglar,' I told her, 'and I think he can give you some real trouble.'

She raised an eyebrow. 'Why?'

'I've run into him before. I don't know what he's after, but I think it's more than your twenty-five thousand dollars.'

'What do you mean? What would he want?'

'Tell me what you know about a guy named Arnold Saydecker.'

That made her blink. 'What are you talking

78

about?' She frowned. 'That's not his name—is it?'

I drank my coffee. 'No, that's not his name.'

'Well, what's the name mean?'

'Nothing—if you haven't heard of him.'

'I haven't.' She sipped from her cup. 'Do you think that man, whoever he was, was after my twenty-five thousand dollars?'

'He could have been—if that's all you've got that might interest him.'

'What's that mean?'

I got up. 'I don't know what that means. I don't know what I mean at the moment. If I do, I'll let you know. Thanks for the coffee, and watch yourself. Don't let that ape-faced guy get close to you.'

'Don't worry.'

'I do worry.' I went around and patted her on the shoulder. 'I have a feeling you know more than you're telling me and I don't think that's smart. In which case, I hope you'll be lucky.'

When I got to the other side of the counter, she said, 'What should I do if he calls again or leaves another message in my mailbox?'

'Call my office. I agree with you. If you're going to make a blackmail payment, you shouldn't do it alone.'

CHAPTER TWELVE

Eileen was rhythmically pounding the typewriter when I pushed open the reception room door. Without interrupting the flow of words from machine to paper, she said, 'You need a band-aid.'

I felt my chin, but the blood had dried. 'Just a scratch.'

'It seems that every time you come in you're carrying another wound.'

'Veronica has sharp teeth. Here's a little job for you. Call Solly at the Motor Vehicle Department I'd like the names and addresses of all car owners in this area with two letter license numbers followed by two-three-five.'

She wrote it down and looked up the MVD number in her address file.

'Just this area,' I repeated. 'This city and, if there aren't too many, a ten mile radius.'

'There might be a lot?'

'Six hundred and seventy-six possible combinations. I hope some of them live elsewhere.'

Eileen had an answer for me when I came back from lunch. There were four such registrations in the city and three more in surrounding towns. The names and addresses of the four city dwellers were on one piece of paper, the other three on another.

I thanked Eileen and she said, 'Thank Solly's computer. He said if they had to do it by hand, he'd tell you to come do it yourself.'

'Send him a bottle of brandy and charge it to office expenses.'

I sat down at my desk and looked over the list of four. One was a woman, one man had an address near the docks where the slums were. A second man had a car that didn't match the one ape-face was driving. The third man's car did. If I got a look at the car, I could verify it. And if I verified it, I was going to bounce the owner off the walls and get answers to all those questions Veronica kept ducking.

I rubbed my hands and fondled my gun in its holster, but I didn't let myself overindulge. I only had clues. I didn't have certainty.

Let's not waste time, however, in speculation. At half-past one, I was off to the races. I circled the address and returned the slip to Eileen. 'Next port of call,' I told her.

She noted the marking. 'Male, huh? And what kind of scars are you going to come back with this time?'

I told her it should be peaches and cream, not that I believed it, but she does tend to worry. I mean, she tries to hide it and all, makes with the jokes, pretends all she cares about is getting paid, that sort of thing. But she's got a maternal streak—most women

81

do—and she can't help but wonder whether little boys will remember to look up and down before they cross the street and take care of themselves, the way little boys like to pretend they don't do—because they want to bug their mothers. Freud will tell you where it all comes from. I'll tell you where I was going.

'Four-thirty,' I relayed to Eileen. 'No, make it five o'clock—quitting time. If you haven't heard from me by quitting time, you go into Phase Three.'

'Phase Three,' she repeated. 'Thank you. What's Phase Three?'

'Haven't I told you? That's where you dial 911 and holler for help.'

She scowled at the address and at me. 'I wish I knew when you're kidding,' she said. 'I'm only twenty-three and already I've found a gray hair.'

I leaned toward her thick mop. 'Show it to me.'

'I can't. It's in a formaldehyde bottle back home.'

I kissed the top of her head and she didn't balk. Sometimes she's skitterish and makes you keep your distance. Other times she wants to be petted and becomes quite docile. You have to know the mood—not her mood, *the* mood. Right now, *the* mood permitted touching and the kiss was accepted.

After that, it was out and away and I drove

for the fourth listed address with a certain amount of anticipation. And damned if, halfway there, I didn't get the smell of doughnuts passing an all-night diner. I paused long enough to circle the block three different ways, hoping to hear a sump pump. There was no such thing in the area, but that smell triggered memories. It was identical to what I'd encountered on that remembered ride two nights ago. With all due respect to the talk about not counting your chickens, I was starting to salivate.

The address of the house was fifteen minutes away. That was encouraging, but the house itself was the whole ballgame. It was a large, hidden structure, set back behind a long gravel drive, though the drive wasn't as long as it had seemed when I was lying on the floor of the limousine.

I didn't take the car in there, of course. I left it in the street beside the drive. Next I reconnoitered the surroundings, the low, wrought iron fence, the enormous shrubs which choked the view, the winding gravel roadway that curved and disappeared.

I hiked it, walking tall, but not flaunting myself. If I were seen, I wanted to be taken for a misguided salesman, not a thief.

And there, at the end, parked on the grass near the house, was the car that had almost wiped me out that morning. Bulls-eye, first try. Go to the head of the class, Simon Kaye.

A garage was under the trees and I tried that next, keeping out of sight of the house. There were side windows and despite the gloom of the interior, the limousine it housed looked very much like the car I'd taken the ride in Monday night. I couldn't see its backseat floor carpet, but I'd guess it was the one that left marks on my cheeks.

I was on target and there was only one question. At two thirty on a Wednesday afternoon, how many people were in the house? Three men had taken me for that ride. Was that the lot, or had others been left behind? I wanted to know how many I owed a beating to. If I couldn't get them all, I'd settle for the leader, the tough guy with the ape-face—give him enough for the lot of them and let him pass on his own kind of vengeance at his leisure.

I ducked low and crept along the side of the house, listening at the windows, hearing nothing. Ape-face's car was to hand. He should be inside. How many others were with him was the question.

There was one way to find out. I rang the bell, leaning on it heavily, and stood inside the screen door, gun in hand. I waited five seconds and rang again, insistently. I'd made sure no one inside had seen me and nobody would know who had come acalling.

The door opened. It wasn't opened so much as it was yanked. The guy on the other side was mad. He didn't like loud doorbells in the afternoon and he was going to—

That was, until he saw my gun. He'd been so bugged by the doorbell, he hadn't stopped to think who might be ringing it. It was ape-face, who else? He was wearing a knitted shirt, summer slacks, and he wasn't armed. The poor, stupid sap.

I shoved my gun in his gut and pulled him up close. He'd looked pretty scary back in Monmouth Park in the middle of the night, especially with a gun, two helpers, and that low-brimmed hat he was wearing. He was an ominous figure on Veronica's fire escape, and scary as hell behind the wheel of his car, trying to run me down in the alley.

But up against my chest, his shirtfront in my hand, his eyes agape and six inches lower than mine, he looked like a baby rabbit.

I hit him with the heel of the gun and he screamed. I mean, he really screamed. I didn't hit him as hard as I got hit, but I hit him in the right place. I broke his cheekbone and blood came through the wound. I turned the gun around as a hammer and hit him in the mouth. It smashed his lips and knocked out two of his teeth. He went against the far wall and sat down. I wasn't stunning him, only hurting him, so his eyes were wide and clear and he got the full effect of the pain.

He tried to speak, but had to stop to spit out the teeth first. 'Whaddaya want?' he cried out. 'I ain't done nuthin.'

I closed in on him fast. I wanted him as a shield if he had friends around. I jerked him to his feet. 'Who else is here?'

He blubbered.

I hit his broken cheek and he whimpered. 'Who else?'

'N-n-nobody.'

'Who else?' I raked the gun against his bleeding lips.

'I swear.'

I gave him the gun butt in the belly. He gagged and his knees sagged. I had to hold him up. 'If there's any trouble., you get it first. You understand?'

'There's nobody here. I swear it.'

Blood was running down his chin and throat, staining the knitted shirt. More blood streamed down his cheek and soaked into the loose collar. I liked the look of it. He wouldn't come my way again for a long time.

I straightened him and marched him to a couch, keeping him between me and the hall to the rest of the house. I threw him on it and got down beside him on one knee. I whacked him three more times because I felt mean. I wanted to punish him, but I made sure I didn't knock him cold.

'Now we're going to talk,' I said. 'You're going to talk. You're going to babble like a Goddam brook, or else you're going to die. Do you like the sound of that?'

86

He was groggy now, but not so groggy he didn't know what he was up against. 'Don't hit me again,' he begged. 'Please don't hit me.'

I clubbed him and started blood flowing from his scalp. 'Don't remind me,' I warned. 'Now talk. Start by telling me about Monday night. Tell me what you thought I was carrying when you pulled the snatch.'

'Monday?' He cried some more. 'I don't know what you're talking about, honest to God. I never set eyes on you before.'

'Maybe it was the bag over my head, huh? Maybe that's why you don't recognize me?' I raised the gun butt again. 'Here go the rest of the teeth.'

'No, no!' He twisted his face away.

'And something else you're going to tell me is, what you want from Veronica Dean.'

He kept his face turned. 'I don't know any Veronica Dean.'

I clubbed him and his cheek split wider. 'You're going to talk before I'm through. You're going to tell me everything I want to know. It's up to you how tough you want to make it on yourself.'

'I can't stand the pain,' he moaned in answer. Already his cheek was swelling up like a balloon and turning violent shades of black, blue and purple. His mashed mouth was ballooning too and he was developing a lisp.

'You don't know what pain is. I've only just started on you.'

'Please. Don't hit me again. I'll die.'

'What'd you pick me up for the other night?'

'It was a mistake. I swear. It was a mistake.'

'It sure as hell was. Who was I supposed to be?'

'I don't know him. We were supposed to meet him. You came instead.'

'Meet him? You mean waylay him?'

'Yeah, yeah, that's it.'

'And do what to him?'

He swallowed and groaned. 'Rob him.'

'Of what?'

Ape-face licked swollen lips. 'Money. He was supposed to be—'

I hit him where he hurt and he screamed. 'Play it again, Sam. You weren't searching me for money.'

Heavy sobs came out of his chest and it was hard to understand him. 'It was a piece of paper.'

'That sounds more like it. Tell me about the piece of paper.'

'I don't know about the piece of paper. I never saw it.'

'Don't play cute or I'll hit you again. What was on the paper?'

It really hurt him to have to tell. 'It was a map.'

'A map of what?'

'I don't know. I was only supposed to get it.'

'Who had the map? Who were you supposed to take it away from?'

He cringed lest I give him another belt. 'You. We thought you had it. We didn't know the guy. We only knew he was supposed to come along the edge of the park.'

'Who searched my condominium?'

He cowered further. 'I did,' he said, weeping. 'I didn't steal anything. I didn't touch anything. I was only looking for the map. We thought you might have hidden it before we got to you, and picked it up later.'

'Who's the "We"?'

'Me and my gang.'

'And your boss.'

'No, I'm the boss.'

'Who told you I was the wrong man? Who told you to take me back to where you dropped me? Who told you to search my condo while I was playing bodyguard to Veronica Dean? How did you know I would be away all last night?'

'Nobody. Please. I took a chance.'

I threatened him with the gun butt. 'You're taking a bigger chance right now. You know Veronica Dean. You know that she's being blackmailed for twenty-five grand and you knew she hired me for protection when she made the pay-off. What were you doing on her fire escape? Did you think you could snatch the dough?'

'No, no,' he shrieked. 'I don't know anything about the blackmail. I didn't make those calls.'

'You're lying. It's a complex scheme, but you know all the parts. Somebody set me up and somebody's setting her up and you're going to tell me who and you're going to tell me why.' I reminded him what I could do if he didn't by shoving the gun butt under his nose. I'd've liked knocking out a few more of his teeth, but I was afraid then he really wouldn't be able to talk.

'Oh God,' he wailed, 'what am I gonna do? I can't tell you. They'll kill me.' He half turned his face toward me, fear in his eyes—fear of my response. At the same time, he was terrified of the alternative.

'They'll kill you?' I snorted at him. 'What do you think I'm going to do to you?'

'I'll be dead. They'll really kill me. Honest to God.'

'You can get away from them,' I told him. 'You can't get away from me. They don't have to know you told me, but you're damned well going to.'

'They'll know. They'll know.'

As I say, I'd placed us on the couch so that I could cover the hall to the rest of the house. What I didn't cover, and what my back was to, was the coat closet near the front door.

That hiding spot hadn't occurred to me until I heard a faint creak and, simultaneously, ape-face's eyes looked over my shoulder and widened.

I swung around. The closet door was ajar, not wide enough for me to see inside, but enough to reveal the gun muzzle pointed our way.

The gun went off even as I looked. I don't know for whom the bullet was meant, except that I didn't receive the impact. Even as it fired again, I was dragging ape-face across me as a shield, and trying to switch my revolver from a club to firing position.

The gun in the closet kept firing. The bullets might have been meant for ape-face, but I knew some had to be aimed at me. No assassin would overlook the guy who could shoot back.

I thought my luck would hold out, that I could draw a bead and blast the closet before I got hit. It didn't work out that way. I took a wallop in the head that felt like a beanball and I was out cold almost before I felt the pain.

CHAPTER TWELVE

My first throught was, 'Damned if Jack McGuire isn't right. There *is* a God, there is a Heaven, and there must also be a Hell, and where am I?' My second thought was that I'd only made the fire-and-brimstone segment of after-life. I hurt too much to be in Heaven. I was hot, too. That went with the territory.

I opened my eyes and the surroundings were too earthlike for death. I was in the same large room I last remembered. I could tell by the ceiling and the upper sections of wallpaper. When I lowered my eyes, I saw familiar furniture. Just beside me, in fact, was the couch upon which I'd battered an ape-faced man whose name I didn't know. I'd sure as hell had it in for him, though, and I couldn't, at the moment, remember why. Let it pass. If I were really still alive, it would come back to me.

But I'd been shot. Someone had been hiding in the coat closet and let me beat up on ape-face until—? Until some certain moment when he'd decided enough was enough and he opened fire intending to silence us both.

In the process, I'd taken a bullet in the head, or I thought I had. I slowly put a hand to the spot. It was sore and tender, but there was no hole. That meant, as best I could reckon, I was still alive.

I got some of the fuzz out of my mind and lifted myself to my elbows for a better look at life. I was on the floor of the large room and ape-face was lying across me, pinning me down. The blood on his battered lip had dried, the flow from his scalp wounds had stilled. The broken cheek and the big wounds there were wet, but they'd stopped bleeding. Fresh blood lay moist in the gashes.

The reason blood no longer ran out of him was because his heart had stopped pumping. Ape-face was dead. From the red holes on his upper torso and the stains on his knitted shirt, he must have died the moment the gun started firing from the closet.

What do you call that? Irony? Someone else had been with him when I banged on the door—a trusted friend. And the trusted friend had taken refuge in the closet while ape-face dealt with the unwanted visitor. And when the visitor dealt with ape-face instead, the trusted friend didn't come to the rescue, he decided on death to us both.

Putting two and two together as best I could, the unknown party hiding in the closet was ape-face's boss. Who else wouldn't want his identity revealed? Who else would see me as a threat?

I'd think about that later. The important thing was to find out about myself. Sitting full up, I discovered I suffered from no more rigors than a sharp pain above my left temple. The rest of me was in better than average shape.

It took a bit of work to shove the dead man off my lap and pull myself to my feet. The sore area around my temple consisted of a swelling, a surface wound, and dried blood.

I'd been flattened by a bullet which had creased my skull. It had ricochetted instead of penetrating. Lucky me. A fraction of an inch is what life is all about. Life and death, that is. But that's Jack McGuire's worry. The important thing was that I could function and prepare myself for Fate's next pitch.

And what would that be? In the distance was the sound of police sirens. Could they be coming here? If they were, I wasn't going to play host.

First off was a quick search of the body. I didn't evaluate what I found, just stuffed it into my pockets. And not a moment too soon. The sirens were close now, coming in the drive. What the hell was bringing the cops this soon after a murder?

I did a fast canvas of the coat closet. It contained nothing but coats. There were no expended cartridges on the floor to indicate that an automatic had been used. A revolver then?

I went out the back door when the squad cars screeched to a stop in front. While their occupants coped with the problem of entry, I wove my way around to my heap via a properly circuitous route.

After that it was turn the key in the ignition and get the hell away. I hadn't learned what I'd wanted to, but I'd kept out of trouble and I'd kept from being killed. The latter benefit was no fault of mine, however.

My next haven was my condo, from which I phoned Eileen of my safe arrival, and said I'd see her in the morning.

After that, I sat down with the stuff I'd taken from ape-face's body. He'd carried a gun, but I left that for the cops. What they got on a ballistics check might be interesting.

Of my own haul, only the wallet was of any value. Well, maybe the keychain might mean something, if I could find the locks the keys fitted. The wallet contained half a dozen hundred dollar bills, half as many fifties, and an assortment of lesser denominations. He looked ready to pay cash for his pleasures, which went with the fact he carried no credit cards. Maybe he couldn't remember his parole number.

He did have a driver's license, though. It was his. It bore his picture for proof. A name went with the picture: Joseph Tanner. The address was the site of his murder.

The prize was a note scribbled in a flowing hand, giving the name Arnold Saydecker and his address.

CHAPTER FOURTEEN

I phoned Veronica just after five saying I wanted to see her. That's one fickle woman. Half the time she clings to me, the other half she doesn't want me dirtying her carpets. This was one of the latter times. I was to get lost, she didn't need me, the blackmailer hadn't called, life was a bowl of cherries.

'The blackmailer's what I want to see you about,' I said, pressing on, undaunted.

Neither him nor my unexcelled masculine charm were tickling her fancy right now. She announced with unflattering abruptness that she had another engagement and if I had something to tell her, I could do it over the phone. The implication of her tone further suggested that, if that were my intent, I be quick about it.

Such treatment stabs my male chauvinist heart. It also piques my curiosity. True, the message that Tanner was dead could be delivered in phone language, but I wanted to tell it to her face to face so I could watch her eyes. Moreover, I wanted to witness her response to the slip of paper bearing Arnold Saydecker's name and address. Would she recognize the writing? She claimed she didn't know the name, but I take a lot of convincing. Women have been known to lie. Men have done it too. In short, I was after all kinds of goodies and here she was, going all female on me with that, 'I've got another engagement' bit.

I gave her the 'cool' approach, played the 'disarm with charm' game. I gave her an affable tone. I said, 'Maybe another time,' hung up, and was inside her vestibule door, ringing her bell, in less than twenty minutes.

It appeared that Veronica really did have another engagement and thought I was it. I didn't have to announce on the intercom that I was delivering a package. She buzzed the lock release and let me in.

The elevator was waiting but when I got off at her floor, she wasn't posing against the doorframe in welcome. This time, the door was closed and she already had a guest. Through the panels came the shrill sounds of bitter female voices. Being a good detective, I drew close and listened.

'When I'm paying the dough, you're going to do what you're told,' came the dulcet tones of Veronica's voice.

The other woman uttered a lower decibel four-letter word.

'Pick up your bag and get out. I told you you aren't staying here.'

'But I have no money.'

'You got here, didn't you? Where'd you get that money, or shouldn't I ask?'

'I cashed in my equipment for a one-way fare.'

'You should've bought a round-trip. You aren't staying in this town.'

'I have to stay. I don't have the carfare to get out. Do you want to give me the carfare, sister dear?'

'I'll tell you what I want to give you. All

97

right, here's a fifty. And I don't want to hear from you again east of Chicago. You understand?'

There was a mocking laugh from the other girl. 'It must be a very heavy date you've got. Are you afraid to introduce me, dear sister? Do you keep me in school because I'm younger and prettier than you are, or because you wish I was dead?'

'Don't tempt me,' Veronica snapped. 'School will do. Chicago will do. Anyplace will do that's a thousand miles away from here.'

'Sure it will,' the sister said. 'Because you're walking the only good road and you want all the other traffic to keep off.'

'Goodbye, and go as far as that fifty bucks will take you or you won't get any more.'

Sister gave Veronica a four-letter parting remark and opened the door.

What she wasn't expecting was to find me on the other side, and her first reaction was a double-take. Her second was to smile.

She was the girl whose picture graced Veronica's bureau, but the picture didn't do her justice. In real life she was a kind of minor league Veronica Dean, not as tall, not as knowing, not as old, not as authoritative. Her face was a little wider, and so were her eyes. The eyes were a pastel green with brown multiflecks. They were the kind of eyes that made me realize I'd never identified

98

Veronica's—at least not for more than colour. This girl was not as slender. She was a little more buxom, a little more bosomy, a bit heavier on the scales, and caring less.

Her smile was bright and welcoming and reminded me that I'd rarely seen Veronica smile. She was carrying a suitcase, wearing a blue linen dress with a white collar which gave her a fresh-from-Sunday School look the smile belied. 'Well,' she said, 'no wonder Veronica wanted to get rid of me. I would too.'

Then Veronica discovered I was in her doorway. 'Where the hell did you come from?' she exploded in raw fury. 'How did you get in here?'

Samantha's eyes grew wide with interest. 'Oh, you *aren't* her date?'

Samantha was cute, but Veronica was my baby. 'I told you I wanted to see you,' I said to her and walked in.

Samantha, intrigued, said, 'I want to listen,' and tried to follow.

Me, Veronica couldn't stop. Samantha, she could. She gave the girl a shove back into the hall and slammed the door in her face.

I said, 'You're so pretty when you're angry.'

She turned on me, wishing she could give me the heave-ho too. Since she couldn't, she menaced me with snarls and threatened my life. There was a quality about her as dangerous as a cornered ocelot and she meant me to know it.

I laughed instead. 'You're good,' I said. 'You're hard as nails. Maybe you think if you act tough enough and angry enough, I'll go away. Is that what you think?'

That defanged her. She shifted gears and tried patience. 'Look, I told you, I have to go out.'

'That's right, I remember. Who's the guy? What're you going to see him about?'

She chose not to answer that, circling instead to sit down on the couch. Her purse was there and she put it in her lap. She bowed her head and stared down at her shoes, her lowcut dress showing a lot of cleavage. I don't think, however, she knew or cared. She'd found out that I could resist her and she didn't work useless tricks. 'All right,' she said, resignedly, 'what is it you want?'

The girl was a chameleon. 'I have to say,' I told her, regarding her with shameless interest, 'for a girl who, twenty-four hours ago, desperately needed my help, you act as if the world's in your pocket. What's happened to you since yesterday?'

She gazed up with innocent eyes. I noticed them now. They were slate and opaque. 'He hasn't called,' she answered. 'The blackmailer hasn't called. I think maybe he won't.'

'Why? Doesn't he want that twenty-five

thousand dollars any more?'

'I think maybe you frightened him away.'

'Who? The man on the fire escape?'

She nodded. 'Yes, isn't he the blackmailer?'

I closed in and stood over her. 'The man on the fire escape was named Joseph Tanner. What's that mean to you?'

If I hoped she'd betray something, she didn't. She only shook her head.

I gave her his address next, with the same result. She looked away, but not before her eyes betrayed the sharp light of curiosity. 'How did you find all this out?'

I ignored that and kept on with my own line of questionig. 'He lived a long way from here. He went to a lot of trouble to come up your fire escape. There's a reason for his making the trip and I want to know what it is.'

I must have touched something for her eyes flashed fire. 'If I knew, I'd tell you. Do you think I like creeps on my fire escape? Do you think I like hiring detectives to help me pay off blackmailers?'

That made me laugh again. 'I just saw you and your sister in action. Do you still want me to believe you'd pay twenty-five thousand dollars to protect her?'

'How my sister and I act together has nothing to do with what we'd do for each other.'

101

'Save it.' I sat down with her so my eyes were on a level with hers, level and unavoidable. 'You've been telling me nothing but lies since yesterday afternoon. Now we're going to change all that.'

I took her wrist and a panic came into her eyes. 'You're crazy,' she cried in a voice that had a touch of shriek in it. 'What do you want with me? I haven't done anything to you. I only hired you to make a pay-off, now you accuse me of doing things to you. What have I done? What am I supposed to have done?'

She made it sound good. That was the trouble. I didn't believe her, but I couldn't disprove her. 'What's the map about?' I asked.

'What map?'

She was struggling in my grip and her eyes were still worried, but they didn't flicker. The map question didn't elicit a tip-off that she held secret knowledge.

I let her go and showed her the paper with Saydecker's address on it. It was my last weapon. 'Tell me whose handwriting that is.'

She wasn't frightened, now that I'd let her go. A girl can really feel helpless in the grip of a man. It can provoke fear out of proportion to the threat. 'Arnold Saydecker,' she said, reading the name slowly. She shook her head. 'No, I don't know him.' Her eyes were serious and convincing. 'I don't know the writing either.' She kept on with the serious, cross-my-heart approach. 'Where did you get this? Can't you please tell me what you think I've done, what this is all about?'

The door buzzer rang. The party she was expecting had come. It made her jump and for a moment, fear shaded her eyes. Then she was on her feet, muttering that she had to go, hurrying around the corner to the intercom phone. This time she didn't press the release button, she said, instead, into the mouthpiece, that she'd be right down.

I was waiting beside her when she turned away. I took her face in one hand and tilted it up my way. 'I'm going to give you a word of warning, Veronica.' I was very serious for I wanted her to understand. 'Something's going on that involves that guy Tanner, and the guy named Arnold Saydecker. It has to do with a map and it's not a pleasant business because both of them have been murdered. They've messed with me as well, and I'm going to mess back. I think you know more about it than you're telling. If you do, I'm going to come back for you and you're going to be in real trouble. If you don't know anything about it, you're also in real trouble because there are other people who think you do.'

I gave her one last chance. 'Do you want to level with me, or watch me go?'

She said, with her face still in my hand, her slate eyes wide, 'I don't know anything about

103

anything. I swear it.'

I released her, patted her cheek and gave her a grim smile. 'Good luck, sweetheart. One way or another, I think you're going to need it.'

She was in the doorway watching, when I went to the elevator.

CHAPTER FIFTEEN

A large limousine was waiting at the kerb when I got outside, its engine purring and a chauffeur behind the wheel. Ogling it, standing in the sunshine beside the door, suitcase at her side, was Veronica's ousted sibling, 'I didn't think you'd be long,' she said. 'I'm Samantha, Veronica's younger sister. I'm sure she's never told you about me.'

'I've heard the name,' I said and told her mine.

'Are you a beau of hers?'

'I'm a private detective, doing a little investigating.'

She drew closer. 'Investigate me. I'm fun to investigate.'

'Come along. That's what I had in mind.'

She giggled, but tarried. 'That car,' she said. 'Do you suppose that's waiting for Veronica?'

'I would guess.' It was a car like the one that had kidnapped me, but it wasn't the same. The plates were different, the look was different.

'Do you have a car?'

'Right over there. Three cars back.' I picked up her suitcase.

She put a hand on my arm. 'I want to follow her.'

'Veronica?'

Samantha nodded, her eyes glistening. She looked at the luxurious car again. 'I want to see where she goes.'

'So do I.'

That sold her. We got into my heap together, I chucking her suitcase in the back. I said, 'Tell me about yourself. Then you can tell me about Veronica.'

'There's nothing to tell,' Samantha said. 'Veronica tries to bury me in schools.' She laughed. 'Veronica says it's to turn me into a lady. The real reason is she's afraid of me. You want to know something else? I've spent my last day in her damned schools. I got myself thrown out. You know why?'

'Robbing banks?'

That made her giggle. 'Not for that. Not for flunking, either.'

I clucked. 'You mean you don't rob banks?'

'That's crude. Not that I'm against money. But there are easier ways to get it.' Her eyes

105

danced with sudden excitement. 'Look at that.'

It was Veronica coming out the door and the chauffeur leaping to hand her into the comfort and luxury of the limousine's rear seat. Samantha drooled. 'That's living. Can you imagine having a rich man send a big car like that around to pick you up, with a chauffeur too? And she's only six years older than I am.' She turned my way. 'I'm going to get that too,' she said, and made a quick evaluation of my clothes. 'Do detectives make much money?'

'Not enough for cars like that.'

'Damn,' she said. 'What kind of cars then?'

I told her my heap was four years old and it was all I had.

'Wife and children eat up all you make?'

The limousine started up and glided smoothly from the kerb. I said, 'You ask too many questions. Start answering some.'

'Look, they're going away. Aren't you going to follow?'

'Yes.'

'Well, when? They're going to get away.'

'No they aren't.'

I pulled from the kerb when they'd gone a block, programming my departure to the traffic, and came up a car behind at the first light. Samantha said, 'This is exciting.'

The limo took by-pass roads to escape center city traffic and picked up Welsh

Avenue, a broad thoroughfare heading north, flanked by large homes and small lawns. Traffic moved fast and was broadly spaced so I tarried well back.

Beside me, Samantha was quiet and staring. This was not the time to discuss her history. She was too concerned with finding out where big sister was going and what kind of a man Veronica had hooked. She thought Veronica's life was the heights, but she hadn't seen Veronica's look of fear when the buzzer sounded. It was the wealth that stirred Samantha's curiosity, it was the fear that spurred mine.

A police siren sounded behind us and the rear view mirror reflected flashing lights. A patrol car came up fast, drew even and didn't go past. Two cops were in it, and the one in the passenger seat was waving me over.

I cursed and pointed ahead and shouted through the open window, 'I'm on a case. I've got business!'

The cop motioned again and he had a gun in his hand.

That was enough of that. I pulled over.

Samantha, crestfallen, watched the limousine disappear in the distance. 'What's this all about?' she grumbled.

'Who knows?' I kept both hands on the wheel in plain sight. If the police approach a motorist with drawn guns it doesn't mean it's a traffic violation, it means they think he's armed and dangerous.

Their car pulled to a stop behind mine and the armed cop got out. He kept his gun pointed at the ground, but it was ready. He came to my window and looked in. 'Simon Kaye?'

'That's right.'

'You'll get out of the car please.'

'Get out? What the hell for?'

'You'll get out and put your hands on the roof of the car.' He gestured with his gun.

'What are you doing, arresting me?'

'Let's say we have orders to bring you in. Young lady, you'll get out too, please.'

CHAPTER SIXTEEN

Sergeant of detectives Don Lasky was running the show at headquarters that afternoon. I had a feeling he would be. He came out of the office when the patrolmen marched Samantha and me through the doors. The one who had searched me put my gun and wallet on the desk.

I said to Lasky, 'What is it this time, jay walking?'

He didn't answer, just turned to the others and said, 'Put him under the lights.'

The squad car driver had Samantha in tow. he said, 'This young lady was with him.'

'Yeah,' Lasky answered. 'I know. I'll talk to her in my office.'

I was taken downstairs to a small, unadorned room which contained a ground level window near the top, a square table, a few chairs, and a couple of Kleig lights. The cops who'd brought me in went out again and it was two other men who were in charge now. One was Harry Dunkin, a paunchy veteran whom I knew from my own days on the force. I said, 'What the hell's bugging Lasky besides the itch to throw his weight around?'

'I don't know,' Harry said. 'If I did, I wouldn't talk about it. I think he thinks you've done something illegal.'

'Am I under arrest?'

'I don't know. I didn't know the word was out for you till they brought you in. What've you been up to, Simon?'

'Damned if I know.'

Harry lighted a cigarette for himself, then, as an afterthought, offered his pack. I shook my head. 'Thanks anyway.'

'I thought you smoked.'

'I've given it up, more or less.'

'I wish I could.' he picked up a tin ashtray from the table.

The other cop, younger and new to me, rested one foot on a chair seat and remained silent. Harry paced and smoked, I sat. We spent twenty minutes like that.

Then Lasky, with two goons for armor, came in, all business. He turned on the Kleig lights, adjusted them so I could feel their heat, and said. 'You want to tell us about it?'

'About what?'

'A man named Joseph Tanner.'

'Aren't you going to read me my rights?' With the lights in my face, he, Harry and the unknown cop were shadows. Even so, I could sense his irritation. 'All right,' he said, knowing he was in front of witnesses. He rattled off the legend that's printed on cards to be read to or given to prisoners apprising them of their right to remain silent, to ask to have a lawyer present, and the rest that has been devised to cope with the Miranda Decision. He had it memorized and rattled it off like playing the Minute Waltz in 50 seconds.

I said I understood my rights and now I wanted to know what the hell made them think I knew somebody named Joseph Tanner.

'You gonna deny you were in his house this afternoon?'

'Whatever gave you that idea?'

'The girl you're with, Samantha Dean. What's she to you?'

'Look, Lasky,' I said, 'I don't like it here. I don't like being picked up by your cops and brought in any time you feel like scaring civilians. If you want any information out of

110

me, bring in my lawyer.'

Lasky grew soothing. 'Well, now, we wouldn't do that unless we arrested you. Do you want us to arrest you?'

'Do what you damned well please.'

'I thought we could talk a little first, have sort of an unofficial friendly conversation—avoid all the legal folderol. That way, when we're through, you can just go on about your business without any complications—like having to hold you in jail until your lawyer gets a writ and that sort of thing.'

'Oh, Christ,' I complained. 'Knock it off, will you? You're making me vomit.'

'Of course, If you want to be hard-nosed about it, we can be hard-nosed too. We can give you a helluva rough time if that's the game you want to play. If you want to answer a few simple questions, you can straighten us out on a few matters and you'll be helping us cops solve some problems.'

'What kind of problems?'

'Like who killed Joe Tanner.'

I laughed. 'What the hell would make you think I'd know who killed Joe Tanner? I don't even know who he is.'

'He's a petty crook—well, not too petty. He's got a couple of armed robbery convictions and a couple of other things he didn't get convicted for. He's no loss to the world. Whoever bumped him off was doing us a favor.'

'You're looking for the killer so you can give him a medal?'

'Well, hell, Simon, you know we have to find the killer whether we're glad he did the job or not. But I don't think anybody killing the likes of Joe Tanner would get more than a slap on the wrist by any judge in this area.'

'And you have some idea that I'd know who it is?'

'Something like that.'

'Something more like the idea that maybe I did it myself?'

'He wouldn't be the first guy you've killed.'

'He's not the first, nor even second. He's not on the list.'

'You were visiting him this afternoon, though, and suddenly, he shows up dead—and it's right after you left. Only right after you left.'

'Coincidence,' I said.

'What'd you fight with him about?'

'I told you. I don't know the guy.'

'Then what were you doing at his house?'

'And where the hell did you get that piece of information? Who told you I was at his house?'

'Well, now, you don't think we're going to identify our sources, do you?'

I couldn't help thinking about it, wondering who, besides Eileen, knew I'd gone there. The person hiding in the closet—Joe Tanner's murderer—knew, of course. The odds favored the murderer as the one fingering me.

I was trying to keep my face blank but those lights are bright and the cops were watching me closely, hunting for signs that I knew what they were talking about.

'You were there,' Lasky said, to cement it. 'I want you to tell us what happened. Who shot him?'

'You know, you interest me,' I said. 'Somebody tells you I was at such and such a place at such and such a time. It's a hot spot. It's going to make you drool. So you lap it up and come chasing me on the taxpayers' money, and wrestle me down to your dungeon and try to beat a confession out of me. I thought you were a smart cop, Lasky. I thought, when you got a tip, you might take the trouble to check it out first.'

'The tip was from a reliable source, Kaye. A *very* reliable source.'

I laughed. 'From the way you tell it, your informant *saw* me in Joe Tanner's house. If your informant was there, then he must have seen who killed Joe Tanner. Or maybe he's the killer himself? You ever think of that, Lasky? Maybe the source of your information is the murderer.'

That was more than he could stand. He stepped in and whipped the heel of his fist at the side of my jaw, all the while mumbling gutturals that weren't words, but reflected his condition.

He didn't catch the side of my jaw. It was hard to see against the lights, but the guidance I needed was reflected by the shadows. I threw up my arms and ducked my head. At the same time, I planted my feet against the floor, bracing myself in the opposite direction, so that when I countered, my weight would be behind my move.

I swung a blind fist with everything I had. If I'd missed, I'd have dislocated my shoulder. If I'd hit a solid, material object, I would have shattered my hand. I did neither. I made contact with flesh and bone. There was enough give to save the hand, enough substance to save the shoulder. Sometimes my fist have broken bone, but I didn't feel the fatal sag this time. The bone bent, but did not break.

There was no chance for the pleasure of assessment or an enjoyment of the sensation. I was seized and yanked and struck, and I felt pain in a number of different places all at once.

I'd come out of my chair to throw my haymaker and there was something about the speed and roughness with which I was manhandled that told me I'd struck gold, that the defense corps was frantic, trying to make up for the havoc I'd wrought. I didn't care. They could beat me into limbo. I'd plastered Don Lasky and flattened him cold.

Lasky's two goons were pinning me in the chair and hammering me in frustration, but all I did was laugh. They could have killed me and I'd have laughed.

CHAPTER SEVENTEEN

By the time Lasky revived and was able to sit up, I was barely conscious. I think his flickering eyelids saved me from extermination. The goons were going at me like dogs after a wounded elk and they'd have had me out of there in not much longer, except for Lasky coming around. Then they got on their knees to him, propped him, and tried to plant him so he could see what a battered mess they'd made of me.

I didn't feel like laughing, but I laughed anyway. Even if Lasky didn't hurt as much as I did, he was enjoying it less.

Lasky didn't look at me and he shoved at his boys. 'Get away,' he snarled. 'Get me some water.'

Harry came between Lasky and me, bending near to my face. 'You shouldn't have done that,' he muttered. 'Lasky's not going to forget it.'

'It's done,' I muttered back. 'I want my lawyer. Call my lawyer, Harry. I want him to see—' I had to stop because my mind was fogging. I might have taken more punishment than I realized. I tried to make my head stand still, but Harry was gone.

Then Lasky was on his feet. The lights were a baleful glare and I couldn't see well. He was still shadowy, but I knew the substance was there. I'd felt it when I hit him and I knew exactly where to strike the shadow to hit him again. They weren't holding me now. They thought the only direction I could move was down to the floor. They wanted to see me fall. I braced my feet instead. I don't know if Lasky caught it, but his minions did because they came into the glare and pinioned my arms to the chair. They were offering Lasky *carte blanche*.

I gathered my wits together enough to say out loud, 'Call my lawyer. I want my lawyer to see me, right here.' I didn't know if I was making sense or not, but I repeated it. It was my only weapon. 'I want my lawyer right now. I want to talk to my lawyer.'

Lasky approached. As best I could make out, he was rubbing his jaw and needed support. 'You think you can play fast and loose,' he muttered. 'You wait and see.'

He went away and a door closed.

I sat, fumbling with my brain, squinting my eyes against the glare. The damned Kleig lights never leave you alone. How can you sort out your thoughts, make plans, care for your future? I was too battered and nerveless to function efficiently. All I could do was clamp my teeth and wait for my lawyer. He would look after me. Not for love, but for money. That's what he was paid to do.

The lights went out and I felt almost cold. For a couple of moments it seemed like midnight and then the gloom of the underground room came into view. A cop I didn't know helped me to my feet. I didn't get a good look at him and I couldn't read his badge number, but his arms felt strong, and, at the same time, gentle.

'You really pasted him,' he said. 'I don't think you were smart, but it was beautiful.'

'Thanks. Do I know you?'

'No, and don't quote me.'

'I wouldn't. Is someone calling my lawyer?'

'We'll see upstairs. Can you climb the stairs?'

I said, 'If I hold on to the wall for a second and get my bearings.' He let me lean against the whitewashed brick and the scenery came into focus. After a bit, I said, 'Okay, I'm ambulatory.' I proved it by going the rest of the way without help.

Topside, across from the desk, Samantha Dean was sitting alone on the wooden benches. Her hair was brushed and neat, her dress wasn't wrinkled, her purse was tidy and in her lap. She looked as if Lasky had served her tea.

An uneasy query crossed her face at sight

of me, however. They hadn't been serving me tea and it showed. My tie was twisted, I was bruised, mussed and wobbly.

The cop who was my seeing-eye guide led me to the desk. Another patrolman was behind it and there was no sign of Lasky. They passed words and the desk man, who was in shirt-sleeves, said no, my lawyer hadn't been called, did I want a phone?

I shook my head and rubbed my sore jaw. My body had taken most of the punishment but my face had some touchy spots too. 'Let it go,' I said.

The patrolman leaned over the desk to hand me a manila envelope and a receipt. 'Sign that.'

I opened the envelope. My gun was there and my wallet. I holstered the gun and went through every bit of the wallet. Nobody had slipped a fiver out of it or anything else it contained. I know because I know everything I carry, every bill in my wallet, every coin in my pocket. It's a habit.

I put away the wallet and signed the receipt. The cop who thought I threw a beautiful punch said, 'Sorry to detain you. You can go now.' His badge number was 471 and he wore a blue name-tag over it which said, 'Mike Delaney.'

I turned and Samantha came over. 'Gee, what did they do to you?' She straightened my tie and smoothed my clothes.

118

'My arm-wrestled in the basement. What did they do to you?'

She told me as we went out together, she holding my arm. Lasky had questioned her in his office, wanting to know how long she'd known me, what I'd been doing that afternoon, what she knew about me. 'I told him I didn't know you at all, only your name and that you were a private detective my sister had hired.'

The fresh air was reviving and, by the time we reached my car, I thought I could drive. In fact, I was functioning well enough to last till bedtime, if bedtime wasn't too late. I didn't intend that it should be. Right now my watch read nearly eight o'clock and I gave myself a couple more hours. Strangely enough, despite the beating, I was hungry.

Samantha slammed the passenger door and I asked, 'What are your plans?'

'I don't have any,' she said with a twinkle.

She was bright-eyed and ready for life. I wasn't. 'That fifty dollars your sister gave you won't last long.'

'I don't think it'd last out the night.'

'Do you want to go back there?'

'No.'

I shifted gears. 'I'm hungry. Let's go eat and then I'll drop you at a hotel.'

We had veal Parmigiana and chicken Cacciatore at a small Italian restaurant I know of where the food is good, the prices reasonable, and where I wouldn't get stared at because I was bruised and rumpled. They know me there. I'm known in a lot of places in this town, in fact. Detectives circulate, especially bachelor detectives.

Over the meal and the wine I got what I wanted out of Samantha. Unlike her sister, she didn't try to lie to me. She didn't know how, for one thing. For another, she was too busy trying to vamp me.

The bank robbery bit? It was a total fiction. Samantha didn't even know how to drive, let alone handle getaway cars. The rest of the stories were also out of Veronica's imagination—Samantha and drugs, Samantha and bad company, Samantha and crime. They were nothing but lies apparently concocted to keep me out of my condo for the night.

That's not to say that Samantha, at seventeen, was any angel. Her cute face and buxom figure no more spelled holiness than her blue linen dress with the white collar meant she went to Sunday School. But her proclivities at age seventeen were along the lines of sex rather than crime and Veronica kept her in school not to reform her but to confine her. Samantha was proud to tell me that she laid virtually the whole male segment of the senior class before graduation, as a for-instance. In fact, she confessed that her ambition was to lay them all, but one guy wouldn't break down and another she couldn't find. But two misses in fifty chances wasn't a bad score and she was ready to take a bow.

One guy talked, though, and the lid almost blew off. There were some anxious moments as to whether or not she and the male population of the senior class (with the two male exceptions) would graduate. One way or another, a lot of cement was laid over a lot of cracks and graduation went through as scheduled, nobody in charge of blowing whistles being any the wiser. It was after that that Veronica started embalming her in far-off girls' schools.

But drugs and bank-robbing? That made Samantha laugh with a bitter note. 'My dear sister,' she said. 'She really loves me. What would she make up something like that for?'

'That's my question.'

As for Veronica paying a blackmailer to keep Samantha out of jail? That was even funnier. 'Jail?' Samantha snorted. 'Hell, she'd win both ways if she could put me in jail. It would pen me up better than school and it wouldn't cost her a thing.' Samantha stopped eating and only toyed with her food at thoughts like that.

'Why'd you come here to her?'

'I had no other place to go. She holds the purse strings.'

As for the story of her visit, she got to Veronica's in mid-afternoon but no one was home. So she sat on her suitcase and waited. When Veronica finally arrived and found her, she threw a fit. They didn't stop fighting until I rang the bell.

'Know anything about that date she had—the guy with the limousine?'

'Only that someone called her in the middle of all the argument. That's when she decided to give me the heave-ho. I was trying to talk myself into her guest room and I thought I was winning. Then she got the call and that was that. She had to go out, she told me, and I was going to go out too.' Samantha's eyes gleamed. 'Now that I've seen the car that got her, I'm not surprised. If I had a guy like that on my string, I wouldn't want a pretty kid sister in my life either.' Samantha sighed. 'I wonder how she does it.'

We left the restaurant at half-past nine and my next mission was to find a parking place for my passenger. I gave her a spiel about the Rivoli Hotel. It was her best bet, I said. The rooms were small and the TV was only black and white, but the prices were the best for its class. The sheets might be frayed, but they were clean, and there weren't any cockroaches the last I'd heard. As an added plus, I said, I knew the manager and that was worth a 10 per cent reduction.

Samantha made faces through all of this and at the end said what I knew she was going to say, and what I was trying to keep her from saying: 'Don't you have a bed in your place?'

The issue had to be joined. 'Yes,' I said, 'but I don't take in boarders.'

'I don't have to be a boarder.'

'I know.'

'I don't even have to dirty clean sheets.'

'I heard you.'

She put a hand on my arm. 'Perhaps we could make an arrangement?'

I put her hand on her knee. 'The answer is no.'

'I can't afford even a cheap hotel.'

'You can afford this one.'

'For one night, maybe two nights. Then what do I do, walk the streets?'

I was tired and battered. I wanted to get to bed fast. Staying up made me cross. Still, I couldn't help laughing. Twenty-two is a great age. Disappointment is unheard of. There's nothing you can't achieve. I remember it well. It's even better if you're female and beautiful. She'd been dumped onto the sidewalk by her sister, but that was no tragedy to Samantha, only the trigger that opened her bag of tricks. From there she'd managed a ride in the direction she wanted to go. The ride was aborted, but that was of small consequence. She'd followed it up with a free dinner, now she was trying to negotiate free lodgings. True, she expected to have to produce a little sex in return, but she didn't like sleeping alone to begin with. Thus, she was trying to win on two fronts simultaneously. And, given a foothold like that, by morning she'd be entrenched in my domicile and in a week, she'd be charging me rent. I didn't stay a bachelor thirty years by playing that game.

And that 'walk the streets' bit? That was to inspire guilt feelings. If she had to become a prostitute, it would be my fault.

So, as I say, I had to laugh, she was very young and the bloom still hadn't left her cheeks, but she'd been around more than she showed. No wonder Veronica threw her out. Girls like her were a real threat.

Samantha got huffy at my amusement and, when I pulled up in front of the Rivoli, said, 'What are you laughing at? What do you think's so damned funny?'

'You.' I reached across to open the door for her. 'I don't really think you'll have to walk the streets,' I told her. 'Not with all your talent.'

She gave me a cold eye, but she dutifully slid off the seat and retrieved her suitcase from the back. She leaned in the window, looking very serious, and very beautiful. 'Thanks for the dinner,' she said. 'And thanks for everything else you've done—and haven't done.'

She turned on her heel, picked up the suitcase, and headed for the hotel doors, her hips swinging. I watched her, and she knew I watched. There was an extra fillip in her stride.

I swung around and aimed the heap for my condo, but I didn't think I'd seen the last of Samantha.

CHAPTER EIGHTEEN

It was quarter-past twelve and I hadn't been asleep more than an hour when the doorbell rang. If there's one thing worse than a phone ringing in the middle of the night, it's a doorbell ringing in the middle of the night. I came to an elbow swearing and the swearing wasn't because I was angry, but because I was worried. Remember telegrams? It's the same thing. Telegrams when you weren't having a birthday, phone calls and doorbells that wake you up, all spell bad news.

I got into robe and slippers, wondering what this bad news was about, turned on lights and padded downstairs through the kitchen and foyer. I switched on the porch light and opened the chained door to its limit, and the bad news was Samantha Dean, her eyes agleam. Did I say I hadn't seen the last of her? I thought I'd have to wait at least until dawn. But no. That was her forte. She was more unpredictable than the rest. That made her the most dangerous.

125

She was carrying only a purse. Her suitcase wasn't in view. That meant it was only a visit? She wasn't attempting a belated assault on my condo stronghold—maybe? I risked it and unhitched the chain instead of closing the door. 'What now?'

In she came, clutching my arms as if she'd discovered the wheel and was preparing me to spread the word. 'Simon, you'd never guess!'

She didn't wait for me to make a guess, but walked on through the condo. 'Oh, isn't this nice!' That was in reference to the sunken living room lying in darkness two steps down. She swung around to assess the dining nook and kitchen. 'So spacious, but tasteful and compact.' She smiled my way. 'I wish I had a condo.'

'You'll probably have one by next week.'

She came to me. 'Listen, you'll never guess. You're a detective? Well, I'm a detective too. Would you like to hire me?'

'What did you detect, that your hotel has no rooms?'

She clutched my arms again. 'Do you know that car we tried to follow this afternoon?'

'Yes.' I detached myself and put water on the stove. Keep busy and she couldn't climb on me.

She approached from behind and her breasts brushed the back of my pajamas, just contact, not pressure. 'I found out where it came from.'

I got out cups and saucers, putting them on the table. She followed and resumed contact. 'You wanted to find out, and I found out for you.' She ran her nails down my back. 'Aren't I good?'

I turned around, almost into her. 'You're great. Who's the guy?'

'Oh,' she said, backing off, but not far, 'I couldn't find that out. I only found out where he lives. I've got his address if you want it.'

'I want it.'

She recited it and it meant nothing. The street belonged to the town and the locale lay in the limousine district, but that was all. If Samantha was as new in town as she claimed, the address was probably valid. On the other hand, Samantha was into strategics worthy of three-dimensional chess.

Nevertheless, I nodded and wrote the address on my shopping pad. When I turned around, she wasn't there. Instead, her voice floated down the staircase. 'Hey, it's nice up here.'

Suitcase or no suitcase, I should have closed the door on her. She was as hard to get rid of as lice.

I sighed and turned off the stove, but didn't put away the coffee cups. I'd set them back on the shelves after I pitched her down the storm porch steps. First things first, and I climbed the carpeted staircase to fetch her.

There's two bedrooms up there with a

127

connecting bath. The master bedroom overlooks the woodlands, the guest room, the condo area. She was in the master bedroom, of course. I had a feeling she'd have her dress off and be fumbling with her bra hooks, trying to beat me under the covers, daring me to pry her out.

Not so. Instead, she was going through the wallet I'd taken out of Joe Tanner's pocket. It and the rest of what I'd cleaned from his body were on top of my dresser in open view. I hadn't been expecting company.

'Well, well,' she said. 'This is the man who was killed this afternoon? This is the man the police hauled us down to headquarters to question us about—the man you were talking to Veronica about?'

I took the wallet away from her and put it back on the bureau. 'Be a nice little girl, or papa is going to knock you through that window over there.'

She grinned. Big tough guys didn't frighten her one bit. She had perched herself in the catbird seat and knew it. For a twenty-two year old, she had thirty years' worth of savvy.

She sat down on the bed, hands on her knees, and cocked her head. 'Aren't you going to say hello?'

'I'm saying goodbye.'

Her smile grew. 'Don't you want to know how I found out where Veronica's boyfriend lives?'

128

'Sure,' I said. 'I've got nothing better to do.'

'After you dropped me at that stinking hotel, I decided you could go you-know where.' She rose and toured the room, stopping at the window and its black view of the nighttime forest. 'Say, you wouldn't have a joint, would you?'

I shook my head. 'Try the hotel.'

'You're mean. I have the feeling you're trying to get rid of me.'

'Do you want me to spell it out?'

She sat against the sill. 'I haven't finished my story, sir. You wouldn't want me to go without telling you my story.'

'By all means, finish your story.'

'Deciding that I didn't want any part of that crumby hotel, I thought it would be worth my while to go back and see what my dear sister was doing. She loves me, you know. She keeps me buried alive she loves me so much.'

'Get on with the story. I want to go to sleep.'

'I took a cab over, but she wasn't back yet. So I hung around and, lo and behold, here comes the limousine, back with Veronica. I knew it was the same limousine even before she got out of it. You know how?'

'No.'

'It had the same license plate. I noticed what the plate said back this afternoon. I'll bet you didn't notice what the plate number was.'

'Of course not. Detectives never notice things like that.'

'So Veronica got out and do you know what I did while that was happening?' She grinned at her perspicacity. 'I hailed a cab at the stand near by. I'll bet you didn't notice there's a taxi stand near the door to the hotel.'

I limited myself to a grunt this time.

'I'd already worked out my plan of attack. I knew it'd be useless approaching Veronica, so my goal was to follow the limousine and I had one of the cab drivers warned that I might be needing his services.' She laughed with the pleasure of conquest. 'Do you know what? He passed up a fare—let the next cabbie take it—just so he'd be on hand when I needed him.'

'Cabbies are all heart.'

'And when the limousine pulled away after dropping Veronica, my cabbie followed him, and he went where I told you. What do you think of that?'

'What time was this?'

'Aha, you *are* interested. I thought you'd be.'

'Which is why, as soon as you saw where the limousine went, you had your cabbie rush you over here so you could tell me what a good detective you are?'

'Gee, you're smart.'

130

'And right now, he's waiting down below to rush you back to that hotel you hate so much.'

'Now you aren't so smart. Now you don't sound like a detective at all. You don't really think a cabbie on the make is going to watch his meter tick while the girl shacks up with another guy, do you?'

'No, but he might want to pick her up when she comes out on her ear.'

'If you're going to throw me out on my ear, do you mind if I take Joe Tanner's wallet along for a keepsake?'

I laughed. 'What kind of school did Veronica send you to? Fagin's Finishing School?'

'A girl who's left on her own a lot learns how to take care of herself.'

'You're not just surviving, you're amplifying.'

'I presume that's a compliment.' Samantha moved from the window, my way. 'So I guess I proved to you I'm a valuable ally. Now that you know who Veronica's boyfriend is, what are you going to do?'

'Where's your suitcase?'

'I checked it at that fleabag hotel you took me to. God, do you have lousy taste. But I didn't check myself there. I don't have a room.'

'And you don't have a cab.'

She shook her head.

131

'But you do have fifty dollars Veronica gave you.'

'Oh, no. I spent that on you—tracking down that limousine.'

'I've heard a lot of lines in my time, but yours gets the iron cross for arrogant effrontery.' I took her by the arm. 'Your sister could learn from you. I'll tell her to look you up. Write me when you know where you're going to stay.'

I marched her to the head of the stairs, but no further. The doorbell rang loud and long and, down below, there was thumping and beating on the condo door.

CHAPTER NINETEEN

Samantha turned to me, wide-eyed and uneasy. 'What's that?'

'Cops,' I told her.

'Cops? I didn't call the cops, honest. Why do you say cops?'

'Because only cops come at you that way.'

I left her at the head of the stairs, went down to the front door, slipped the chain back on, and opened up.

Yes, it was cops. And, as I expected, it was the worst of the cops, Detective Sergeant Don Lasky himself.

He was in front and he showed hardly a

132

sign of the blow I'd flattened him with a few hours earlier. My face was bruised and puffy but all he had was a slight swelling along the jaw line. He sneered when my features appeared in the opening, but not because I looked like raw liver on the hoof. It was my red-bloodedness he was after. 'Don't tell me you're actually home? You aren't out screwing some broad?'

He's great with one-liners. I said, 'What's your role tonight, picking up prostitutes?'

'Picking up murderers.' He thrust a paper through the opening at me. 'Read that and weep. And get the damned chain off this door or we're gonna break it down.'

I looked at the paper in the dim light. It was a search warrant. The cops had been given the legal right to go through my apartment, poke into everything I owned, and take whatever they wanted to away with them, giving me a receipt in the process.

That really blows my cool. It's an invasion of privacy—a legal invasion, but an invasion all the same. It's like being burglarized, coming home and finding your rooms ransacked. Other people may be able to handle such things but I relish my privacy and guard it jealously.

When I saw the warrant, I wanted to blast every one of the cops out there on the storm porch. Especially, I'd've liked to blast Lasky, shoot the grin off his face with a load of

133

buckshot.

Unfortunately, there are laws, and what I had to do was try not to let Lasky know he'd really got to me this time. I gritted my teeth but forced a smile and tried to appear relaxed. I unchained the door, affected a 'take your time, be my guest' attitude, and opened up.

No sooner was the chain off than in they came like a tidal wave. I almost got bowled over by the influx. Lasky was third in line, preceded by two ardent TPF guys (meaning they belonged to the Tactical Police Force, which blankets an area in a hunt for clues), and followed by a third.

Lasky dallied to gloat. 'It took us a while,' he said, as he followed me into the kitchen, 'but we finally got a judge to see it our way.'

'See what your way?'

'Well, well,' he said, observing the setting on the kitchen table while his lackeys switched on lights and roamed the living room. 'Cups for two, eh?' He picked one up and turned it under the light. 'Unused. The party hasn't started yet.' He grinned maliciously. 'You expecting a late guest?'

'Knock it off before I knock you off. What're you doing here? Don't you have anything better to do than harass innocent citizens?'

'Innocent?' He couldn't help sneering again. 'Simon Kaye innocent?' He almost spat in my face. 'What could you be innocent

134

about?'

I doubled a fist. It was the way to treat him even if he was Authority. 'Where do you want it, you sonuvabitch? If you want a lawsuit on your hands, I've got a lawyer who eats creeps like you for breakfast.'

Lasky leaned close to show me his teeth. 'Tough guy. Well, you want to know why we're here? I'll tell you why. There's a guy at the morgue right now—guy named Joseph Tanner. You haven't forgotten Joseph Tanner have you?'

'We went through all that down in your basement this afternoon. You didn't have anything to hold me on then and you don't now. Why the hell aren't you home in bed?'

Lasky only laughed. He'd been smoking cigars and his breath would fumigate a flophouse. 'I'll tell you, Simon,' he exclaimed with the glee of certainty. 'When we searched the body of Joseph Tanner, it was clean. There was no ID, no coins, keys, notepads, nothing in his pockets to give him away. In fact, we couldn't swear that it was Joseph Tanner until we got a check of his fingerprints back from Washington.

'So the question is, what happened to the things a guy like Joe Tanner would normally carry in his pockets—wallets, keys, change, and all that?'

The sonuvabitch had me nailed. I'd forgotten about Tanner's belongings up on

135

the bureau. Dammit, I hadn't covered my tracks and now I was really in the soup. The search would reveal that I possessed everything that was missing from Joe's pockets. It would be back to the police station and another grilling, and there's no telling how much my lawyer could do for me now.

Lasky gloated. 'What's the matter, Kaye? You look a little ill. You wouldn't be guilty of robbery, would you? Robbery with a little murder thrown in?'

In spots like this, the one thing you never do is throw in the towel. You tough it out to the end. ('What's that? Joe's wallet is on my dresser? I wonder how it got there. It must be a plant!') Never admit anything to anyone but your lawyer.

I shrugged and yawned. 'It's been a long day and I have to get up in the morning. Search as long as you want, but if anything's missing when you're through, I'll see you in court.'

I started past him for the stairs.

He didn't let me get away with it, of course. 'Don't be in a hurry, Kaye,' he said, shoving his bulk in my path. 'I'm sure you won't mind keeping me company until my men check the upstairs.' He summoned one of them, a guy named Paulson, and said, 'Mr Kaye's pretty anxious to go up to his bedroom. Case it but good.'

Paulson took the steps two at a time and

was no sooner out of sight than there was a high-pitched shriek and a very feminine voice saying, 'How dare you come in here? Who the hell do you think you are?' followed by a mumbled male response.

Lasky grinned wolfishly. 'Surprise, surprise,' he said, and he hurried up the stairs like he'd won the lottery.

Needless to say, I was on his heels.

Samantha was sitting on the side of my mussed-up bed dressed in a pair of my pajamas, the sleeves and pants legs rolled up high enough to let her hands and feet show. It hung on her like a tent but, even so, she looked cute as hell. As for her clothes, they lay tossed in the easy chair. She hadn't had time to fold them, but that was okay too. It gave the effect that she hadn't wanted to take the time.

Meanwhile, Paulson knew his duty and was doing it. He ignored the girl and was prowling the room, probing the contents of drawers, checking under cushions, under Samantha's tossed clothing, the underside of the furniture, getting down on his knees to look under the bed and dresser.

Lasky was more interested in my guest. 'Well, well, Miss Samantha Dean. I thought you told me this afternoon you didn't know this man.' He looked from her to me and his face grew ugly. Had he been taken for a ride? 'I think,' he went on, advancing closer, 'you and me had better have another talk.'

I said to her, 'Don't tell him anything. Don't even answer him.'

'Sez you,' Lasky told me. He went on to the girl, 'Maybe you'd like to come back downtown with us. We can give you a good time down there.'

'He can't take you out of here without arresting you,' I told her. 'If he does that, refuse to talk until my lawyer arrives.'

Samantha was a good girl. She compressed her lips and stared steadfastly at the detective.

Lasky didn't like that. He looked around the room himself. Samantha's purse was in the chair with her clothes. He picked it up before I could stop him. With his back to me, he opened it and all I could do was tell him what he already knew, that the search warrant didn't entitle him to go through any property but mine. It didn't matter to him that nothing he found there would be admissible in court. He was after information and if he found anything useful, he'd manage—or the lawyers would manage—the necessary tricks and ploys to make it admissible.

What he was groping for and hoping for was Joe Tanner's wallet, but the only wallet in the bag was her own. It was when he was trying to go through that that I yanked Lasky around, using my foot to trip him, and threw him to the floor.

Paulson rushed at me, and the other TPF

138

officer, just coming up the stairs, came from the other side.

Meanwhile, I'd rescued Samantha's purse and leaped with it back against the wall. 'Nobody touches this purse,' I said, holding it out like a shield, 'or I'll knock heads together. This is private property belonging to the lady, not to me.' I pointed at Lasky, now on his knees, holding a wrist he thought he'd sprained. 'He knows that. But he insists on ransacking her private property. You two, both of you, and the girl, are witnesses.'

Lasky got up, but his cradling of his wrist and pretense at pain were for effect. He'd found the information he was seeking—that Joe Tanner's wallet wasn't hidden in her purse. Because of that, he was less assertive and less willing to take me on in a battle over her wallet. 'The bed,' he said, pointing. 'Pull the bed apart.'

Samanatha rose and moved beside me while the two men dutifully pulled off the covers, lifted the mattress and checked the pillows.

They had no luck and since the rest of their search was failing, Lasky felt ever more out of place. It appeared all he'd done was stumble into the middle of a love-nest and all his work and all the overtime had been expended following a wrong star. He was so sure I'd been in on Joe Tanner's killing! I wished I knew who or what had convinced him.

They left at last, the TPF men wordlessly,

Lasky sullen. For once he didn't have a threat to toss over his shoulder when I closed the door.

I went back to the bedroom. Samantha had remade the bed and was sitting on the edge of it where the covers had been neatly turned down. It was the same position in which Paulson had found her.

'You're all right,' I admitted. 'You're more than a little okay.'

'I heard him down in the kitchen and I knew I had to do something.'

'Where'd you hide everything?' I looked. 'Not the pajama pocket?'

Samantha nodded and pulled out a handkerchief and, after that, the keys and change which the handkerchief had silenced. She was grinning with pride.

'And the wallet?'

She pulled up the pajama top and revealed it folded over the drawstrings tied tight around her slender waist.

I drew her to her feet and kissed her.

She melted and she wasn't supposed to. We were both in pajamas. I let her go and she smiled. 'Now do I get to stay here tonight?'

What could I say? She hadn't checked into the hotel. I was just as glad. It was too late and too much trouble to take her there anyway. 'All right. You can have the guest room.'

She slipped under the covers instead. 'Here

140

would be just fine.' She pulled the wallet from her waistband and held it up. 'I don't need to keep this any longer, do I?'

I don't know that she'd really have betrayed me to the police if I didn't do as she said, but I wasn't in the mood right then to put her to the test.

'Be my guest,' I said, but I wondered, as I climbed in beside her whether I could get rid of her before she ate me up.

CHAPTER TWENTY

'Hey, Simon, how much money do you have?'

'None.'

'You've got a nice place here. You can't tell me it's free.'

'I don't have money the way you're talking about money. I told you, private detectives don't make money.'

Samantha was lying under the sheet and I was getting dressed. It was warm in the room, even with the windows open, but I'd just taken a cold shower and was cool. Samantha's pajamas were on the floor beside the bed where she'd kicked them during the night. She didn't wear nightclothes in hot weather, she explained.

Samantha stretched bare arms above her

head. 'I wish you had money,' she said. 'If you only had money, you'd be perfect.'

To tell the truth, Samantha was a doll, but I was glad I didn't have the money she wanted. She was the kind of girl who could smother a guy, emasculate him, bloodsuck him. I tied my tie in the mirror and looked at her reflection. No question, she was beautiful. And she knew her way around a bed as Jack Nicklaus knows his way around a golf course. That was the thing about her. She wasn't in the learning stage. It was like catching a tiger by the tail.

She caught my eye in the mirror and I said, 'I don't need money to be perfect. I'm perfect already.'

Samantha ignored that. She looked out the window and luxuriated, stretching and twisting under the sheet. 'What about blackmail?' she said, catching me in the mirror again.

I slipped the tie knot into place and turned around. 'What about blackmail?'

'You've got wealthy clients, haven't you? They confide in you. They tell you all kinds of secrets. I'll bet if you utilized your resources, you could make tons of money.'

'It's not that easy.'

'It's not that hard. Look at me. I've got you blackmailed. I can tell the police you've got Joe Tanner's wallet. You're in a vice. I made you bunk me with you against your will. I

142

made you make love to me. I can make you do anything I want.'

'Sorry, sister. The police aren't going to find Tanner's wallet any more. That piece of blackmail has run its course.'

She shook her head. 'I don't think so. You see, I can not only tell them you had it, I can tell them what was in it.' She gave me her rapacious smile. 'I wasn't born yesterday.'

'You weren't born last year either.' I patted her on the head. 'You're a cute little trick, Samantha. If you're lucky, you'll live to a ripe old age—like, maybe, twenty-five.'

She caught my hand and held it. 'We'd make a good pair, you and I.'

I took my hand away. 'Except I don't have money.'

'We could make tons of it—you and I together.'

'I think you can make tons of it all by yourself.'

I prepared breakfast and she came padding down the stairs in the buff. 'You got some coffee I can have?'

'First you have to put on some clothes.'

She didn't like that. She wanted us to make tons of money together and she was working on the together part. 'It's hot,' she complained sulkily.

'It's morning and I have to go to work.'

She picked up a piece of toast. 'I'll get dressed, but you have to pour me some coffee

143

first.'

'After.'

'You forget I know you've got Joe Tanner's wallet.'

'You forget I don't give a damn what you know.'

We glared at each other. She put the toast down and went back up the stairs. I didn't see her again before I left.

After checking into the office and cleaning up the routine odds and ends, I took myself over to the Hall of Records. It was another hot day with only a scattering of cumulus in the sky. The Hall of Records, which is the home of all the city's files, papers, documents and what-have-you, is a large granite, nineteenth century temple, built back when cities had pride in their identity and wanted the populace to have pride in them too. The halls are wide, the ceilings high, the place an oven in summer, even with air-conditioning, the heating bill enormous in the winter. 1888 is the date on the cornerstone and it was a different world back then.

What I was after was the tax-assessor's office. That's where the identity and assessed value of every piece of property in town is kept—who owns it, how big it is, what shape it is, and all the rest. Joe Tanner had been killed in a certain, large, isolated house on a certain street in town and I had a hunch the house wasn't his. I wanted to know the name

144

of the owner.

The name of the owner was someone called Newman Olds. That meant nothing to me. The address, however, did. Surprise, surprise. It was the address Samantha had given me last night. It was the estate to which she'd followed the limousine.

I tooled my heap back to the office pondering the meaning of that interesting discovery. Joe Tanner had been on Veronica Dean's fire escape yesterday morning. Joe Tanner had been killed in a house owned by Newman Olds that afternoon. Newman Olds' chauffeur had picked Veronica up late that afternoon and brought her home again late that night.

Veronica claimed she didn't know Tanner, only that he was hanging around. She claimed she was afraid of him. Veronica also told lies.

Joe Tanner had searched my condo and my office while Veronica kept me away on a phony blackmail story. Joe said he was looking for a map. Never mind what he was after, the point is that he knew I wasn't going to be home that night. How did he know? Was he in cahoots with Veronica? Or was this Newman Olds back of what was going on? Maybe Tanner and Veronica were both puppets on Olds' string?

★   ★   ★

I walked into the office at quarter of twelve and Eileen wasn't behind her desk. The outer door was unlocked, but the reception room was empty and the door to my inner office was closed. That made me stop. If Eileen had gone in there, the door would have been open. If she'd gone to lunch, the outside door would have been locked.

Besides, the place was too silent. The stillness was so heavy and waiting and ominous you could hear Eileen's philodendron grow. I left the hall door open and drew my gun. Next I tiptoed to my office door and stood beside the jamb. Even putting my ear close, I could detect no sound. But someone was there. I knew it as surely as I breathed. At least two people were behind that door—maybe more. One of them was Eileen. She was being very still. I wondered what they'd done to her.

I twisted the knob with my left hand as softly as I could. When the knob was turned to the stop, I put my foot against the panels, then let fly.

The door kicked wide and banged against the hat tree in the corner. As it swung, the room came into view. A guy with a gun was sitting on the radiator by the windows. Another guy, pinning Eileen in my chair, holding a hairy hand over her mouth, was crouched behind my desk. It was almost subliminal but as I saw the men, I knew their faces. They were bent-nose and golf-cap, the other two who, with Joe Tanner, had kidnapped me last Monday night.

Bent-nose, on the radiator, leaped to his feet. The trouble was, he'd been careless. He'd been sitting there, dangling his leg, holding the gun in his lap, figuring I'd enter the reception room full of innocence, move slowly, make noise, give him plenty of warning. He thought he had plenty of time to get set.

That was his first mistake. I came in with my gun at the ready. His was not. What he should have done was drop it and put up his hands. Instead, he tried to recoup and get off a shot. That was his second mistake—the fatal one. He gave me no choice.

I fired twice, one-two, half a second apart, the bullets hitting half an inch apart. They caught him dead center in the upper body and I'd have to guess that at least one of them got his heart. I couldn't tell because the impact knocked him back and he went right out through the open window.

That left golf-cap and I swung his way. He'd been caught napping too, like bent-nose-out-the-window, but he had time to draw, and he held Eileen as a shield.

I had no shot, but he sure as hell did. Eileen kicked and struggled and spoiled his aim, but he got one off before I could jump back out of the doorway. I poked an eye and a muzzle around the frame and said, 'Drop it and put your hands up.'

He was behind my chair and behind Eileen, with his left arm around her throat. He poked his gun over the top of the chair, close by her ear, and I ducked as another bullet whistled. He was going to be tough. He had a gun, he had a hostage, and he didn't bluff. Nor could Eileen help the cause. She was pinned in place and couldn't get at him, while he could peer at me from beside her face. I had as little to shoot at as he did and a miss would be fatal.

'Okay, Kaye,' he said. 'Throw your gun in the door or your secretary gets it.' He turned his gun and held it to Eileen's head. She didn't say anything. Through all of this she hadn't broken silence; she hadn't screamed, she hadn't cried. Now her face was very white and her eyes very large. She was holding still.

I hesitated, but I knew he wasn't bluffing. He said it again. 'Throw in your gun and come in here with your hands up. You think I won't let your girlfriend have it? I got nothing to lose. It's gonna be you or her, punk. Take your choice.'

'Leave her alone,' I said. 'Let her go and I'll throw in my gun.'

'Throw it in first, Kaye. I'm gonna give you ten.' He said a slow, 'One.'

I let him get to seven, studying him, evaluating him. He wasn't giving me clues

148

and I couldn't risk Eileen. That's when I pitched the gun on to the carpet and said, 'All right, let her go.'

He beckoned. 'In here, big boy, with your hands up high.'

He was using his gun to motion me and Eileen spoke up for the first time. 'Don't do it, Simon,' she cried out. 'He'll kill you.'

He tightened the arm around her throat, cutting off her wind, and he pressed the muzzle against her temple. 'Cute, huh? How'd you like a bullet through your brains?'

I came through the door fast. 'You touch a hair on her head—'

That brought his gun around, all right. He wasn't threatening her any more, but he damned near gave it to me. I'm not sure why he didn't except, perhaps, he thought he might have trouble getting away.

'Hands on your head,' he said and it was a half shriek. He was afraid I wouldn't stop in time and he'd have to plug me on the spot.

I skidded to a halt and did what he said. I could only see Eileen peripherally for my attention was on that big black muzzle looking ready to open up some messy holes in my stomach.

He moved from the desk then, keeping the gun steady, dragging Eileen by the arm. He detoured to the radiator, over by the window, and took a quick glance out to see what had happened to his friend. He didn't dare lean far enough and long enough to see anything, for he was sweating. He was in a big-time spot with no support. He was afraid of me, even when the weapons were on his side, and a hostage too. He gestured me over near the desk. I was in his way and he wanted to get around me.

I was very obliging. I didn't want to disturb him. My eyes, though, were on Eileen. She was thinking and it made me nervous. I was afraid she might grab for his gun.

That would be a good ploy if he were in a last ditch situation and the game was lost in any event. But there was no point in her trying for his gun if I couldn't get to mine. And mine was lying on the carpet, closer to him than to me. In fact, it was at his feet and he was debating bending down for it. If he could stuff it in his pocket, I couldn't get it. On the other hand, to hold the girl with one hand, his own gun in the other, squat and try for another gun—that might give a desperate man a fancied opportunity. And, as I say, he was afraid of me.

He decided to leave the gun where it was. He kept his own trained on me, he kept Eileen gripped by the arm, and he backed to the doorway. That gave him his escape route and it might also give him his best chance to kill me and get away.

And don't get the idea that they hadn't

come there to kill me. It was an ambush, the same as in the park Monday night, except that this time they weren't after the wrong man. This time, Simon Kaye was the target.

My options were narrow. In fact, they were non-existent. I could duck behind the customer's chair, but that didn't stop bullets. I could dive out of the window *à la* bent-nose, but golf-cap could nail me with at least two slugs en route. In addition, he had captive Eileen in tow to make me behave. Under those conditions, he could fire when ready and all I could do was wish I wore bullet-proof vests.

Out behind the guy, the door to the hall was open, as I'd left it. And now, through it, strode two matched thugs who looked like they picked their teeth with ten-penny nails. They were new in the game for I hadn't seen them before, but in my business you get a lot of strange looking specimens showing up. Private detectives get almost as much variety in clientele as psychiatrists.

They were bulky and wore jackets and brimmed, plastic-mesh hats, and they came in like Tweedle-Dum and Tweedle-Dee. They pushed the door wide and stopped simultaneously, like mirror images, at finding themselves facing a slowly retreating man holding a girl and a gun, while I stood with my hands raised in the room beyond.

The two thickset newcomers reached, as

151

one, inside their jackets for shoulder holsters and Eileen's captor, sensing something amiss, turned at the same time.

He saw the men going for their guns and did the only thing he could. He yanked Eileen in front of him and rammed his gun in her back. 'Get outta my way,' he yelled, 'or I'll shoot.'

The newcomers froze and looked at each other, their hands inside their lapels. The guy with the gun was panicky now. He didn't know what to do except hold on to his hostage.

But he, like bent-nose, had made a mistake. He let me out of his sight. I dove for my gun.

He heard me and turned back. His gun came around and, at the same time, Eileen clawed for his face and kicked for his groin.

He fired at me and missed. It was close enough to singe my scalp, but it was still a miss. That was Eileen's doing.

My first slug caught the shoulder of his gun arm. I aimed wide to make sure I didn't hit the fighting Eileen. It didn't cripple his trigger finger, but it did knock him off balance. He half staggered toward the reception desk and Eileen was fast after his gun. He knocked her away, which was his second mistake, and the fatal one, for it gave me a clean shot. I killed him with a bullet in the chest, halfway between his diaphragm and his collarbone. This time there was no question about its hitting the heart.

He crashed on to his back beside Eileen's desk and by the time he hit the floor, I was on my feet, tucking my gun in the holster, catching Eileen. She was too feisty to fall, but she looked rocky and I thought this was a time she might like having her hand held.

She let me hold her tight, and she even held me tight, but it was only for a moment. The two new guys were watching. They'd taken their hands out of their jackets now and eyed us and the body on the floor as if this had been take thirteen of a horror movie they were producing. Except that they didn't know the cast of characters. Tweedle-Dum said, 'You're Kaye?'

'Yeah.' I asked Eileen how she was feeling and she answered by disengaging herself.

'Who's he?' Tweedle-Dum jerked his thumb at the body on the floor.

'I'm about to find out,' I told him, and knelt to do a search. I said to Eileen, 'Better get on the phone to the police. This is going to shoot the rest of the day.'

The two squat men with their hats and coats and heavy features, both with mustaches, stood over me in silence while I lifted the dead man's wallet. 'Name's Luke Benzi,' I announced and Eileen wrote it down while waiting for the cops to come on the line. I recited the address and she jotted that, then started announcing herself to the desk sergeant at headquarters.

Luke's wallet had some money in it but not an assassin's pay. Not even an advance on the job. The pay-off would have come, I guess, when he brought in my scalp. Well, he didn't deserve an advance. He and bent-nose were a couple of amateurs. Had they been pros, I'd have been dead by now.

It was the newcomers who were the pros. They stood by, watching me go over the body and they listened to Eileen reporting the shootings to the police.

'There was another, went out the window?' Tweedle-Dee said when Eileen hung up.

I said yes and went through the rest of the dead man's pockets, putting the contents on the desk while waiting for the two men to make their move. They were in no hurry. They watched Eileen get herself a cup of water from the cooler to calm her nerves. They picked up Luke's wallet and went through it after I did, and they watched Eileen resume her seat. She was nervous about them. She knew they carried guns and she didn't know what it was about. She eyed them as they went through Luke's wallet and noted that I hadn't put up a squawk.

When I was finished and stood up, was when she asked the men how she could help them. They gave her scarcely a glance. 'We want to talk to him,' one said, indicating me.

The other said, 'Out in the hall.'

She chewed a lip, looked at me and said nothing. I told her to record the items on the desk and make sure the police knew they came from the dead man's pockets. When I went out in the hall with the men, she gave me a parting glance that had a sense of longing in it. She was saying she thought I needed help, but she couldn't give me any. I knew I needed it too, but I didn't want to quarrel with the two gentlemen who had saved my life, not in front of her. She hadn't been hurt yet, but if another fight broke out, she would be.

In the hall, Tweedle-Dum stood a little behind me, Tweedle-Dee a little in front. Tweedle-Dee held out his hand. 'Let's have the gun.'

I didn't argue. I very carefully slid it from my shoulder holster and handed it to him, butt first.

'We're gonna go for a little ride,' he told me, and jerked a thumb. 'You were smart not to make a fuss in there.'

'Yeah,' said the other. 'Saved us from having to hurt that cute little girl.'

They led me to the elevator.

CHAPTER TWENTY-ONE

The ride was in the same limousine which had taken Veronica away the preceding afternoon, with the same chauffeur behind the wheel. If Samantha and the tax assessor had their facts right, we were en route to the abode of a man named Newman Olds, who owned the house that had become Joe Tanner's final resting place. What the hell, Olds didn't have to send a couple of his hoods after me, I'd've been going to see him this afternoon anyway.

The Olds estate was out of town—not far out, but enough for the guy to spread himself over a few hundred acres without having to buy up and knock down a dozen office buildings. It was close enough to the city proper for the roads to be still paved and buses still running, where Mr Olds felt safer behind ten foot stone walls than chicken wire fences.

We rode through a stone gateway with a sentry box on the side, got a wave from the sentry, and followed a wandering drive through half a mile of woodlands before encountering the cared-for part of the estate and the low-slung, modern ranch that centered on the grounds. Through it all, the trip was conducted in silence, the chauffeur tending to his driving, the twin thugs sitting in back, one on each side of me.

The car pulled up, not at the front door, but at a bowered walk along the side of the house. Everywhere the trees were large and the house was speckled with shadow.

I was led from the car along the bowered path. Birds fluttered in the leaves and a black cat, lying on sunny stones, scampered away at our approach.

In back of the house the area was clear and bright sunshine poured down on a swimming pool, formal gardens, and a miniature golf course. A couple of girls in scanty attire basked on towels on the flagstones surrounding the pool, and a muscular male with a tousle of curly hair bounced on the diving board, showing off a flat stomach and an athletic physique. The girls weren't watching, they sunned their backs and talked together.

Over at the miniature golf course, a plump graying man with thin hair, a splotchy face, and purple varicose vein tracks running down spindly white legs, played a round with a buxom, peroxide blonde who was almost growing out of her white, two piece bathing suit. The man wore tan Bermuda shorts and a Hawaiian sports shirt that was a cross between a rainbow and a sunset.

He was the major domo, the one to whom the thugs led me, and he smiled as if I were the King of Siam paying a call. 'Mr Kaye,' he said, without waiting for introductions, 'what a happy pleasure to have you here.' From the way he held out his hand, you'd have thought I was selling him my yacht.

I stuck my hands in my hip pockets and looked from one to the other. The brassy blonde had a well-developed roll of fat around her middle and her thighs were dimpled. She stood as tall as the Major Domo too, though she only wore scuffs. While she wasn't old, her eyes had a worn out look to them and while her smile of welcome was as broad as his, it didn't carry the same candle power. It was a tip to her background, too. It was a chorus girl smile.

'Permit me to introduce myself, sir,' the soft, balding man said, passing over my disinclination to shake his hand. 'My name is Newman Olds. And these—ah— acquaintances of mine—' he indicated the thugs, '—You've met them?'

'Encountered them,' I said. 'We haven't been formally introduced.' I was studying Mr Olds now. His eyes were a hard brown. Otherwise, he could have been a coupon clipper, a retiree who made his money some easy way; a soft, gentle type who never learned what it was to struggle, who got his swimming pool from Sears-Roebuck for trading stamps, and wouldn't have the faintest idea that the two 'acquaintances of his' carried guns. All except for the eyes.

'Well, yes,' Mr Olds said with sadness tinting his tone. 'I'm afraid they do rather rush into things without a great deal of finesse. The one on your left is Murray and the one on your right is Theodore. I hope, in their eagerness to oblige me, they have not been impolite?'

'Nothing more than fracturing their skulls would take to avenge. Theodore happens to have a gun of mine,' I added.

'Oh, that won't do. That won't do at all.' Mr Olds motioned. It was nothing much, a slight turn of the palm, and, miraculously, the gun was back in my hand. It was a well disciplined crew Mr Olds controlled. You don't fool around with a gang like that.

I returned the gun to its holster and Murray and Theodore, Olds' version of Frick and Frack, stepped back a pace, but remained at the ready. Compared to their casually attired boss, the Doomsday twins looked like IBM repairmen in their ties and jackets. They also looked as if they could derail a locomotive barehanded, which was something to keep in mind.

Mr Olds picked up his putter and took aim at his golf-ball. He paused and looked up at the blonde. 'Or is it your turn, Love?'

She said, 'Yours,' without hesitation. She knew her place.

The interplay reminded Mr Olds of his

manners. 'Oh, Mr Kaye, I don't believe you've met my friend, Lavinia—Lavinia Gould? Love, this is Mr Kaye.'

Lavinia Gould gave me the obeisance required of the ménage. She said it was an honor and a privilege to make my acquaintance. She said it well, made it sound as if she'd taken my photo to bed with her in childhood, but she didn't care any more about me than about whose turn it was on the miniature golf course.

I gave her the same line back. Everybody does it. It's the grease that oils the wheels, except that I didn't have to make my pitch as good as hers. I wasn't performing for anybody but myself.

Newman Olds was pleased. He concentrated on his golf shot. Well, let's say he *looked* pleased. Let's figure he didn't acquire a miniature golf course through tipping his hand. What came through from his performance was that the game was going his way. He didn't *really* have to sink this next putt to gain Nirvana. Nirvana was already in his oversized pockets.

'I hear,' he said, 'you had a little trouble down at your office just now. A couple of hoodlums were killed?' He stroked the ball. It missed the hole and bumped against the backstop. He took it well, didn't break the club over his knee or anything. In fact, he didn't seem to notice. What he was after was my report on the killings.

I said, 'I beg your pardon? Did you say "two" killings?'

'That's what I heard.' He took a second golfball from his pocket, set it and aimed again.

'You've got good hearing.'

'Oh that?' He waved a disinterested hand. 'There's a police radio in the house.' He putted again and missed again.

Lavinia giggled.

Newman Olds said, 'You better lose ten pounds if you want to laugh at me.'

She kissed him on the cheek. 'Ah, sweetheart,' she said. 'Are you sore because you're losing?'

There was a time when he would have melted, but that time wasn't now. Cuteness isn't bewitching in elephants. Brains weren't her long suit and obviously she'd forgotten that it was her body that had put her where she was. Maybe she was relying on Olds' memory but that was wearing thin. I saw the expression on his face and cringed for her.

'What'd the police radio say?' I asked, to keep the conversation going.

'Oh, that?' Olds moved on to where both golfballs lay within two feet of the cup. 'All I know is that two punks named Luke Benzi and Leo Chard were killed in your office a short time ago. The police, as of the last message I've received, don't know any more

161

than that—except that you aren't there to talk about it.'

He showed me he could grin. His teeth were white and even, as phony as his smile. 'I'm sorry if Murray and Theodore have unwittingly interfered with police procedures, but I presume that you don't mind?'

'You presume one helluva lot,' I answered. It was about now that my choler began its rise. 'I'm going to have to talk to them now or later. I'd rather have it now.'

'Oh, come,' Olds responded as if I were being difficult. 'I'm sure you and I have more interesting things to say to each other than you and the police—you and a Detective Sergeant Lasky, for example—do.'

He was showing off. That bit about Lasky was tossed in to impress me. It was his way of saying he didn't need a police radio. He had a direct pipeline to the department itself. Headquarters would brief him on demand.

It's not a one-way street, though. Life is a game and any number can play. He was feathering his arrows, which is what any smart little kid on Hard Row Street is going to do. But I grew up there too and I know the rules as well as he does. Out on that putting course, Olds and I were estimating each other, but he was underestimating me—not because he was dumb, but because he didn't realize how much I knew.

I said to him, 'Does your in with the police

162

tell you who Luke Benzi and Leo Chard are and what they were doing in my office?'

'Only that they're a couple of local toughs. You mean *you* don't know what they were doing in your office?'

I said to him, 'Let's skip the inquisition. You brought me here. I suppose you have a reason. What the hell do you want?'

Though I was irked, he remained placid. He stroked the first ball into the cup and moved to the second. 'A man named Joe Tanner was killed yesterday afternoon. I understand you knew the gentleman.'

That was an interesting disclosure. I said, 'Is that more of the crap you get from the cops? You ought to upgrade your sources.'

His bland eyes met mine from his putting stance. 'You mean you don't think they know what they're talking about?'

'That's what I mean. They seem to make the same mistake you do. They thought I knew him too.'

Olds put the second ball into the cup and bent to remove the pair. He stepped off the putting surface. 'Funny thing,' he said. 'But they got a call about a shooting at a certain address in town and when they—'

'Who made the call?' I interrupted.

'I understand it was a woman neighbor. She didn't give her name.'

'I see.' I watched Lavinia line up and sink the ball, first shot.

'Hee, hee,' she chortled. 'That's ten you owe me.'

Olds shrugged and went on with his story. What he wasn't telling me was that he owned the house in question, nor how the hell some woman neighbor could have known where the shooting came from. There wasn't another house within a hundred yards. 'When the police arrived,' he continued, 'they noticed a car was parked near the drive that led to the house where this Joe Tanner had been killed. And, being proper cops, they duly noted its license number. When they checked it out, they found the car belonged to you.' Olds turned his very shrewd, very dark brown eyes on me. 'Do you blame them for placing you on the scene?' He watched Lavinia stoop to remove her ball from the cup. She crouched and though she weighed too much, she was graceful. 'Of course,' he went on to me, 'no one is accusing you of complicity in Mr Tanner's death. The bullets weren't the same caliber as your gun, so you have nothing to fear from that.'

'Which is by way of saying it's all right for me to confess I was there?'

'That's right.'

'Sorry to let you down. I don't know a thing about it.' Then I said, 'But since you do, maybe you'll tell me who the hell this Joe Tanner was. Who, besides me, is supposed to know him? Who, besides me, is supposed to want him dead?'

'That's the question,' Olds answered, walking to the next hole and setting down his ball. 'Who would want him dead?'

Lavinia started feeling his trousers and exploring his pockets. He said, 'What are you doing?'

'Looking for money.' She found his wallet and he took it away from her. She said. 'You owe me ten.'

He fished out a ten and held it towards her while repocketing the wallet.

She stepped closer, clasping her hands behind her back. 'Aren't you going to stick it in my bra?'

'Stuff it yourself.' He turned to me. 'I hear tell, though, that there's some kind of a map.'

'I've heard that rumor too.'

Lavinia took the bill and tucked it in her bra. She was pouting, but he ignored her. 'I also hear,' he went on, 'that there's a big payment waiting for the guy who can produce it.'

'That's one I haven't heard.'

'A lot of money for the person who can produce it. No questions asked.'

'Did Joe Tanner have the map?'

Olds shrugged and addressed his ball. Properly hit, it would go through a loop-the-loop and up a ramp to where the hole was. 'I don't know if he had the map or not. If he did, he doesn't have it now.'

'You think the killer took it?'

'It's certainly a possibility.'

'And you think I might be the killer and I might have the map.'

Olds gave me a watery smile. 'There's that possibility. You'd be a rich man if that were the case.'

'How rich?'

'How does a hundred thousand dollars richer sound to you?'

'You'd pay that for the map? What's on the map?'

Lavinia took Olds' arm, kissed him on the cheek and laid her head on his shoulder. 'C'mon, honey. Play with me. You can talk while you putt and I want another ten dollars.'

Olds disengaged himself. 'Patience, my dear. A little patience.' He did eye the lay-out, however, as he continued. 'I didn't say I wanted the map,' he stated, wanting me to be clear on that point. 'I'm only saying there are those who'll pay that much for it.'

'What's the map of, I asked you.'

Olds shook his head. 'I don't know that either.'

'But you'd pay me a hundred grand if I gave it to you to—give to the party that wants it.'

'That's right. Or pay the money to whoever could produce the map.'

'But if you don't know what the map's of,

how are you going to authenticate it? What's to keep me from drawing lines on a piece of paper for you?'

Olds stroked the ball firmly. It whipped through the loop and on to the hole area, bouncing off the wooden rim, kissing the opposite rim and coming to rest an inch from it. He'd have to push-put from there and Lavinia chortled. 'Of course,' he said, moving over to study his lie, 'there are those who do know what the map's about. It would be verified before payment would be made.'

'Well,' I said, 'it sounds like a lot of money for a piece of paper. Tell me something. Is the only reason you think I've got it because my car was parked near Joe Tanner's house?'

'I don't know who's got it. I'm only making inquiries—'

'For the person who wants to pay a hundred grand, I know, I know. Now let's forget the funny business and get down to cases. Who's Joe Tanner and who's Veronica Dean and what are they to each other?'

Olds lifted an eyebrow and said, 'Veronica Dean?' as if it were a new kind of breakfast cereal.

Not so Lavinia. She said, 'That bitch!'

For a moment, Olds almost lost control. He made a motion. It was slight, but it was also clear that if he'd carried it through, he would have knocked her head off with his club. She let out a little gasp and then her knees started to shake. He turned his back on her and said to me that he didn't really know what I was talking about, that all he knew about Joe Tanner was what the police reported, and maybe I'd tell him who Veronica Dean was.and why I was interested?

'I'm interested,' I said, 'because she came to see you yesterday afternoon and didn't get home until late last night.'

Behind him, Lavinia's eyes widened. That was something she hadn't known before. She was pale beneath her tan and her knees still shook. She said, 'Newman, I don't feel well. I think I'll sit down.'

He paid her no heed as she wobbled off toward the pool. He looked from me to Theodore and Murray, who stood like statues. He didn't say anything and I tried to read his mind.

It was at that moment that an elderly servant, in a white jacket and black trousers, came out of the house, past the pool, and over towards Olds.

Olds saw him coming and some of the tension went out of the scene. He turned and waited. The man moved with a deliberate walk and the bent knees of age. He didn't speak until he reached his boss and had come to a complete halt. 'It's the gatekeeper,' he announced. 'There's a girl wanting admittance who says her name is Samantha Dean, Miss Veronica's sister.'

CHAPTER TWENTY-TWO

Newman Olds swallowed the news with little grace. First, he didn't know Veronica had a sister. Second, he could no longer pretend he didn't know Veronica. Reluctantly, he said, 'Let her through.'

The servant nodded and went away. Olds gave a sign and Murray turned on his heel to go form a welcoming committee. Theodore stayed on guard. I was bigger than Olds and armed as well.

Olds turned to me. 'Were you aware, Mr Kaye, that Veronica had a sister?'

I watched the servant by-pass the swimming pool. The muscular man was in the water, splashing around, the two bathing beauties were on their backs now, toasting their fronts, and Lavinia had slouched into a beach chair on the near side and was observing the swimmer.

'Yes,' I said. 'I know about the sister. What I don't know is how much you've told Veronica about the map.'

'I? Why would I want to tell her anything about a map?'

He was playing the innocent again. Games like that irritate me and I said, angrily, 'She's in on this map business and I know it as well as you do. And if I guess right, what she knows she learned from you. What was she, Lavinia's predecessor, or do you still keep her around? I'd guess Veronica would be a prickly burr to handle and I'd guess she'd pick your brains as well, but I know you didn't call her over yesterday to hold hands. She came when you whistled, but she was scared to make the trip.'

'Really, Mr Kaye,' Olds smiled, 'I've never known anyone who could jump to such extraordinary conclusions.'

'Dammit,' I snapped, 'for somebody who wants to pay a hundred grand for a piece of paper, you sure as hell pretend a lot of innocence. Whom do you think you're kidding? You know what the map is, but you don't know where it is. That much even I can figure out. What I can't figure out is why you think I've got it. That's not something you picked up from the cops. Is that some kind of story Veronica fed you?'

Olds sighed. 'I might as well be frank with you, Mr Kaye. yes, I do have an interest in the map. Yes, I will pay one hundred thousand dollars for its return. No, I do not know who's got it or where it is. I thought perhaps you did. Since you don't, or since you claim you don't, which is the same thing, I'd like to make you a proposition.'

That was more like it. 'Shoot.'

'The offer of one hundred thousand dollars stands. You're a private detective. You do jobs for hire. You track down people and things. I'd like to hire you—on a contingency basis—to go after that map. If you can track it down and deliver it to me, that's what I'll pay you—a hundred thousand dollars. Again, as I said before, there'll be no questions asked. You get me the map, I give you the money. How does that appeal to you, Mr Kaye?'

'It sounds great,' I answered, 'except you've rigged it so the offer doesn't do me any good unless I already have the map in hand.'

'How so?'

'You know how so. If I don't have it, then I don't know anything about it. I don't know why it's valuable, I don't know who's likely to have it. A detective can't find something without knowing what he's looking for.'

Olds stroked his chin for a moment, trying to decide whether enlisting me in the cause would be worth the investment. Obviously, the fewer the people who knew what the map was, the better.

At length he smiled. 'Mr Kaye,' he said, 'I like you.' He bent over his golfball and evaluated his next putt. 'Yes, I like you very much. You're an astute man, Mr Kaye. You're very astute. And I like young, astute people like yourself.' He moved the golfball a few inches with his foot to give himself more putting room.

'You know what I'm thinking?' he went on as he lined up his putt. 'I'm thinking you're

171

trying to get me to do your work for you. That's how smart you are. You'd like to collect that hundred thousand dollar reward without having to expend any effort.' He raised a cautionary hand to silence me without even glancing up to see if I was prepared to speak. Silence fell. He stroked the ball and it rolled three and a half feet into the cup.

'Yes, Yes,' he went on, advancing to retrieve the ball. 'But I don't blame you, Mr Kaye. That shows how clever you are. And I appreciate cleverness.'

Now, with the ball in his hand, he turned and smiled. 'But you see, if I had all this information you're asking me to provide you with, I wouldn't need your help. I could retrieve the map myself and save the hundred thousand dollars. Does that make sense to you?'

'None of what you're telling me makes any sense to me.'

'Ah, dear me.' He shook his head. 'What I'm saying, Mr Kaye, is that all I can offer you is money, not information. The information is something you'll have to acquire from other sources. And I'm sure you're resourceful enough to ferret out those other sources.'

'In short, you don't want me to know what the map's about?'

'In short, Mr Kaye, the question you have

to answer is not what the map is, but who has it. That's the question I can't answer. It's the question I'm willing to pay a hundred thousand dollars to get the answer to. If you want to take a crack at making that sum, I'm giving you my blessing. Do we understand each other?'

I said, 'Yeah, I get the message. I'll come back when I've got the map and, meanwhile, you can hustle up that hundred grand.' I jerked a thumb. 'Do you want to tell Theodore here to have your chauffeur give me a ride back?'

Newman Olds did not balk. He said. 'Theodore, would you see the gentleman to the car and tell Harry to return him to his office?' He gave me his friendliest smile. 'I hope when next we meet, you'll be giving me a map and I'll be giving you a cheque for a hundred thousand dollars.'

I muttered something that sounded serious, but we both knew that was a laugh. This was the Monday night kidnapping all over again. He found out I didn't have what he wanted and he was returning me to my point of origin. Though the modus operandi was the same, the guy behind it had to be different. Newman Olds wouldn't be kidnapping me twice for the same reason.

On that bowered path beside the house, Theodore and I encountered Murray escorting Olds' newest guest, Samantha. She

173

was as bright and shining as a goldpiece in a coalbin. I was expecting her, but she wasn't expecting me and her jaw sagged for a moment as if she'd fallen off a cliff. I gave her my very best smile and said, 'If you play golf, you're in.'

She blinked and stopped and looked at me and said, 'If you wonder why I'm here, I'm looking for a job.'

She wasn't wearing the blue linen Sunday School dress with the white collar for her job interview. This was a thin summer frock that was shapely and low-cut. Her slip showed through the material and it was good she had the slip on because you could tell she wasn't wearing anything else.

I was mean. I patted her on the shoulder and said, 'I think you'll be hired.'

CHAPTER TWENTY-THREE

I had Harry the chauffeur let me off a block from the office. It was pushing two o'clock and I'd been gone two hours, but I wanted to reconnoiter the area before I checked in. When Theodore and Murray had taken me away, two dead bodies were cluttering up the premises and dead bodies draw policemen the way they draw flies. I didn't feel like talking to any policemen just then. I'd have to do it in time, but I wanted it to be my own time.

The premises looked pretty clear to my wandering eye. The alley under my window, where Leo Chard had come to his end, was clean and empty. The body was gone, the alley had been swabbed of whatever was left, and the signs of that had long since dried. It was as if it had never happened.

In the office building lobby, no policemen and no reporters waited. It's a grubby building to begin with, not the spit and polish, spacious, stone floored lobby type that goes with high-rise, big-city downtown buildings. This is a brick structure, six stories high, built in 1910, and the latest renovation was the push-button elevator they installed in the mid-fifties. It's serviceable and it's kept reasonably clean and there actually is a man on all-night duty after five o'clock, at least according to the brochure. (He didn't stop Joe Tanner from ransacking my files, so maybe he's a myth.)

Anyway, the lobby was free of cops and the press and there was only the normal afternoon traffic going in and out. I took the elevator to my floor and went down the hall to the office door. It's pebbled glass with my name on it and the fact that I do private investigations, and we keep it closed but unlocked during business hours.

That's the way it was right then, which was the way it was the last time I'd approached it—back when the shoot-out took place. I couldn't help thinking about that as I turned the knob, and I couldn't help wondering if Eileen would be seated at her reception desk when I walked in, or what would be the case. Maybe there'd be more assassins. Maybe a squad of strong-armed cops would be waiting behind the door to take me down into their dungeon again. To tell the truth, right then I didn't feel up to another session under the bright lights, or another run-in with Don Lasky. I shook myself for I didn't like the feeling. Don't tell me I was over the hill at thirty?

I opened the door and it was the way I wanted it to be. There was only Eileen.

She was sitting behind her desk, but she wasn't the real Eileen. There wasn't the ready smile, the quick, sure movements, the brightness. Instead, she stared blankly at a case folder, making some mechanical markings on it with a pencil, going through motions, her face pale and frozen, her eyes lusterless.

When she saw me enter, her lips parted, her eyes widened, and some life came back into them. For a moment, I could have been a ghost. 'It's you?' she whispered and her face bore a querulous expression, as if she didn't really believe it.

I closed the door and said, 'What did they do to you?' I was worried. I hadn't wanted to go off and leave her.

She stared at me. 'You're back.'

I went to her. 'Are you all right? What happened? What have they done?' She touched my face with tender fingers. It was one time when my face wasn't full of bruises and lumps. I'd not only returned, I'd returned untouched and unbattered. She said, 'You're all right? I didn't know what happened to you.'

Then she started to cry. I'd never seen her cry before. I'd hardly ever even seen her eyes water.

I said, sure, I was all right, and took her in my arms. She wept and even let me kiss her hair. Kissing is usually a no-no.

She pulled away then and sat back down, wiping her eyes with the heel of her hand. 'I'm sorry,' she told me. 'I'm all upset today. I don't know what I'm doing.'

I held her hand. She still let me do that. 'You've had a bit of a time,' I said.

'Oh, not all that much. It's foolish. I can't explain myself.'

Not all that much? Just being held hostage, watching a couple of bodies get created. Then her boss gets whisked away and she's left to handle the police all by herself. If she'd been someone else, I'd have sent her home for the day, but you don't insult Eileen like that. I got the brandy bottle from the drawer of my desk instead and poured two inches into a

177

paper cup. I held it in front of her. 'Drink like a good girl.'

She almost laughed. 'Oh, my Lord, look at it all! What do you think I am?'

'It's all right. Half of it's mine.'

I sipped some and then she sipped. I was on a knee in front of her, she in her chair. I said, 'They give you a bad time after I left? What happened?'

She touched my hair. 'You're all right? They didn't do anything to you?'

'Is that what bothered you?'

'You usually come in all banged up. People beat up on you an awful lot, Simon. And that's when you go out on a case on your own. When two men come in and take you away—' She paused and said slowly, 'I thought maybe you weren't going to come back at all.' She tried to smile and sipped more of the brandy. 'And I couldn't even tell the police who they were. All I could say was that you'd been kidnapped.'

'And what did the police say?'

'They didn't believe me. They thought you'd killed those men and fled.'

I got off my knee and sat on the corner of the desk and had another swallow of brandy, passing the cup back to her. 'And what else did they say?'

'What did those men want with you? What happened to you?'

'Those men,' I told her, 'took me to the lair

178

of a man who owns the house where a guy named Joe Tanner was killed yesterday.'

'Joe Tanner? I read that name in the paper.' Her eyes widened. 'Does that murder involve you?' She laughed when I nodded and she had a touch more brandy. It was warming her now. 'I should have known,' she said, shaking her head. 'What murder in town doesn't involve you?'

'Those two men who tried to ambush me here this noon—they were part of Tanner's gang. I should say, rather, that all of them were part of somebody else's gang.'

She sipped a little more and laughed a little more. 'It's crazy. I think you're making it up. Tell me more.'

'The guy's name is Newman Olds and the whole thing has to do with a map.'

'Map? A treasure map?'

'It must be because it's worth a hundred thousand to him to get his hands on it. He thought maybe I had it. That's why he sent his hoods for me. But he decided, after he got me there, that I not only didn't have it, I didn't know what it was all about. So he let me go again.'

'Just like that?'

'Pretty much just like that. Once he decided I was an innocent bystander, he clammed up, so I don't know what it's all about, except that it seems to be at the bottom of everything that's been happening.'

'Including the man named Joe Tanner? Including those men who came in here to kill you?'

I said yes, and told her about being kidnapped by the three of them three nights ago, that they seemed to think I was carrying the map back then.

'But you weren't? So why would they come here to kill you?'

I shrugged. 'There's a hundred and one things about this case I don't know, but I'm going to have to find them out because I'm getting tired of being pushed around and beaten up and threatened by everybody who comes by.'

She shook her head and she wasn't smiling now. The effects of the brandy wore off pretty fast when I said that. She bit a lip. 'I don't like it when you talk that way. It makes me wonder when I won't be coming to this office any more because you'll be dead.'

She couldn't laugh, but I could. I finished the brandy and said, 'That won't happen for a while. I still have payments to make on my condo.' I kissed her forehead because she was in a receptive mood this afternoon. 'Now tell me what you did today.'

CHAPTER TWENTY-FOUR

Once again I had to have my session with the police. This time, though, Sergeant Lasky wasn't on the case and I was working with a more receptive crew. Dan Saxton had the killings and I gave him what I knew, including the names of the witnesses, Theodore and Murray, and the name of their employer. Dan knew of them, said Newman Olds had some shadowy areas in his background but that if his fingernails were suspected of having dirt in them, the cops didn't know where the dirt came from. Talk of maps didn't mean a thing to Dan. Nor did the cops know of a tie-in between Joe Tanner and the two guys I'd knocked off a few hours earlier. The cops, he said, had accepted Eileen's testimony that they'd entered and seized her and that my actions against them were in self-defense. It would be investigated further, but they weren't going to charge me with anything unless contradictory evidence came up.

I said, 'Thanks a bunch,' and wanted to know what they had on the body that had been found in Monmouth Park three nights ago, the one they had no ID on, the one to whom Father McGuire had administered last rites?

Saxton got out the file and went through the papers slowly. The FBI had come up with a name for the guy—Elias 'Mutt' Stark—plus a number of aliases. He came from the midwest and was wanted on assorted armed robbery charges and suspicion of murder.

'Midwest? You don't know what he was doing here in the East?'

'Yeah, killing Arnold Saydecker. We haven't made it public yet, but it was his gun that did the job.'

'Or the gun that was found on his body.'

'His gun. He'd used it before.'

As for who had done him in, the police had no idea.

'What do you figure for a motive?'

Saxton shook his head. 'We don't know. We'd figure someone stole off of him what he stole from Saydecker, but Saydecker's manservant says nothing was taken.'

'It might have been something small—that the manservant didn't know about?'

'That's possible, but there were plenty of valuables out in plain sight that he could have picked up, including a diamond ring on Saydecker's finger which would fence for a couple of gees.'

'Then what's the motive for the murder if it isn't robbery?'

'Vendetta,' Saxton suggested. 'We don't know much about Saydecker—where his money came from, but we think there're some unsavory elements to it—mainly because we can't trace his sources. So a guy like that is bound to have enemies.' Saxton sat back and put a hand on the open file. 'Consider, Simon, that the guy was a recluse, lived here nice and quiet, been here only a couple of years and we don't have a past on him, and the vendetta theory makes sense.'

'Vendetta?' I said. 'Let's see—a guy named Mutt Stark is paid by Saydecker's enemies to rub him out. He does the job while the manservant's out, doesn't touch a thing in the house, just turns and walks out. Good thinking except that, once outside, something funny happens. He's murdered and cleaned out—left with nothing on him but the gun. That spoils the story.'

'Not necessarily. Mutt Stark probably had empty pockets to begin with. All he needed was his gun.'

'How'd he get to Saydecker's then? Where'd he come from? Where was he staying?'

'How about with the guy who hired him—who brought him to town?'

'And who offed him? The guy who hired him? Instead of picking him up? So he couldn't talk?'

'We don't have a theory on that yet,' Saxton answered, shaking his head.

That was as far as he could waltz that one around and we left it at that. What the police were doing about my case, he said, was looking into the backgrounds of Benzi and Chard, trying to find out the reason for the assassination attempt. I wished him luck, but on the basis of what they were coming up with on the Saydecker and Mutt Stark murders, it didn't seem likely.

I gave the office a final check before going home and, sure enough, the reporters were there. The word had been leaked that Simon Kaye had resurfaced. I pleaded ignorance about most things, partly because I don't believe in tipping my hand, mostly because I *was* ignorant. Even so, I didn't get away from there for an hour.

Then it was home to the empty condo. Samantha had gone to Newman Olds and hadn't come back. I hadn't expected her to. Nevertheless, I had to admit I missed her. She was young and beautiful and hot as hell and had the rather charming faculty of knowing exactly what she wanted in life. What she wanted in life, unfortunately for guys like me, was money. And she made no bones about it. She was after men with million a year incomes and private detectives like Simon Kaye were only way stations—overnight resting places along her path. She'd be deadly to live with, but I wouldn't have minded another day or two of her company before she flew off to higher and better things. But Samantha wasn't a girl for wasting time.

So I had a quiet night and a lot of sleep and a chance to collect my thoughts.

* * *

Despite my reticence with the press, Friday morning's paper ran an extravagant article identifying the hoods I'd killed as associates of Joe Tanner who'd been killed the day before. And, courtesy of pipelines to the police department, the article went on to reveal that Simon Kaye had been questioned about the Tanner murder. That sure as hell made it sound like the vendetta Saxton was talking about. What was interesting was that no mention was made of Theodore and Murray and the fact that my benefactors were in the employ of Newman Olds, who owned the house wherein Tanner was murdered. If you're a big-shot like Olds, you can keep your name out of the paper. If you're a little-shot, like me, you can get smeared by innuendo and the innuendos in the article were about an inch thick.

If the papers were operating in the dark and painting black on black, so were the police. That was the problem. Everybody was laboring in the dark. Meanwhile, I was tired of being pushed around and the only person who could do anything about it was myself.

As a first step, I had Eileen make an

appointment for me with a man named George Geary. Geary was the manservant who'd found Arnold Saydecker's body, the one who'd been out for the evening when the murder took place, the one who told the police nothing had been stolen.

Saydecker and Mutt Stark were in on this thing in some manner or other. The only way to explain Joe Tanner, Leo Chard and Luke Benzi kidnapping me was that they mistook me for Stark. They didn't know what Stark looked like, perhaps, but they sure as hell expected him to come their way and they sure as hell thought he was going to be carrying a map.

And where would Mutt Stark get a map? From Arnold Saydecker, of course. And whom would you talk to about the late Arnold Saydecker's map but the only person who knew the guy—his manservant. It was as simple as adding one plus one plus one plus one. (Sometimes it's that simple.)

*   *   *

George Geary was younger than I expected. He was also more hard-boiled. He had dark hair, mustache, a slender build, watchful eyes. He looked more like a protector than a caretaker and I began to think I was on the right track. Put his age in his middle thirties, whereas Saydecker was in his late forties, and

186

you got a picture.

The late Arnold Saydecker's abode was a spacious nineteenth century collection of rooms, part of a millionaire's mansion that had been broken up into apartments. There was a marble vestibule with sweeping stairs, once one got by the buzzer locks on the outer doors. The number of apartments was four and Saydecker's was the right wing on the second floor. It was a dwelling that George Geary now treated as his own.

Geary was in a lounging jacket and though he looked too much like a hitman for the get-up, he behaved as every inch the lord of the manor, born to the silver spoon, or lately inheriting it. He had a firm handshake, the kind of grip that tries to make you wince. He was shorter than I by about three inches, and his hand was small. But his eyes were bright and he seemed to count on vim and vigor, as if they were what would take him where he was going in the world.

It was eleven in the morning and the sun was streaming through tall windows from which heavy velvet curtains had been drawn.

George Geary brought me through a well appointed, cluttered living room—too much furniture, elegant though it was, and not enough room to move between with comfort, and into a study which, again, created the same effect by containing, perhaps, one more chair than it should have.

The appointments, however, were excellent, though the point of interest was that the bookcases contained no books, only knick-knacks. Arnold Saydecker had been a doer, not a thinker.

Geary seemed eager to impress. He offered me cigars from a large humidor on the study desk as if he'd bought them himself and had dispensed them to favored guests for more years than he'd been alive. He did it well, but acting wasn't really his profession and the way he smelled the box before he made the offer, as if afraid they might have gone stale, spoiled the myth he was trying to establish.

He did other things wrong too, like offering me a drink when I declined the cigar. As I say, it was only eleven in the morning. he seemed disappointed when I refused, as if he needed the sustenance himself but didn't want to betray it by drinking alone.

All in all, he was trying to act as Saydecker would act, having watched the man for—well, that was something I wanted to find out—just how long had he been Saydecker's manservant?

There was one other thing wrong with the set-up. That was the faint aroma of perfume that floated in the air of the living room.

★   ★   ★

'Well, sir, what can I do for you?' Geary

finally said, coming to rest uneasily in the highbacked chair behind the desk with its back to the windows. He was welcoming me as someone he could do business with, as if I could throw next month's rent his way. He hadn't balked when Eileen phoned for the appointment, which was unexpected. The police had interrogated him about Saydecker's death, the ripples had spread out and receded. All he had to do was hold still and all troubles would vanish. Yet here he was, willing, almost eager, to welcome a private investigator. What did he think I wanted to talk to him about? How did he think I could do him any good?

He was expectant, but his guard was down, and I bombed him fast. I said, 'I'm representing a party who's interested in the late Mr Saydecker's map.'

Geary must have jumped a foot—well, two inches? Then he put on his wide-eyed innocence mask. As I say, he wasn't good at deception. He wasn't good at much except muscles. So he said, 'Map?' and gave me his bland stare, and you could see him posing and wondering: 'Is this bland enough? Should I lift the chin a trifle more?' He planted a smile on his face that made him look like an ostrich. 'What map is that?'

'Oh come on,' I said, acting irritable. 'The map Mutt Stark killed him for. Don't pretend you don't know about it.' Of course this was a guessing game on my part, but when a guy like George Geary is giving you leads to follow, you follow them.

Geary studied me for several seconds, except he wasn't studying me, he was making believe he was studying me. Actually, he was trying to decide how to respond. What came out was about what I'd expect. 'What makes you think Mr Saydecker owned a map?'

I sat straight in the chair and shot it at him. 'The hell with the crap, Geary. Saydecker had a map and you know it. And now it's gone. Mutt Stark took it from him last Monday night, the night you were out—or at least you say you were out!' I paused to let that one sink in and it was sinking like the setting sun. Glimmers of understanding streaked the sky, a little rosiness tinged the clouds, but it was all downhill. 'Listen,' he said. 'Mr Saydecker got killed. I wasn't here.'

'At least that's your story.'

Geary sat forward. 'Yes,' he hissed. 'That's my story. The cops can't prove otherwise and neither can you. So take it and run.'

'I'm not going anywhere. I'm not interested in where you were when Saydecker got killed. I don't care who killed Saydecker and I don't care who killed Mutt Stark. But I am interested in what happened to that map. It's worth a lot of money to whomever has it. But you already know that. So I should think you'd want to get it back.'

I was taking shots in the dark with that speech but I couldn't have been missing by much from the way he was responding. He nibbled his mustache and finally said, 'What's your interest in the map?'

'I've got a client who wants it. He's willing to pay fifty thousand dollars for it. If you knew where it was, for example, you could make a quick fifty grand, tax free.'

Geary wasn't biting. He snorted. 'Your client's a piker.'

'How much of a piker?'

Geary decided not to answer that one. 'Who's your client?'

That wasn't the kind of thing I answer. I smiled and said, 'You know better than that. Tell me what you want for it and I'll see what he'll pay.'

Geary shook his head. 'Me? I don't have the map. I don't know anything about it.'

'You know *all* about it. You know what the map is. You know Saydecker had it. You know it's not there now. Don't tell me you don't know anything about it.'

'The guy who killed Mutt Stark must've taken it.'

'And I think you know who that was and how to get hold of it again.'

'That's a lie.' He lifted himself half out of his seat. 'If I knew who had it, I'd go get it.' He sat back and smiled. 'As a matter of fact, I thought you had it.'

That was from out of the blue. 'I?' I gave him a short laugh. 'Where'd you get that idea?'

'The papers this morning. The shoot-out in your office. Some of the names in the articles had to do with the other half of the map.'

He put his elbows on the desk and rubbed his hands. 'Let's put it this way. What would you say if I told you I had a client who'd pay fifty thousand dollars for the other half of the map, the half your client's got?'

CHAPTER TWENTY-FIVE

George could sure make a party interesting. I couldn't tear myself away. Right now, he was throwing me some tasty tid-bits, but I didn't think he had anything he intended to sell. He only wanted me to tip my hand.

That made it a battle of wits, for I wanted him to tip his. Already he'd given me information. There wasn't one map. There were two halves and you had to have them both for the map to be any good.

The way I put two and two together, Newman Olds had one half, Saydecker the other, and Olds paid Mutt Stark to bring him Saydecker's half. That made sense to me. Newman Olds was that kind of a guy.

Somebody else, however, loused up Olds'

plans by killing and robbing Stark and that somebody was the 'client' George was talking about.

Without straining my brain, I could also guess that the whole map was worth many times one hundred thousand dollars. Big bucks were involved here, the kind of money people kill for—the kind of money a lot of people can get killed over. I could count five already, Arnold Saydecker, Mutt Stark, Joe Tanner, Luke Benzi and Leo Chard. And the two pieces hadn't even been put together yet.

Why Tanner was killed and why Luke and Leo made me a target, I couldn't guess, but it was all of a piece. It had to do with the map. If I lived long enough, I might find the answers. That looked like my only way out.

'Fifty thousand dollars?' I said to George Geary. 'You'd pay fifty grand for my client's half of the map?'

'My client would pay it,' Geary corrected.

'I think I could get my client to accept,' I said. 'That sounds like a fair price.'

George's eyes hooded. If I was talking about what he was talking about, those weren't the right answers. 'I'd have to get a look at the map,' he said. 'To verify it.'

'That can be arranged. You're capable to making the verification yourself?'

He hesitated and then shrugged. 'Of course.'

'You and Mr Saydecker must have been a

lot closer than servant and master.'

'I protected his interests. He trusted me.'

'Except for Monday night. You didn't protect his interests very well that night.'

George's mouth became a tight, hard line. 'I wasn't here,' he snapped.

'Arnold's tough luck.' I gave him my knowing look. 'On the other hand, a break for you. Now you have control of his half of the map.'

That brought him to his feet and for a moment I thought he'd jump me. He leaned forward, his face red, his fists doubled and called me names instead. You'd have thought I'd insulted his mother. The essence of his message was that Arnold Saydecker was his friend and if he'd been around when Stark came, he'd have killed him.

I waited till he'd cooled a little. 'But you weren't here,' I reminded him. 'So somebody else killed Stark, right? Who was it?'

He went back to his chair. 'I don't know what you're talking about,' he grumbled. 'If I wasn't here, how the hell would I know who killed him?'

George hadn't been born with a lion's share of brains but at times like this, he could be almost insufferable. 'I don't know how the hell you'd know, but whoever killed him took the map and you're telling me that the holder of the map is your client. So who the hell's got the map?'

George put a smile on his face and turned cute. 'I never said I knew who had the map,' he answered. 'I was only saying "if." I wanted to see how much you knew.' He shook his head, maintaining the smile. 'And you don't know much at all. You don't know what the maps are really all about and you don't know how much they're worth.'

'That's right,' I agreed. 'All I know is that neither half is worth a dime by itself, but you put them together and the combination is worth a mint. But I know who's got one half and if you know who's got the other, we can do business.'

George stretched wearily and got to his feet again, covering a yawn. 'That's right,' he said, going to the door to let me out. 'If the person who has the other half of the map should contact me, I'll be in touch.' He pulled the door ajar and waited for me to rise up and go through it. 'But you better understand one thing. I don't know who killed Mutt Stark and I don't know what happened to the half of the map Mr Saydecker had. I don't know anything at all.'

CHAPTER TWENTY-SIX

The weekend passed and Monday came around. Nobody called me, nobody shot at me, nobody hit me on the head, nobody tried to make me produce pieces of map that I didn't have. It was a restful respite. I could almost think those adventures belonged to my past.

It wasn't due to last. At ten o'clock, Newman Olds called. He interrupted Eileen in the midst of serving us our mid-morning cup of brew from the office Silex. He was pleasant and full of good will, treating me as if I were his investment banker. How were things with me, he wanted to know? And had I had any luck tracking down the map? It was only a form of greeting, he wasn't expecting a report. He was calling, he said, because he wanted to see me. It was a matter of business—he'd like to acquire my services. If I could come out right now, we could settle the business arrangements and he'd be delighted if I'd stay on for lunch.

Lunch with Newman Olds wasn't my idea of Happy House so I said I couldn't stay that long, but I'd be glad to pay him the visit. I didn't know what kind of project he wanted to hire me for, but it wasn't so pressing that he sent his hoods around to collect me. He was letting me drive there on my own.

I tooled over in the heap, arriving about quarter of eleven and had to pass inspection by the guard in the sentry box at his gate. The guard came forth, all spit and polish, asked my name and recorded my license plate

196

number, but didn't try for a strip search.

I left the car in front of the long, low-slung ranch and Theodore appeared from the arbor walk to lead me out back again.

Today, the same pair of bathing beauties were sunning themselves beside the pool and the same muscular man was practicing his dives. You got the feeling they were hired for decoration, to give the place that lived-in look.

There was Newman Olds, over at his miniature golf course again but, surprise, surprise, the girl with him wasn't the blonde and sulky, bulging-out-of-her-bikini Lavinia Gould. This time it was a trim and pert, dark-haired, green-eyed vixen named Samantha Dean. She had a putter in her hand, a happy smile on her face, and she looked as if she'd won the Pulitzer Prize. Well, maybe she had, because Newman Olds looked pretty pleased with himself too.

I came to them with Theodore at my shoulder—big, tough Theodore, who shadowed you close enough so you could feel his breath. He knew how to intimidate. And I stopped far enough away so that Olds wouldn't offer me his hand again. I smiled at Samantha, who was wearing a tight bikini that exposed the exact amount of skin that the most liberal censor would permit and I said, running my eyes over her, up and down, 'You're looking well.'

Olds said, 'I believe you two know each other?'

'We've met,' I acknowledged. If Samantha wanted to tell him exactly how well we had known each other, that was up to her.

Olds lined up a putt and sank it. He stepped aside while Samantha, wearing a pair of sandals as her only other garb, tried her hand and missed. 'I'm not as good as the last girl,' she said with a smile and a shrug. 'At least at golf.'

'Only at golf,' Olds assured her with a Cheshire Cat grin. 'That's another ten you owe me.' He held out a hand.

She giggled and winked at me. 'Now where do you think I could carry any money?' They were sure one cute couple, having themselves a picnic, playing games for me.

'Whatever happened to the other girl?' I asked. 'She fall down a sewer?'

'Oh, she's around,' Olds said. 'Somewhere. She's probably home.'

'She has a home?'

'Yeah, the other side of town.' He reached over to whack Samantha on the fanny when she bent to pick up her ball and she screeched and giggled. I turned around to see how Theodore was relishing the horseplay but he looked like a cigar store Indian.

'I don't see Murray,' I said, wondering if he'd fallen down a sewer too, but I didn't really believe it.

'He's around,' Olds said. 'Why don't we sit down?'

We didn't go to the umbrella stands by the pool where the people were, but over to some lawn furniture under the trees. Olds sprawled on a chaise longue, making room for Samantha so he could pat her thigh and wedge the tips of his fingers inside the edges of her bikini bottom. Since it fitted her like skin, that was as far as he could get, and even then he was cutting off circulation.

I didn't know whether it was pleasure in his prize or whether it was love in bloom but he couldn't keep his hands off her and she seemed more than pleased by his helplessness. Me, I wouldn't shake the creep's hand. There was something about him that reminded me of sludge and slime. But he did have money and that's what Samantha had said she was after. I trusted she'd play her cards better than Lavinia.

I faced them in an aluminum chair and Theodore came to the edge of the shade and remained standing, his arms folded across his chest. They weren't taking my gun away, but they weren't forgetting I had it. Theodore was braced and ready.

'The last time we met,' Newman Olds began, 'we had a discussion about a map.' He smiled and waited, so I smiled and waited.

'In fact,' he went on, 'I authorized you to be my agent in the matter.' He paused for my agreement.

'More or less,' I said.

'True,' he acknowledged. 'There was no set fee, no formal arrangement. I merely said I'd pay you a certain sum of money should you chance upon the map and bring it to me.'

I waited some more.

'Something has happened since then,' he continued after caressing Samantha's thigh for an eternity. 'I have been in contact with the owner of the map—perhaps I should, more properly, say the *holder* of the map. We are in the process of negotiating a purchase price. It is my desire, as you know, to acaquire it.'

I nodded and looked at Samantha. She was staring at the ground, accepting the stroking, but acting quite bored. How her patrons made their money didn't concern her. Her juices only started flowing when it came time to spend it.

Newman Olds worked his fingers under the part of the bikini that came over Samantha's hip, then had trouble getting them free again. 'What I need,' he said, 'is a go-between, a—what do you call them?'

'Intermediary?'

'Yes, that's it. An intermediary. And when I discovered this, I immediately thought of you.'

That was as believable as a blind eye-doctor. However—'And what would being your intermediary entail?'

'You would become the liaison between me and his liaison. He's paranoid and does not choose to deal with me directly. At present, his intermediary contacts me and negotiations have gone on that way. I've now decided it'll be to my benefit also to have an intermediary. Matters will progress much faster if there's someone in front of me, paving the way.'

'Sounds all right,' I said. 'You want me to relay your messages to whomever the other guy's contact is, and report back what he tells me?'

'That's the essence of it.'

'What about when the deal is made?'

'Well, yes, of course, I'd need you for that.'

I smiled drily. That was what it was all about, of course. He didn't need somebody to speak for him, he needed someone to deliver the payment and collect the map after the deal was made. After all, this wasn't like buying a painting or a washing machine where everything's on the up and up. This was akin to paying ransom—like the phony deal Veronica hired me for. In such cases, one has to be sure the right amount of money is being paid and that the object being purchased is the genuine article. There can be an element of danger in such situations for each side is eager to double-cross the other. That was why Newman Olds was after an intermediary. He wanted someone from outside his organization to run the risks.

Well, that's my business, as long as I get paid in advance and the payment is of a magnitude equal to the risks entailed.

'Okay,' I told him. 'If the deal gets concluded within a month, I'll handle it for five thousand dollars.'

He smiled. 'You come pretty high. This is really a simple chore. It shouldn't take more than half a dozen hours of your time.'

I said, 'I'm not charging by the hour, I'm charging by the risk.'

Olds pooh-poohed it. 'Risk? Really, there's no risk involved.'

I got up and said, 'Let's not haggle about it. If you want somebody cheaper, you shouldn't have any problem finding someone. Run an ad.'

Interestingly, he didn't put up a fight. 'No, no,' he said. 'I want you. If it's five thousand, it's five thousand.'

Fine, I told him. As soon as the check cleared the bank, I was his boy.

But I went back to the office deep in thought. A lot of suckers would have handled the chore for one tenth of what I was charging. Why was it so important that he should hire me?

CHAPTER TWENTY-SEVEN

I didn't get through work until half past five and I was alone when I locked up the office. It was hot in the halls and in the elevator. A small fan over the elevator controls is the landlord's only concession to summer.

The lobby doors were propped open to let some air circulate and, beyond them, pacing the sidewalk in a light, sporty dress that did a lot more for her figure than a bikini, was Newman Olds' recent lady-friend, Lavinia Gould.

I gave her a smile and she came over. It really was I she'd been waiting for. 'Do you have a minute, Mr Kaye? Could we go somewhere and talk?'

I suggested Lupone's Bar, a block away. She had a car at the kerb, but we walked. Her make-up was bright and fresh, her fingernails red and gold, her dress attractive, her step sprightly, but her face was forlorn. We took a table at the back where the light was poor but the clientele sparse, and I ordered. She took a Bloody Mary and I said, 'Beer.' She wanted to pay but I told her Pete Lupone only took money from me. I lighted her cigarette and said, 'What's on your mind, Miss Gould?'

'You should call me Lavinia, Mr Kaye.'

'What's on your mind, Lavinia?'

'Newman's given me the air. You may not know it, but that's what's happened. He's given me the old heave-ho.' She inhaled deeply on the cigarette and rubbed a tip of ash into the tray.

I didn't know what I was supposed to say, or why she wanted to tell me. 'I'm sorry to hear that,' I answered. 'It's that new girl, Samantha Dean?'

She nodded. 'I understand you know her.'

'We've been introduced. It doesn't go much further than that.'

'He took one look at her and went bananas. She meant him to.'

'She has a way of getting what she wants.'

'I suppose,' Lavinia sighed, exhaling more smoke, being careful to blow it away from me. 'I should have seen it coming. I don't mean her, of course. I couldn't see her coming. If I had, I might have been able to do something about it, but nobody saw her coming. All of a sudden she just arrived. What I mean is, my days were numbered. I knew it when I took up with him. I mean, I displaced her sister. You know her sister?'

I nodded.

'That's right. You asked about her. Newman didn't want to tell you he knew her. I shouldn't have said anything. I was too sure of myself, like a damned fool. That's what I mean. I beat Veronica out for him. So I should've known it'd be just a question of time before somebody beat me out. The trouble is, you always think it's going to be tomorrow, or the day after. You never think "today"!'

She had some more of her cigarette and waited while Pete served our order. Then she stared morosely at her Bloody Mary. 'I'm only thirty,' she said. 'I was older than Veronica, but I beat her out. I still look good. I always study myself in the mirror to look for wrinkles. Of course I did put on some weight. I put on twenty-five pounds in the two years I was numero uno. But Newman only laughed. He'd tell me I was getting tubby but he'd laugh. I thought he didn't care, that maybe he liked girls who were pleasingly plump. And he liked it that I was feisty. I'm not that way, really. Inside I'm scared. But Veronica was pretty fresh with him and stood up to him and got what she wanted out of him and I watched her and I decided that's what he liked—you know, tough girls, not wilting violets. So I practiced being tough and standing up to him. And it worked.' She nodded at me and said, 'Veronica was like what you say her sister is—good at getting what she wants. Maybe she was too good. Because Newman ditched her for me and, like I say, she was younger. Some people might think she was prettier than me too, except I think she's got hard eyes. I wouldn't trust her myself. So Newman gave her the air

205

and put me in her place.' Lavinia mashed out her cigarette, took the celery stalk from her Bloody Mary (Pete almost never gets asked for a Bloody Mary, but he's read the book and he's going to do it right) and licked it. 'And now,' she added gloomily, Veronica's kid sister has done it to me.' She shook her head. 'And there's not a damned thing I can do about it. I can't compete with her for looks or age or figure. I'm over the hill. I had my thirtieth birthday five weeks ago and I cried all night. Newman didn't know what the hell was the matter with me and I wouldn't tell him.'

I sipped some of my beer and made sympathetic noises. This was all very interesting, but I still didn't know why she was telling it to me or why she should want to. We hadn't said two words to each other heretofore. I said, 'Where do you go from here, then? Do you have any plans, any more in the bank?'

'Oh,' she said, letting me light another cigarette, 'I don't have to go anywhere. Newman will still take care of me. He's loyal. He's, you know, full of—you know— integrity.'

'He is?' I could see Olds being full of integrity—about a thimbleful, if you had your finger in the thimble.

'Yes,' she said, nodding as if she knew. 'Like Veronica. He still takes care of her.'

She thought about that for a moment, then quickly said, 'I don't mean he sleeps with her—except he might. I mean, you say he called her to his place one night last week. So maybe he did. It's, you know, like a harem.'

'Harem?' I said. 'Are those girls who sunbathe by his pool part of the harem?'

'Not them,' Lavinia answered quickly. 'They're nieces and the boy is a nephew. They don't count.'

'Then who *is* in the harem?'

Lavinia sipped a little of her drink and had another drag on her cigarette. She munched some of the celery and talked while she chewed.

'First there was Veronica. Well, I shouldn't say first, you know. There must've been lots of women before Veronica. He isn't, you know, all that young. He's in his fifties, if you want to know. But when I came around, Veronica was his number one girlfriend. That doesn't mean he didn't have a lot of other girls on the side. Someone like him, you know, with lots of money to spend, he can have any girl he wants. And he wants a lot of 'em. I mean, when he first started taking me out—I was dancing in a revue in the Paramount Club back when they were, y'know, still putting on shows. And he was dating—and laying—half the girls in the chorus line. But, as I say, Veronica was his steady date. Me? I was just one of the rest of the bunch. But I watched Veronica and tried to figure what she had that got him, and then I practiced the same techniques and pretty soon he moved her out and me in as his steady date. I don't mean he moved me into his house or anything like that. But he set me up in an apartment, rent paid, and that was where I kept my things. But I'd be on call. That was the name of the game, see? He wanted female companionship but mostly he wanted it from one special girl.' Lavinia shrugged and drained her drink in a hurry so she could have another. I wasn't half through with my beer, but I didn't have her problems.

I signalled Pete for a refill and had her go on.

'Newman supports Veronica,' she told me. 'He pays for her apartment and gives her money. That's what I meant about his, y'know, being loyal. He might even sleep with her now and then.'

'True loyalty,' I said.

'I mean it,' Lavinia insisted. 'And he's got me set up in an apartment too. And just because Samantha's in and I'm out doesn't mean that I'll never see him again, or that he won't want my body again. It just means he won't want it as much.' She sighed heavily as the significance of the statement weighed on her. 'A girl,' she said, 'when she starts to lose her looks—when she passes thirty—when she finds a man wants somebody else instead of her—when she reaches the point where her body can no longer provide for her, she's in real trouble.'

Lavinia seized Pete's second Bloody Mary and downed half of it before she could stop. Then she slapped the glass sharply on the table, stared into what was left and said, 'You don't know, because you're a man. Men believe women have it made. Men believe women can have anything they want because they have the proper internal plumbing. Men think women live in the catbird seat because they can withhold or dispense their favors at their pleasure. That's a wonderful fiction, Mr Kaye. Thass a wunnerful—' She paused as her voice slurred. She took a breath. 'What I'm trynna say is—that maybe, from where the man sits, he thinks the woman's got it made. But from where she—where the woman sits—it's not like that at all. Because I'm a woman, I'm supposed to get anything I want. All I have to do is pull down my pants. The world is my oyster because, whatever it is I want, all I have to do to get it is pull down my pants. Neat trick, huh? But what happens if you pull down your pants and nothing happens? What if the men don't come running? What if there's another girl pulling down her pants and they're all going to her and nobody pays any attention to you?' She was starting to weep. She finished the second drink and bit her lip and shook her head.

'Y'see,' she said, 'this is something a woman can't explain to a man. He won't know what she's talking about. All he thinks about is getting laid. Women are sex objects and all he cares about is what's inside their pants. And what he doesn't think about is, what about the women who want to show off what they've got, and the men don't give a damn? Do you know how this scares the living be-Jesus out of a girl? All of a sudden, the fail-safe gimmick doesn't work any more. So what's she gonna do for an encore?'

She reached out a hand to touch mine. It wasn't to find a new bed, she was only seeking company. 'Newman doesn't want what I have to offer any more. So what do I do? I don't know how to do anything else but what I do. I guess I'm a whore, but I'm not a prostitute. I don't have the training to be a secretary or a teacher. I can't be much more than a waitress—unless there's a man who's interested in me. And, at the age of thirty and five weeks, I discover that that's where it is. I'm dependent, for my survival, on a man—any man.' She snorted. 'And men think women are in the catbird seat. It's the men who have the women by the short hairs.' She shook her head and a tear fell. 'And all the women's lib in the world isn't going to change it. It's hell being a woman.'

I decided I'd have a double martini and signalled Pete. By the time it arrived and he took away my empty beer glass, Lavinia was after a third Bloody Mary and cursing Newman Olds in a guttural monotone.

I lighted another of her cigarettes and took one for myself. 'I notice,' I said, 'that Newman likes to keep his pet of the month, or is it playmate of the year? close at hand—even when he's conducting business.'

'Oh, hell,' she complained. 'When I first took over Veronica's place I felt like a bird in a cage. He wouldn't go anywhere without me. All the time he'd be discussing business with one jerk or another, he'd be doing everything but sticking his hand inside my pants. In fact, I think there were times when he was even trying that. You wantta talk about dirty old men? That Samantha bitch is going to learn what it's like to have star billing on Newman Olds' Hit Parade.'

'What's this map business of his all about?'

Lavinia picked up her new Bloody Mary when I signed Pete's check. She put her celery stalk on Pete's tray and told him, 'You take this. I'm not a rabbit.' He smiled and looked her over in a way that said, 'Can you be sure?' and returned to the bar. To me, she said, 'What map business?'

'He's negotiating for a map. You must have heard about it. You were there when he and I were discussing it.'

Lavinia shook her head. 'That was the one thing I learned to do right—what I think

211

Veronica was doing wrong. I didn't pay any attention to his business. To me it was gobbledygook. I don't have a head for that kind of thing. Y'know something?' She leaned forward over the table, knocking over the ashtray with her elbow, but never spilling a drop of her drink. 'The way the world was meant to run is very simple. Men are supposed to go out and do whatever it is they do to make money. Women are supposed to take down their pants to oblige the men when they're through making money. And the men, for the privilege the women provide them, are supposed to give the money they make to the women. Or, at least enough of it to keep them happy.'

I patted her hand. 'A nice thought. Too bad it doesn't work.'

In response, Lavinia said, 'It would work if men reacted properly when a woman pulled down her pants. It's the damned men.' She raised her Bloody Mary glass. 'Here's to Samantha Dean. May her reign last a day to my month.'

CHAPTER TWENTY-EIGHT

Along about half past seven, Lavinia was into her fifth Bloody Mary and getting maudlin. Hell, she'd been maudlin. Now she was getting downright drunk.

Of course, I could have shipped her home after the second drink, but that wasn't what she'd come to me for. If I couldn't whisk my magic wand and make Samantha disappear, at least I could provide a shoulder and that was her minimum need. Give her less and she'd fragment.

So why was it my shoulder? Don't ask me, except that I knew Samantha. And why did I hold still for it? I'm not that full of the milk of human kindness. What if Lavinia did fragment? Why should I care? I didn't even know the girl, nor did I care for her. She was a dumb blonde who wouldn't have appealed to me the best day she ever knew—and those were behind her. Nothing against her, we just weren't on the same wavelength.

I did have a selfish reason though—at least I did at first. Lavinia had hung around Newman Olds for a good two years. She had to know what he was about—at least she ought to know something on the subject. And, since Newman Olds seemed due to occupy some of my future, and since I regarded him as a dangerous man, any little tidbits I could pick up would be all to the good.

So I was willing to ply Lavinia with drinks and listen to her tale of woe and, frankly, be Goddam glad I wasn't a woman. And then the point was reached where she was too rocky to be entrusted to her car.

I brought her a meal to sober her up, but it didn't help much. Lavinia stopped crying enough to tell me what life with Newman was like. The description would have gone big in the pornographic market, but it didn't illuminate the side of Newman Olds I was after—his source of income, his methods, his contacts, his power. You win some, you lose some.

I drove her home in her car when we'd finished eating. She still was too sloppy for self support. She showed me her building and I took her up in the elevator. It was in the same rent category as Veronica's—plain, middle-class, furnished. It was, claimed Lavinia, where she spent her time until Newman wanted her to grace his own abode. Then she ran and graced it. There was a familiar ring to the tale. It was Veronica's situation all over again, except Veronica seldom got wanted any more. The one time I saw her summoned, a look of fear had crossed her face.

Lavinia staggered when I opened her door and almost took a header on to the living room floor. I have a feeling she was make-believe drunk because I hadn't given her a drop in two hours. But who's to say? Sometimes, once you cross your own threshold, all your stays let go and there's nothing left to hold you up (or in) any more.

214

I caught her and brought her to her bedroom. She was starting to weep again and stroked my jacket and wanted me to know that she'd tried to do right by Newman, that he had no cause to reject her like that.

I told her that God never promised us a rose garden, that we'd opted out of Eden and the good die young. Some of them do, anyway.

That made her cry some more and I knew that she didn't want me to go. I also knew that that was what I was going to do.

I hunted through her larder for a bottle of booze and said that she and I would have a nightcap together. Then I poured her a fistful and myself a dainty three fingers and said to her that when we were finished, she was to get undressed and go to bed.

So naturally, she went flat on her back on the bed before she'd half finished. I don't think she was out, but she was pretending to be. So I put her glass on the bedtable and the rest of my own beside it and I hummed her nursery tunes while I undressed her. She managed to help while pretending she didn't know where she was. In a way it was sad. I understood what she'd been talking about back at the bar. She wanted to be wanted and I didn't want her, and what more could she do to promote something than offer her naked body?

It took a while, but I finally found her

nightgown. It took a longer while to get it on her. That was the part where she hindered rather than helped.

I pulled her upright to get her under the covers and she wept again and said, 'What am I going to do?'

That was the imponderable and I didn't try to answer. I tucked her in and held her hand and made her take another slug of her drink. 'It'll make everything look better in the morning,' I told her. Then I put the glass back beside my own and kissed her goodnight and walked out.

I supposed I could have gone through her purse or through the personal effects on her desk to see if there was anything more I could learn about her friend Newman, but it didn't seem appropriate, and while that's no justification, I was sure it wouldn't have been worthwhile.

★   ★   ★

Newman Olds' check cleared the bank on Tuesday and I was in business. Five thousand dollars was a good chunk of coin but I didn't think I'd priced myself too high. If I knew Olds, I'd be earning it.

It didn't look that way in the beginning, though. No calls from map dealers upset my priorities that day and everything was routine. That, I discovered, was only because the map dealer wasn't working a business schedule. He didn't call me until half past ten at night, and he rang my condo.

I was just back from a boxing workout at the gym—Tuesday is boxing night. (If you want to stay in shape, you have to work at it.) The phone was ringing and the voice on the other end said he'd been calling since eight o'clock.

It sounded like George Geary so I said, 'Bully for you, George.'

He didn't like being recognized and pretended he hadn't heard. 'I understand, Mr Kaye,' he said, 'that you've been chosen by Newman Olds as his intermediary?'

'That's right, George. Do you have the other half of the map?'

That brought hesitation, then careful words. 'I am in contact with someone who has a property I think would interest your client.'

He was being careful because to know the owner of the map was to know the killer of Mutt Stark, and he didn't want to acknowledge that. I said, 'Oh, hell, George, stop beating around the bush. You've got the other half of the map that Olds wants. How much do you want for it?'

'I don't have the map,' George insisted. 'I'm only representing the faction which does have it.'

'Yes, yes. All right, it's held not by you,

but by a faction. How much does the faction want for the map?'

The answer was matter-of-fact. 'Five hundred thousand dollars.'

I whistled and then I laughed. 'That must be *some* map.'

'It is.'

'And do you think Olds will pay that much?'

'He will.'

'You've talked to him about it?'

I threw that in because I was curious. And if he meant not to answer, he forgot. 'Yes,' he said. 'Mr Olds knows what the price is.'

That raised the question, for me, why the hell was I being brought into it if George had already talked to Olds himself? All of a sudden, Olds wasn't to be directly involved any more? Why?

'If Olds has agreed to the payment, then we can save a lot of time,' I said.

'I don't know that he's agreed,' George answered. 'He knows that's the asking price.'

'What does that mean, that you and I are supposed to dicker?'

'There's going to be no dickering,' George answered. 'The map is worth twice that. He's getting a bargain.'

'And he knows it?'

'He knows it. After all, he has the other half. He's had it from the beginning.'

'So what do you want from me?'

'You're going to be the one who delivers the money.'

'Me and a truck, huh?'

'You and a suitcase or whatever he puts it in.'

'If he puts it in.'

'He will. He's choking, but he knows it's a bargain.'

'And he just happens to have half a million in cash lying around?'

'No,' George said. 'It'll take him a little time to get it. I'll call you on Thursday. Thursday night, about nine o'clock.'

He was trying to play it like a big-shot—make statements, don't discuss. He said that and hung up with a bang. I mumbled a few curse words into my mouthpiece before I put down the phone. I had a date for Thursday night—dinner and a show and a nightcap at her place. Well, for five thousand bucks, maybe I could show her my etchings.

CHAPTER TWENTY-NINE

If Thursday was D-Day, certain preparatory steps had to be taken. The first was a call to Newman Olds reporting George's asking price of a half-million dollars. Olds swore at the figure as if he hadn't heard it before.

Since I knew he had, this meant he wasn't leveling with me. That was no surprise and it shouldn't be any surprise that I didn't level with him either. I didn't, for example, tell him my opposite number was Saydecker's former valet. I guess I was feeling kindly toward George for I sensed that if Olds knew his identity, he'd figure, as I was figuring, that George was in the game, map and all, all by himself and George would, thereupon, soon suffer the same fate as Arnold Saydecker. It was my belief that the more Olds could be kept in the dark the better for everyone else—myself included.

The second step was Olds' return call saying he'd decided to meet the seller's price. He said it would take him a little time to get the money together and he'd let me know when it was ready.

What was interesting was that the final step came Thursday afternoon when Olds phoned that the money was in hand and all that was now needed was for the other party to contact me about the pickup.

What was also interesting was that, throughout all this, Olds never asked if the seller wouldn't take deeds and mortgage and stocks and what have you in lieu of cash to make up the payment. That he had to convert a half million in holdings to coin of the realm and didn't whimper meant, to me, that this had been spelled out to him in no uncertain terms before I was ever brought into it. In short, the deal had been made and I was only being hired to deliver the goods.

I was to be trusted (for a five thousand dollar fee) to deliver half a million bucks in cash? That was a big laugh.

Newman Olds was able, in two days' time, to convert a half million dollars worth of holdings into half a million dollars worth of greenbacks? That was a bigger laugh.

Simon Kaye was being set up as a patsy. Five thousand bucks Simon Kaye wants? He'd be cheap at twice the price. Goodbye Simon Kaye. Have a good funeral.

The girl I had Thursday's date with didn't cancel out when I had to renege on the show. We had dinner and looked at my etchings instead. I don't have any etchings, of course, but she already knew that.

What she didn't know was why I was restless and uneasy. Here she was, sitting on the couch with the TV on and the sound off, wanting to be friendly and comfortable, and there I was, pacing the floor or perching on the edge of the cushions. I didn't know why I was acting that way either. It was only a phone call, I'd told her. A guy would ring me up to ask if a client of mine was ready for the next step of a business arrangement. That shouldn't prey on my mind, I insisted. She didn't think it should either. But something was wrong and she finally said, 'Why don't you turn up the sound and we can watch the damned TV till the sonuvabitch makes his call?'

I turned up the sound. 'I don't know what the hell's the matter with me.'

'Why don't you pour us both a drink, a good stiff drink?' She'd unbuttoned her dress when she sat down. Now she buttoned it up again.

For some reason I didn't even want the drink. An inner voice told me to stay sober. 'I'll make *you* one,' I said.

'I'm not the one who needs it,' She laughed bitterly. 'I didn't think detectives had nerves. I didn't think you did, anyway.'

I sat beside her and held her hand. We stared at the screen, I didn't know what it showed.

The phone rang and we both sighed. I rose to pick it up and she started undoing buttons again.

It was George, and the conversation went like this:

'Have you contacted the client?'

'Yes.'

'Will he meet the terms?'

'Yes.'

'When will he have the money ready?'

'He has it now.'

'Then we can complete the transaction right away?'

'Any time you say.'

'Tonight then.'

I looked over at my friend on the couch. She had only unbuttoned her dress. She hadn't taken it off. She wasn't going to rush things and her cloudy eyes were studying my behavior on the phone. There was a question as to when I'd give the all-clear signal. I wasn't giving it yet. Right now she could sense there wasn't going to be any all-clear signal.

I gave her a long face and said to Geary, 'If that's the way you want it.'

The girl, who shall be nameless because her identity isn't relevant, hesitated, and reached for the lowest undone button. When I nodded, she did it up again, saw that she had properly interpreted my meaning and slowly reassembled herself.

Geary, meanwhile, was saying that that's the way he wanted it—what he meant to say was, that's the way his client wanted it.

I said, 'Yeah, yeah, the client.

'You will bring the money,' he continued, 'to a certain spot I'll tell you about, where there's an outdoor phone booth.'

This was a replay of the fake pay-off Veronica had rigged. But why not? It's a tactic that works as well as any. I said. 'Yeah, but—'

Geary would not be put off. 'You will wait by that booth for me to phone you there. At that time I'll tell you where we meet to conduct our business.'

I said, 'Don't go off half-cocked, George. I don't have the money.'

There was a loaded pause. 'I thought you said—'

'I said the client has the money. I don't have it. What do you think, he passes that kind of dough around?'

'But you can get it from him tonight?'

'I expect I can. I'll have to check with him first. Why don't you give me a call back in fifteen minutes?'

'No,' George said. 'I'm not calling you again. The next call goes to the phone booth I mentioned. You call your client and tell him the trade's being made tonight. If he wants the map, he'd better give you the dough. How long will it take you to go get it from him and get to the phone booth?'

'I don't know. Where's the phone booth?'

He didn't want to tell me—yet. He said, 'How long will it tak you to be ready with the money?'

I looked at my lady-friend. She gave me a kiss as she went for her things. It was a short evening, but it had been a good dinner and she knew the vicissitudes of a detective's life. Figure twenty minutes to drop her off, twenty more minutes to get to Olds' place, ten minutes collecting the dough (or what he was going to give me in place of dough).

'An hour minimum,' I said. 'From the time I phone him.'

'All right,' he said. 'I'll call you at that phone at eleven thirty. That'll give you over an hour and a half. If you have the money. I'll tell you where we meet. If you don't have the money, we won't meet. Got pencil and paper?'

I said I did and he gave me the location of the phone booth. It was the same booth Veronica had taken me to. Maybe I shouldn't have been surprised. It was in a properly deserted spot. Maybe it was the favorite site for clandestine arrangements.

I laughed and he said, 'You know the place?'

'Yes, I know the place. I'll be there at eleven thirty.'

'Make sure you're alone.'

'I'll be sure.'

CHAPTER THIRTY

I got on the phone to Olds as soon as George had freed the line. Mission to be completed tonight, I said.

That was fine with Olds and when I outlined the scheme, he was not only agreeable, he was pleased.

I dropped the lady and promised her a

better evening next time around and I'd let her know when. Then it was on to Newman Olds' place and now I knew why I'd been nervous. It wasn't a phone call from George, it was the whole arrangement. No matter what George had that Newman Olds wanted, Mr Newman Olds wasn't going to pay George half a million dollars for it. He might pay someone else half a million, but not the likes of George Geary. Newman Olds didn't get to where he was in the world by paying small fry their asking price. George was going to get booby-trapped. And Newman Olds had rigged it so that he wouldn't be anywhere around. It was all going to be done through me.

What was making me nervous was that I didn't know how Olds was going to do it. Give me something I know and understand, no matter how bad, and I'm okay. What I didn't like was this ominous damned shadow.

The sentry waved me through the gate and the old servant let me through the door. Olds was in the darkened living room with Samantha Dean watching the Betamax of a World War II movie. He turned on lights and greeted me like royalty, begging me to give him a minute while he fetched the package. He and the servant disappeared and I was left with Samantha.

She was wearing orange lounging pajamas which became her far better than the blue

linen dress with the white collar. All Olds'
surroundings became her better. She looked
good—like Hollywood in its glory days. No
wonder she was after money. She knew what
it could do for her.

I said, 'Happy?'

She nodded. 'Newman's a great guy.'

Well, each to his own opinion.

Newman came back carrying a suitcase in
one hand and a package wrapped in plastic in
the other arm. He opened the suitcase on the
couch in front of me as if to demonstrate that
it wouldn't explode.

The sloppily wrapped package, he placed
inside it. The package was the size that a half
million dollars' worth of twenty dollar bills
would fill and it fitted comfortably in the 24
inches by 18 inches by 6 inches space of the
suitcase.

I said, 'Want to let me see all that money?'
because I was damned sure what was in there
wasn't money.

'No,' he said. 'You're only a messenger.
You can feel it if you think it's something
else, but you can't see it. I'm telling you what
it is and you're going to take my word for it.'

I felt it. The contents were packets with
elastic bands around them. It was all
paper—no metal objects, no hidden
transmitters or plastic pipe bombs. That was
my main concern.

When I was satisfied, I said, 'All right, now

what?'

He closed the suitcase and locked it with a key. He put the key in his pocket and gave me a screwdriver. 'Your liaison,' he told me, 'will want to count the money before giving you the map to make sure it's all there. He's going to have to break the suitcase open to do that. That's what the screwdriver's for. That's to prove to him that you haven't tampered with it either.'

I said, 'I see,' and rubbed my chin. I was still trying to guess the angle.

'Before you let him open the suitcase, make him show you the map.' He handed me a folded sheet of paper. 'This is the kind of paper it's on and the size it'll be. It will be torn along this edge. The line I've drawn shows the raggedness of the tear. The tear on his map should match this. Also, the tear is across a watermark where I've made those lines. The map will be in black ink and there'll be a signature on it that will match this one.' He handed me another, smaller, piece of paper with a reproduced signature which said, 'I.M. Jenks'. 'The signature will be in blue ink. Make sure it's the same handwriting and not a copy or a tracing.'

'And if I'm satisfied?'

'Then give him the suitcase. Let him open it and count the money. When he's satisfied, make the swap and bring the map to me.'

That was that and it was off to

adventureland. He saw me to the door and bade me godspeed. Samantha stayed behind, turning off the lights so they could go back to the Betamax. Never mind what Lavinia said, Samantha was getting dough out of Olds the easy way. Mine was the tough job.

★   ★   ★

I drove to the phone booth and parked in the shadows, but close enough to hear its ring. Nobody had followed me. Nobody was parked in the area. The occasional passing car paid me no attention.

As for the locked suitcase and the screwdriver, that was another laugh. Olds was a real funnyman. I carry a set of keys that would match most locksmiths and the idea that I'd have to break the suitcase open to see what Olds had stashed inside was a joke. If he'd put real money in there, I could pack off to South America with it on the next plane from JFK. Which is why, of course, I knew what he'd put in there wasn't money.

So, what was it? I had time to kill, I might as well find out. I turned on the dome light and sorted through my keys.

It didn't take a minute. The third suitcase key fitted and I lifted the lid, unfastened the tape that held the plastic wrapping, and spread it open. What came into view were elastic bound packets all right, but not of money. They were composed of cut up newspaper. Olds hadn't even tried to make it look like actual money by putting a twenty at the top of each. The suitcase didn't contain a red cent.

I wrapped and sealed it again and relocked the suitcase. I'd known all along there would be no money changing hands tonight, but the actual discovery left me even more uneasy about Olds' plans for this evening.

Now what was going to happen?

Precisely at eleven thirty, the phone rang and I picked up the receiver. George said, 'Kaye? Do you have the money?'

'Yeah.' What I meant, of course, was that I had what Olds have given me. I could have told George the truth, but that would be betraying a client. Also, I was curious to see what George would be bringing with him. Would the map be phony too?

'You know the Alderbrook Cemetery?'

'I do.'

'Do you know the road that goes around behind it on the north side, it's off Linden Place?'

'Dromara Road?'

'I guess that's the one. Anyway, a quarter of a mile in, on the righthand side, beside the cemetery wall, there's a big oak tree. You can't miss it.'

'I'll find it.'

'I'll meet you there at twelve o'clock.'

I said sure and hung up. That was it. The witching hour.

CHAPTER THIRTY-ONE

I arrived at the oak tree with five minutes to spare, got out of the car with gun and flashlight, and reconnoitered. No one had followed me and there was no one to be seen. I was still itchy. Things were too pat, too quiet, too phony. I had a real case of jitters tonight. I couldn't leave my gun alone.

The car stood just past the tree, parallel to the wall and I leaned against it, looking over its roof, scanning the road. There was nothing to see but shapes and shadows, nothing to hear but the rustling of leaves in a light breeze.

At five after midnight, the glow of the headlights reflected off the distant trees, then lights showed over the grade and George Geary's car pulled in ahead of mine. His windows were open and he said, 'Kaye?'

'Ho.'

He saw me, got out and came around. 'You got the dough?'

'In the front seat.'

'Get it out. I want to count it.'

'First the map, George.'

'First the money.'

I said, 'Forget it. My orders are that you don't get a smell of the money until I'm satisfied the map is authentic. What kind of a jerk do you think Olds is? What kind of a jerk do you think I am?'

'All right. I'll show you the map, but you can't handle it. You don't touch the map until I've counted the money.'

'Suits me. Show me the map.'

Geary slipped an envelope from an inside pocket and opened it in the light of my flash. From it, he produced a folded paper the size of the one I took from my own pocket. 'Open it up.'

He did and held it while I beamed my light over it. There was a crude sketch on it of a road, some trees, an 'X' and a lot of figures for distance and angles. I opened my own paper and matched the ragged line with the torn edge of his map. Perfect.

'What are you doing?'

'Verifying. Now the watermark,' That matched as well.

'It's genuine,' he insisted. 'You think I'd try to double-cross Olds?'

'The signature. Hold it steady.' I matched that and scored another bullseye. It was the real thing all right. 'Okay,' I told him. 'You can put it away.'

I snapped off the flash so my eyes could grow accustomed to the darkness again. The moment of truth was coming up and I had the

232

feeling skyrockets and fireworks were going to explode.

'The suitcase is on the front seat,' I told him in a low voice and got down on a knee. 'Keep low.'

'Why?' he said. 'What do you think's going to happen?'

'I don't know, but I want to be ready.'

'What're you whispering for? You weren't followed, were you?'

'No.'

'Well, neither was I.'

He opened the door and the dome light came on. He took out the suitcase.

'Keep down,' I said. 'I heard something.'

'But nobody—'

I reached over and slammed the door to put us in darkness. I was on a knee by the rear wheel and I'd heard something, a scrape or rustle that wasn't caused by the wind.

Someone was out there—at least one, but I was betting two. I nudged George and scurried from behind my car to behind his. Keep 'em guessing, is my motto.

George followed, but stumbled over a root. It made a noise and the noise was followed by the blast of a revolver firing. There was a flash of flame across the road and the keening whine of a bullet. George had fallen, and the bullet went over his head, but it was close.

He scrambled on hands and knees beside me. 'Jesus Christ!'

I held fire. The shot had come from behind a rock and I had nothing to aim at. I muttered to George, 'You got a gun?'

'Christ, no.'

There was another shot, this from behind the oak tree, right down the line of cars at us. It thudded and we got behind the front of George's car. I said, 'Are you all right?' for we'd been in the open.

'Yeah, I think so.'

'Come on out with your hands up,' a voice said. It came from behind the oak and was Theodore's. That meant the man behind the rock was Murray.

George whispered to me, 'What do you think?'

'They want your map.'

'I don't care about the map as long as I get the money.'

'There isn't any money. It's a trap.'

I peeked above the hood of the car. Through the windshield and rear window I could see the oak. The door post blocked me from the man behind the rock. I steadied my gun and held it on the hood, aimed at the dim outline of the oak.

George cursed Newman Olds softly, but heartily. 'Did you know about this, Kaye?'

'Are you nuts?'

'I can see you,' the voice from behind the oak bawled out. 'Surrender or die!' To emphasize the point, Theodore fired another

234

shot which ricochetted off the fender by George's head.

I said my gun was aimed. I had a bead on the flash and returned fire for the first time, the bullet going through the windshield and rear window of George's car. I didn't know if I hit anything, but I knew I'd come close. Now I ducked low and peeked around the car at the rock. It was too damned dark to make out more than shadows.

It wasn't all shadows long. Flashes flared as Murray cut loose a brace of bullets, but they were two feet overhead. He was aiming at where my gun had been. I let one go in return but I was probably as wild as he was. All right, three shots from Murray, two from Theodore. I kept low and alert, and slipped a couple of cartridges out of the box in my pocket, taking advantage of the lull to replace my empties. If they tried to keep count on me, they'd get a surprise.

On my left, George muttered more curses. 'What're we going to do?' he queried nervously.

'Wait them out. We don't have much choice' Then I told him to stay low but keep an eye on the oak tree. 'I don't want Theodore sneaking in closer.'

'Theodore? You know who they are?'

'Theodore and Murray—friends of Mr Olds.'

George shivered. 'God,' he whispered.

'They're killers.'

I don't know what he thought he was telling me. I said, 'Just keep low and watch the oak.'

With George guarding that side, I concentrated on trying to make sense out of Murray's hiding place. There were bushes and a rock, but that's all I knew. I could aim my flashlight, but that would give him something to shoot at. If I couldn't see him, at least I knew where he was and had him pinned down. My eyes were well conditioned to the darkness now and he'd be a target if he tried to sneak anywhere else.

I won't say I was feeling confident, but I thought at least we had an even chance. Although I couldn't see anything moving where Murray was, I aimed carefully and pulled the trigger. Who knew but that I might make a lucky hit?

I didn't. What I drew instead, were two, three angry and vicious shots my way and the air hissed out of the front tire. Well, that should have emptied his gun, but I was sure it hadn't. He wouldn't have been so eager.

Then I tried the old trick of throwing a handful of pebbles over the roof of the car. They came down with a rattle on the trunk and Murray opened fire again. Did I say his gun was empty? He had plenty of bullets left, or a second gun. What spewed out from the rock was a fusillade.

I thought I could shoot at the flashes, but I never had a chance. One of his wild shots hit the gas tank. George's car exploded and the whole rear went up in the air.

Before it came down, flames were billowing fifty feet into the sky and the whole scene was bathed in a bright orange glow; the road, the rock and bushes across the way, and Murray behind the rock, to say nothing of George and me.

Murray's hiding place was a small rock. Even on his knees he couldn't conceal himself. In the burst of flame and light, I could see his face, the 'O' of his mouth and the expression of astonishment at the fireball, at the way the interior of George's car became an inferno.

Then he saw me, edging away, driven into the open by the searing heat. He tried to get lower and aim his gun, but the rock wouldn't protect him. I fired and the bullet ricochetted off the top by his ear. It was a miss, but it flushed him.

He leaped to his feet and ran into the road, firing my way as he went. He was trying to get across the open to the shelter of the oak.

My first shot missed. He was running like hell and I hurried it.

I dropped him with my second, but still didn't get him where I wanted. He rolled over and was up and hobbling. I don't know if he still had his gun or not, but he wasn't shooting. He only wanted to get away.

That's the thing you don't let happen. I hit him again and he was down again. This time he came up and scrambled on his hands and knees. My next shot caught him as he reached the side of the road, and this time he rolled over on his back and his arms flopped wide. He wasn't going to go any farther. Not ever.

That took care of one, but the heat of the inferno kept driving George and me out into the road where there was no shelter. I kept the flaming car between us and the oak, but we were sitting ducks.

George was on that side of me, though, and when he saw Murray's body, he pulled me the other way and pointed. He was showing me. Theodore, lying on his back on the ground, half out from back of the tree, his face a bloody mask. I was crazy with luck tonight. I'd got him through the eye with my windshield shot.

That was all I needed. 'Quick, into my car, before it catches fire.'

We ran for it and just in time. Already, the door handles were hot.

I pulled out and backed around and we didn't tarry to examine the bodies. George's blazing car was lighting up the midnight sky and there'd be all kinds of traffic on this road at any moment.

We got the hell out.

CHAPTER THIRTY-TWO

I hit fifty heading for town and George sat turned in his seat, staring back at the way the fire lighted up the sky, all the while cursing Newman Olds. 'How the hell did we get staked out?' he wanted to know. 'Did you tip them off?'

I snorted. 'Make sense. I was their target, same as you.'

'That would be like Olds, get you to tell him where we were meeting and then double-cross you, kill you too.'

'What do you think, I've got meatloaf brains?'

'All right, I wasn't saying you sold me out. I didn't think you would. That's why I made Olds hire you. But if you didn't tip them off, how the hell—'

I said, 'What do you mean you made Olds hire me?'

He opened the window for another look when I stopped at a light and I turned around too. The flames were dying and there was only a dim whitish glow against the blackness now. 'Yeah,' he said, turning back. 'We talked last week. You seemed to know something. I needed somebody as a contact. I'd talked to Olds, but I didn't want to deal with him directly. I'm scared of him. He's ruthless and slick and he'll double-cross you no matter what you do. That's why I told him I wasn't going to deal with him, I was only going to deal with you.'

'The two of you knew each other. You think he recognized your voice?'

'No, I was careful about that. And I was careful tonight. I didn't tell you where to meet me except over a public phone and I made sure I wasn't followed. So unless they followed you—'

'They didn't follow me,' I snapped. 'I told you that. Besides, they were there, with the place staked out, before we arrived. They had time to hide where they put their car.'

'I don't get it,' George said, as I started on. 'How did he do it?'

'I don't know, but he had the double-cross set up before I ever picked up his suitcase. Because there's no dough in it. He wasn't going to pay you off, he just wanted you to have the map on you.' I snorted at my own folly. 'He was using me too, the sonuvabitch. He told me to verify the map before I gave you the suitcase. If the map was a phony, no suitcase. Get it? So the moment I give you the suitcase, Theodore and Murray know the map is valid and they open fire.'

'The bastard,' George said. 'Listen, take me to my place. I've got to get to my place.'

'Don't be in a hurry, George, you and I have a lot to talk about.'

240

'Yeah, that's okay, I'll tell you everything I know, but get me home.'

I headed his way and mused about Olds and the double-cross. 'You told Olds to hire me? What did you say? Did he know you knew me?'

George shook his head. 'I didn't tell him we'd ever met. I told him I wasn't going to call him any more, that from now on my client wanted to work through a liaison. That's what I told him. I made sure he understood I didn't have the map, I was only an intermediary. And I said he was to get an intermediary too. I told him my client had seen your name in the paper in connection with Joe Tanner's murder and my client wanted you as the intermediary. And I told him my client's price was half a million dollars and that I'd phone you tonight to find out his answer. I left it up to him to take it from there.'

'That gave him time,' I said. 'He had several days to rig something.' Then I said, 'I'll bet that's it.'

'What's it?'

'Suppose Theodore and Murray are handy, dandy little electricians, or Newman Olds can get people who are? Suppose you tell him last weekend that you're going to phone me tonight? Suppose his boys then rig a tap on my phone line? When you call me tonight, they find out all about the public phone where you'll make your next call and they run out and put a tap on that while I'm getting the suitcase from Olds? When you call me with instructions about our meeting, they're right ready to hightail to the spot and wait. What do you want to bet, George, that my phone line is tapped?'

George smote his forehead. 'Stupid, stupid. I never thought of that.'

'Yeah, stupid. Now let's have it. What's this all about?'

'Get me home, he said. 'It's a long story. Get me home and I'll tell you.'

I parked in front, under one of the trees that lined the sidewalks, and got out. 'Okay, we're here.'

He was slow disembarking on his side and I was impatient. 'The suitcase,' he mumbled. Nothing would do but that I bring the suitcase up with us. I humored him, but without a smile. My nerves were pretty well shot. He didn't look so good himself and he stumbled over his feet. When I tried to steady him, he shook me off, but when we got inside, he held the railing going up the stairs.

His key was steady sliding into the lock, but he slumped into the nearest chair in the living room. I set the suitcase by his feet and went through the rest of the apartment, turning lights on and off.

When I got back to him, he was sprawled and taking deep breaths. 'Where's your girlfriend?' I said.

He pulled himself erect. 'Huh?'

'Last time I was here, you'd entertained a girl overnight. I have to say you switched from servant to master pretty fast.'

'It wasn't what you think,' George growled. 'It was a friend. She said she wanted protection. She used to go with Olds and was on the outs with him. That's what she said, but I didn't trust her.'

'Not Veronica Dean?'

George looked at me. 'You know her?'

'We've met. Did you tell her you had the map?'

'Hell no. That's what I was afraid she was trying to find out. I sent her away.' George gestured at the suitcase. His pasty face was drawn and tired. 'Let's see the money,' he said hoarsely. 'I want to see what Olds gave me.'

'There's no money,' I said. 'I told you there wasn't any.'

'I want to see what's in there anyway.'

I got out my keys and opened the suitcase at his feet. He bent to pick up a stack of cut newspapers, pulled off the elastic, spread the sheaf, and threw it. The bill-shaped papers soared, floated and fell. He did the same thing with a second packet and then a third, all the while cursing Newman Olds in a steady stream. 'I told you he was a double-crosser,' he said. 'But he's not going to get the map.'

I sat on the couch. 'All right, George, you've had your fun. Stop messing up your living room and start talking. I didn't bring you home to watch you play.'

He smiled. 'It's all I've got left.' Then he shrugged. 'Do me a favor. Get even with Olds.'

'Yeah. All in good time.' I pointed at his jacket pocket. 'The map, George. I want to know about the map.'

'It's been a secret for a long time,' he said heavily, 'but it doesn't matter any more, so you might's well know the whole story. Maybe you can make some kind of moral out of it.'

'Not likely, but don't let that stop you.'

He smiled wryly. 'Do you remember the Hillsdale armored car robbery eight years ago?'

'Vaguely. Give it to me again.'

'Armored car robbery.' George helped himself to a cigarette from the box beside the chair, lighted, coughed raspingly and sat back. 'Two guards killed. It was a shipment of nearly four hundred pounds of gold. The price of gold was a helluva lot more then than it is now, but even today it's worth close to two million dollars.'

I was getting the picture, but wanted him to paint it. 'Go on.'

'There were twelve of us worked it,' he

said. 'Twelve guys. Nobody ever got caught, if you'll remember, and the gold was never recovered. Pfft. Everything vanished into thin air.' He sighed. 'That was part of the plan. We were to sit tight until the heat was off. We knew it'd take a long time—years. But we were willing to wait.

'So what did we do with the gold? We buried it. And we made a map, and after we made the map, we tore it in two. One half would show where the gold was buried with relation to a certain road. That's the half I've got. It's the measurement in angles and feet with bearings taken from certain trees, rocks, and other landmarks.

'The other half of the map, the half Newman Olds has, shows where the road is with relation to other roads, with relation to compass direction, the town and all the rest.

'After we buried the gold, we all traveled away together to let it sit. Then we had a farewell party and divided into two groups, one half under Arnold Saydecker, the other half under Morris Jenks. We divided the map. Arnold was the leader of one faction—the one I was in, and Morris was the leader of the other faction. Olds, and those guys you killed tonight, were in the other half with Jenks. The idea was the gangleaders would keep in touch and when the time was ripe, we'd get together, the twelve of us, put the map back together, and go dig up the gold.'

'And what happened?'

'Well, we had our other ways of making money. We didn't retire, of course, and we didn't need that bonanza to keep us alive. We all knew we had to wait before we could do anything. But all the time we were doing the other things we were doing, there was this vision of—well, it was over three hundred thousand dollars apiece back then. Now it's less than half that, but still a neat bundle. And, of course, not all of the twelve survived the next eight years and with each death, the value of our shares went up.'

'Did some of you help the undertaker along that way?'

'You mean, assisted some of the members into their graves? Arnold didn't. I don't know about the other gang, except that all of a sudden, Jenks was dead and Newman Olds headed up the gang.'

I nodded. That sounded like Olds. 'Go on.'

'That's it.'

I shook my head. 'That's not it, because Arnold Saydecker also didn't live to put the map back together. He's dead and you've got the map.' I pointed a finger. 'You killed him.'

George shook his head. 'I didn't kill him, Mutt Stark killed him. I killed Mutt Stark. That's who I killed.'

'Let's hear about it.'

It wasn't something he wanted to discuss

and he looked pained. 'Let's just say Mutt killed Arnold and took the map. I took it back, that's all.'

'Yeah, Johnny on the spot. Come on, you've told me the rest of it. Don't hold back. You killed the guy. I want to know how.'

'All right,' George said unhappily. 'Maybe I couldn't've helped it. Arnold got killed and it was my fault. Maybe if I'd been more careful—but Mutt was one of our guys. Arnold trusted him.'

'I want to know your role.'

'Yeah.' George rubbed his face with a hand. 'I'm trying to tell you. I was Arnold's bodyguard. I lived with him. I was like his valet.

'So when Mutt came, since he was one of us, Arnold and me, we got a little careless. Arnold and Olds had been in contact. It was getting time to put the map together. We were all supposed to get together the next day, the ones from the old gang who were still alive.

'That's why Arnold had the map in the house. He took it out of the safety deposit box that day. And Mutt called up and came over. He had a problem, he said. Something to do with women, he said, and he wanted advice. So we let him up and didn't suspect anything, and when he came in, he pulled a gun on us, took mine, and made Arnold produce the map, and when Arnold did, he shot him and he was going to shoot me, but I got away.

'He ran outside then, but I ran outside the back and I laid for him and got him with a knife and took back the map and my gun and everything else he had, except his gun. And I left him there and when I looked over the stuff he had, I found Olds' phone number. And nobody but Arnold was supposed to have that. So that meant that Olds had put him up to murdering Arnold, that Olds was trying to get Arnold's half of the map and double-cross the guys in Arnold's gang, me and the others. So I got rid of Mutt's stuff and hid my gun and the map and then I called the cops and told them I'd come home and found my boss—my master—murdered on the floor.' He shrugged. 'I figured I let Arnold down, but at least I got the guy who did it to him.'

I said, 'Who are the other members of Arnold's gang?'

George smiled faintly and shook his head. 'No you don't. I don't mind you knowing the names of the ones who're dead, but I ain't gonna rat on the ones who're alive. They aren't gonna get the gold. Nobody's gonna get it. That much is for sure. But at least they aren't gonna go to jail.'

'You want Olds in jail, don't you?'

George scowled. 'I want him dead!' He went through his monotonous string of oaths describing what a double-crosser Newman

Olds was. Then he said to me, 'But you know Olds is part of the gang. You can finger him to the cops if you want, but not the others.'

That got me angry. 'Stop playing noble, George. You were going to sell your half to Olds for five hundred grand. You were going to double-cross the rest of your gang yourself.'

He didn't like that. He sat up straight. 'I was going to sell it to him, yes. Because I knew he'd kill me for it otherwise, the way he hired Mutt to kill Arnold for it. But I would've split the money once I got it.'

I laughed. 'Sure you would.'

He didn't argue. He sighed and lay back in the chair. 'But now nobody's gonna get that gold, and nobody's gonna get the map. It's cost enough lives. It's not gonna cost any more. Because I'm gonna destroy it.' He reached inside his jacket.

'Oh no you aren't,' I said, and rose to my feet. The time had come for me to take charge.

He beat me to it. He withdrew his hand and it wasn't holding the map, it was holding a gun. 'You didn't know I had this, did you?' he said. 'Now you just sit down again. I'm gonna burn this map and you're gonna watch me do it. Then you're going away from here and we'll pretend tonight never happened.'

'George,' I argued, 'use your head.'

'I am, I said that map's cost enough lives.

Sit down, I told you. Don't make me add you to the list.'

I sat and he smiled apologetically, resting the gun comfortably in his lap, aiming it in my general direction. He slid his free hand back inside his jacket for the envelope, but when he brought it out, it was wet. It wasn't just wet, it was soaking. What had saturated the envelope was blood, George's blood.

I started. 'You've been hit.'

He nodded. 'From behind the car.'

'Why the hell didn't you say so?' I started up. 'We've got to get you to the hospital.'

He raised his gun and backed me down again. 'It's too late,' he said. 'There's nothing they could do about it anyway. I knew that the moment I got it. It's all right, though. It doesn't hurt. I wouldn't even know I was hit except that I'm getting weaker. That's why we've gotta stop now. I've gotta destroy the map.'

He put the envelope on the table beside him so that part of it projected over the edge. That way he could set fire to it with the lighter and keep me covered at the same time.

I said, 'Look, just because the map won't do you any good doesn't mean it should be destroyed. The gold ought to be recovered.'

He smiled. 'Getting greedy, Kaye? You think you'd like to share the map with Olds? He'd kill you, you know. Like he killed Morris Jenks, like he killed Arnold

250

Saydecker, like he's killed me. You'd be next. But it's not gonna happen. He's not gonna get this map.'

George held the flame under the corner of the envelope but it wouldn't ignite. It was too wet. He cursed. The lighter flame died and he relighted it. The flame was small. He shook the lighter and tried to light it again, but dropped it instead. He started to lean forward for it, but paused, lest I jump him. 'Move over there,' he said, waving his gun at the far end of the couch. I slid slowly, watching. He was dying fast now.

When he thought I was far enough away, he reached down and groped on the floor for the lighter but couldn't find it. I watched him miss and kept silent.

He pulled himself erect and leaned back. The effort had exhausted him. He fumbled for a book of matches in his pocket, then tried to tear one loose with one hand. He almost couldn't do it.

Lighting it was out of the question. For that he'd need both hands. He hesitated, let go of the gun and scratched it quickly. I braced myself, but he had the gun again. 'Ah, ah,' he said, his eyes gleaming. 'Greedy, greedy.'

With his gun on me, he held the match to the envelope. He held it till the match scorched his fingers, but nothing happened to the envelope.

He dropped the match, sucked his burned fingers and swore. He leaned back, breathing hard. 'Who the hell cares?' he said, and his eyes shut.

I waited, but he didn't move again. I silently got off the couch, moving away from the gun's line of fire. He didn't do anything. I circled behind his chair and felt his neck for a pulse. There was none.

I put the wet envelope in my inside pocket, turned out the lights, and left.

CHAPTER THIRTY-THREE

Trust the police not to pass me over as a suspect any time there's a murder in town. At least this time they didn't get to me until Monday afternoon at the office. By then the papers were billing Thursday night's events as the Mystery of the Century. So were the cops.

Feature this: At half past twelve Thursday night, flames light up the sky from back of the cemetery. Upon arrival police and firemen find the white-hot burning remains of a late model sedan. Also found are the bodies of two armed men, one shot once through the eye, the other shot three times. Ballistics, as of Monday evening's papers, state that all four bullets came from the same gun.

The two men are identified as Theodore Hurtz (shot through the eye) and Murray Leitman (shot in the leg, stomach, and chest). Both had guns in their hands. Two bullets had been fired from Theodore Hurtz's gun, only two bullets are left in Leitman's.

The burned-out car is traced by its license plate to Arnold Saydecker, who had been murdered ten days earlier. Saydecker's apartment has since been occupied by his valet, George Geary. When the landlord lets the police into the apartment, George Geary is found sitting in an armchair in the living room, stone cold dead, holding a loaded revolver in his lap. He has been shot through the side of the chest.

On the floor beside him is a suitcase filled with cut-up newspapers, some of which have been scattered around the room. Oh yes, to add a little extra touch of mystery to proceedings, a completely burnt paper match is found on the rug by George's chair, along with a lighter, and there are burn marks on his fingers.

Then comes the shocker. Ballistics has just learned that the bullet which left Geary dead in his living room came from Theodore's gun back at the cemetery.

And, as a final note, the busy-bee ballistics lab has also determined that Geary's gun was not the gun that fired the bullets into Theodore and Murray.

Now then, how did Geary get from the cemetery where his car was burned, to the chair in his living room? What kind of pay-off was the suitcase full of paper supposed to represent? Who was the gun in Geary's hand aimed at?

Quite obviously, another person or persons were on hand when the shoot-out took place. Someone had to provide Geary with transportation home. Someone had to shoot Theodore and Murray.

Who could that someone be?

Well, background on Theodore and Murray is inconclusive. They seem to be engaged in uncertain lines of work and are business associates of one Newman Olds, whose line of work is also uncertain. Newman Olds would be the logical one to query on the subject. Unfortunately, Newman Olds' house is closed up and Mr Olds seems to have left town for the time being, whereabouts unknown.

Who else is there whom the police might ask?

Who else but Simon Kaye, of course. Wasn't Simon Kaye reported in the neighborhood when Joe Tanner was slain? Didn't Simon Kaye blow down two punks in his own office just the other day? And, in fact, wasn't it Theodore and Murray who helped him? And didn't Theodore and Murray walk off with Mr Simon Kaye, the suspicion being that it was against Mr Kaye's will? And where would they be taking Mr Kaye? Why, to see Mr Olds.

So, if Mr Olds isn't around to give us any help, why don't we ask Mr Kaye some questions? Who knows what pearls of information lie within his ken?

This time, for once, they didn't have anything on me at all. They'd never done a lab test on the bullets I put into Luke and Leo so they had no idea what gun killed Murray and Theodore behind the cemetery. All they could do was play hunches and hope I wouldn't laugh in their faces.

And because they were only guessing, they didn't come at me with their superchargers on, they played it low-key. Instead of Don Lasky, they sent Dan Saxton.

He sat with me in my office, all nice and quiet, and he told me what the cops had and what they didn't have and how puzzled they were. Had I heard the latest—that the bullet that killed Geary had come from Theodore's gun?

I said it was in tonight's paper.

'You know some of these people,' Dan went on. 'Olds, for instance. What about him?'

I said we'd met but I didn't know him that well.

'And Hurtz and Leitman? They picked you up here last week, I understand. What the hell would they be up to?'

'I understand they worked for Olds. Errand boys, messenger boys. Something. Where do you think Olds went, and why?'

'Underground, we figure. We think he doesn't want to answer our questions.'

'What makes you think I do want to? What makes you think I would if I could?'

'You were a cop once. I have to figure you on the side of the law and order.'

I laughed. 'There're a lot of cops who aren't. Some right here in town.'

'But I figure you aren't one of them.'

I sat back in my chair. 'I'll tell you something, Dan. If there were something I knew that would help you in what you're trying to do, I'd tell it to you. If there isn't, I'm not going to open my mouth. Fair enough?'

'We might know better than you whether the information you have will help us or not.'

'You might. But I'm the one who has to make the decision. I'm sure you'll acknowledge that?'

He had to concede the point but it made him sigh for he knew my decision would be that I didn't know anything that would help them out.

The fact was that I didn't. I couldn't even help myself out, and that was my priority. The hell with police department problems. I have *my* problems.

Dan went away in time but the problems didn't. They had to be tackled. Number one on the agenda was how to get my hands on Newman Olds. The cops thought he'd fled to avoid me. He'd set me up—used me as bait in a trap. The trap was supposed to get him George Geary's half of the map and rid the world of George and me at the same time. It didn't work and he knew I'd be after him. What's more, he didn't have Murray and Theodore for protection any more. So he was lying low and I had no way to track him. Samantha? She'd probably gone underground with him. Veronica? Nobody answered her phone any more. Lavinia? I called her and she didn't know what I was talking about. Her voice was half sloshed with alcohol. She wasn't even sure who I was.

Finding the bastard was a problem, though, that should solve itself in time. All I needed was something I was a little short of these days—patience. Wait for a bit and Newman Olds would resurface. Newman Olds would, when his courage returned, come my way again. Because I had something he wanted. I had a million dollar piece of paper with drawings and figures on it. And he knew I had it. Or he would know when he sat down long enough to figure out what had taken place that Thursday night behind the cemetery wall.

CHAPTER THIRTY-FOUR

It happened at half past twelve on Thursday night. Nobody gives a damn that I go to bed at a reasonable hour. They seem to think my condo is a subway at rush hour.

The phone woke me up and a sobbing voice was on the other end. It was Samantha and she didn't have to identify herself. Her voice, even full of tears, has a particular quality that's unmistakable.

She identified herself anyway, just in case I had a short memory, and she sobbed something about Newman that I didn't get.

'What's the matter?' I said, wondering if she were waking me up to say she'd discovered the wages of sin.

'Can I see you?' She was really crying. This was no make-believe. 'Simon, I have to see you.'

'What about?'

'It's about Newman.' She choked on her sobs. 'We had trouble. I'm not with him any more.'

I wasn't in a sympathetic mood. Partly because I don't like being waked out of a sound sleep. Partly I don't like being everybody's wailing wall. Partly why the hell should I care about Samantha's problems? She went with Olds of her own accord.

Nobody twisted her arm. 'Newman's a great guy,' she'd told me exactly one week ago. So he had feet of clay? That's information I'd already collected. 'Lover,' I said, 'There's only one thing I want to hear about Newman, and that's his whereabouts.'

'Please!' It was a plea. 'I have to talk to you.'

'Where are you?'

'In a phone booth.' She sobbed for a couple of breaths. 'I've run away.'

'And you don't have any money.'

'No, no, that's not it. I've got money.'

'Then what the hell are you waking me up for?'

'He's after me. I've got no place to go.'

I have to tell you, the tears were real, but I wasn't believing any of this. You don't run away from Newman Olds. You can get sent away, but you don't run away. 'Call Veronica,' I said.

'She doesn't answer. I don't know where she is. Please, Simon, I have to see you.'

'You want to see me,' I said, 'come to my office in the morning.'

'No, now. I've got to see you now!'

'Why?'

She was sobbing again. 'I can't tell you why.'

I said, 'Forget it,' and hung up.

That worked out just fine. I got her off the line, but my freedom didn't put me back to sleep. I lay there with the light on for five minutes, suspicious as hell, wondering what was going on, what she thought she was doing, what she thought I was going to do.

I sat up and had a cigarette, which I do every once in a while. Then I got up and prowled the bedroom. I opened the door to my closet and took the gun out of the holster that hangs on a hook just inside. Something made me want to reacquaint myself with the feel of it. I'd been using it a lot lately. How many men had I killed the past couple of weeks? It was a staggering figure, even if I were in the business. I was a regular one-man gang. And there'd been a few other murders in the same period for which I wasn't responsible, but which were connected to me nevertheless, guys like Arnold Saydecker, Mutt Stark, George Geary, and Joe Tanner.

I turned out the light, tried again to go to sleep. I couldn't. Samantha was on my mind. I knew hanging up hadn't been goodbye. The question was, what would happen next?

'Next' turned out to be one o'clock. The doorbell rang. I didn't have to be told who it was, and I also didn't have to be told to be careful.

I slipped on a dressing gown over my pajamas and put my gun in the dressing gown pocket. I went down the stairs turning on lights, crossed the kitchen, then out through the foyer. At the door, I said, 'Who's there?'

It was Samantha, of course, and she was still crying. 'Simon, please open the door.'

I switched on the outside light and cracked the door an inch, keeping the chain on. It was raining and she was wet. Her dark hair glistened with droplets, her face was dirty and tear-streaked, she had a swollen, black and blue eye. All she was wearing were those orange lounging pajamas which looked so damned good on her when she was in Olds' lavish living room, but which now, sodden and clinging, in the dull gloom of my storm porch, looked like hell.

When she saw me, she didn't speak, she just put her hands over her face and sobbed brokenly. I've seen sad women in my life, but no one as desolate as she.

I didn't know how she'd got there—she could have walked for all of me. There was no sign of anyone with her, no sound of a car driving away.

'All right,' I said, and undid the chain. I was going to let her in, but I wasn't relaxed. I still smelled trouble. Girls don't sob on my storm porch in the middle of the night for nothing.

It was trouble, all right. The door was no more than half open when it was kicked out of my grasp and in came Newman Olds with an arm locked around Samantha's neck and a gun pointed at my navel.

He entered swearing and I thought he was

going to empty his gun into me before his feet were over the threshold, but he didn't want to make it quite that quick. The fact that I backed off and raised my hands told him he could savor the moment before applying the *coup de grâce*.

In the grip of his vicelike arm, terrified Samantha choked and sobbed. 'He made me,' she cried out. 'I didn't want to.'

Judging from her swollen eye, she'd had to be beaten before she would phone me and her tears stemmed from physical pain as well as the agony of betrayal.

Once in the foyer, Olds kicked the door closed and threw Samantha into a chair. He stood panting, legs spread, clad in an open trenchcoat, and his eyes were wild. He'd made her phone me, he'd made her ring my bell. He'd hidden on my steps and kept his gun on her while she sobbed for admittance. And when I released the chain, he jumped on her, throttled her, rammed his gun into her, and kicked his way inside. I thought I'd been ready for whatever might happen, but I wasn't. I should have been, but I wasn't.

Now he held me at bay while Samantha huddled, wide-eyed, in a chair. She was going to witness a shooting. What of it? She wouldn't be telling anyone for she would be one of the victims. It would be a double murder—Simon and Samantha killed together, and let the cops add that to the mysteries they already had. I could hear them at it: 'Samantha? You remember that broad with Simon when we brought him in on the Tanner killing? We never did find out enough about her: We should have paid more attention.'

The trouble was, there was nothing Samantha or I could do about it. I had a gun in my bathrobe pocket, but my hands were at head height and the muzzle of Newman's gun was as big as a cannon and pointed at my midriff where there was no way he could miss. As for Samantha, she was crumpled in the chair with the fight beaten out of her. Forget it.

Olds was frothing at the mouth. The names he called me and the vituperation of his tone nearly scorched the paint off my walls. He wanted me to know, before he killed me, the damage I had done, the wreckage I had caused to his operation. He was going to plant a bullet in my innards for each and every wrong deed I'd committed—until he ran out of bullets or I ran out of innards.

Not only had I destroyed his operation, I'd frustrated all his plans.

I saw a faint glimmer. 'You mean,' I said, 'you didn't come for the map?'

'No, I didn't come for the map, I came for you.' Then he hesitated. He wasn't as smart as I'd thought. He hadn't doped out where the map had gone, he was only here for

263

revenge. Now the seed had been planted. 'You've got the map? Like hell you have.'

'A present from George Geary. He willed it to me.'

Olds cut loose with more oaths. 'What've you done with it?'

'It'll cost you half a million dollars to find out.'

He threatened me with the gun. 'I'm gonna make you bleed, Kaye. I'm warning you. Where's the map?'

'Nowhere where you're going to find it.' I was playing it tough now, real tough. I wasn't feeling tough at all, but it was my only chance. Feed his greed. Get him worrying about the map, make him realize if he killed me before he got it, he'd be doing himself out of two million dollars which, by now, he wouldn't have to share with anybody.

It worked. I could see the dollar signs come into his eyes. 'Yeah,' he said. 'I figured that too. You made sure the map was genuine before you gave that bastard Geary the suitcase. When they found him with the suitcase, it meant you had the map. So what do you think you're going to do, sell it to me?'

'That's right. You want it, I've got it.'

'I'm not going to pay you for it, Mister. I'm going to take it.'

'Not if you don't know where it is.'

His eyes glinted. 'That's right, but you

want to know something? You're gonna tell me where it is.' He patted his gun. 'Because of this.'

'You've got to be kidding,' I snorted. 'Since you're going to kill me anyway, why should I hand you two million dollars?'

He leered. 'On accountta I think you got a case on the broad here. I don't think you're gonna want to see her get hurt. And I'm gonna make her scream till you cough up the map. So whaddaya think of that?'

I glanced at Samantha. She was dry-eyed now, but her eyes were very large and they were staring at Newman Olds as if she couldn't believe what she was hearing, but knew, at the same time, that he meant just what he said.

We were at an impasse, Olds and I each trying to outbluff the other, each trying to take the trick with a bigger trump. I shook my head at him. 'She's not going to scream at all, Olds. I'm going to tell you that. Because the moment you lay a hand on her, I'm coming for you and you'll have to kill me to stop me. And that's not going to get you your map.'

I could see the wheels turning. I had him on that one and he knew it. I had nothing to lose. I had nothing to lose, in fact, in tackling him right now, forcing him to open fire—nothing to lose, that is, except my life. That was his trump. He knew I'd hang on to life as long as I could, even though I knew he'd kill me in the end. There's always the hope of escape. So, unless he overplayed his hand, I wouldn't self-destruct and would even produce the map for him all in good time just to prolong my life. But he knew he'd have to bargain with me. He'd have to buy the map after all.

He looked at me bitterly. 'What's your price?' he said. 'Remember, if it's too high, it's no deal. I can live better without the gold than you can live with six bullets in your gut.'

'I'll tell you the price,' I answered. 'The girl goes. You let her go.'

He snorted. 'Straight to the police she goes. You better name another price.'

'You aren't going to kill Samantha. That's my price. That's my only price.'

'I'd rather let you go than let her go, and there's no way you're gonna live. Does that spell out my answer?'

'Yep. You going to start firing now?'

He hesitated. Even at deflated prices, four hundred pounds of gold represented a lot of money. Much effort and much killing had gone into acquiring it. It would be a shame to bequeath it to future archaeologists.

I tried to sweeten the pot a little. 'I'll tell you, Olds, if you let her go before you kill me, then she won't be a witness to anything. It'll just be her word against yours that you were ever here at all.'

He was thinking—hard. You could see the lights blinking and tracking behind his eyes, like on old fashioned pinball machines. 'What's your proposition?' he finally grunted.

'You let the girl go, and I give you the map.'

He gave it another moment's thought. 'All right.'

I looked to Samantha, but he shook his head. 'Hold it,' he said, giving the girl a wicked smile as she slowly started to uncoil. His leer came my way. 'Now what do you really think's gonna happen, Kaye? You think maybe I'll let the girl go and then, all of a sudden, it turns out you don't have any map, or you decide you don't want to give it to me? Is that what you think?'

'I've got the map,' I said.

'That's right. And you're gonna show it to me. I'm going to verify it personally before Samantha gets the goodbye sign. You're real cute, Kaye. Real cute.'

And, of course, doing it his way put the shoe on the other foot. I let him see that the map is valid, and he proceeds to gun us both down as he'd planned to do all along. I said, 'If I show you the map first, then where's Samantha's guarantee of safe passage?'

'You've got my word. That's all you need. My word.'

I shook my head, stalling for time, without knowing what I'd do with the time. 'No way.

I know what your word's worth.'

Olds lost patience. He was bound to sooner or later. 'Cut the crap, ' he snapped. 'You're wasting my time. I don't think you've got the map. You're stalling. I've let you live too long already.'

'I've got the map. It's in my possession!' My words came fast. The map was losing its appeal and I had to wave it like a flag to distract him from finishing what he'd come to do.

'Next you'll be telling me it's in your safety deposit box and we'll have to wait until morning.'

'It's upstairs. I can put my hands on it in thirty seconds. I'll go get it.'

'We'll all go get it,' Olds answered. 'We'll all go upstairs nice and slow, and when we get there, you can show me the map. If it's what you say it is, then Samantha can go. If you try anything funny, you both get it. Both of you. Understand?'

I said I understood and he motioned Samantha out of the chair. 'Kaye goes first,' he told her. 'With his hands up at all times. You go second, and I'm holding on to you.' He seized her lounging pajamas by the back of the neck and yanked her in front of him. 'Okay, Kaye, turn around and lead, and put your hands on the top of your head.'

Samantha bowed her head and obeyed. She'd been such a cute, pretty girl when she came into my life, fresh and bold and spirited. She hadn't figured to last long, but a radical change had already taken place. Her face was still, I suppose, pretty and cute, but that's not the impression it now made. It was a sober face, the vivacity gone, the *joie de vivre*. She'd been crying, she'd been beaten, she'd been terrified. She was finding out the hard way that you pay for what you get in this world. She was learning that what she'd bought cost more than it said on the price-tag.

Her lackluster eyes didn't meet mine. She'd betrayed me and she wouldn't look. Well, unless we got a break somewhere along the line, her blackened eye and tear-stained cheeks wouldn't matter. Nobody would think what was left of her was cute and pretty. They'd wrap her up in a body bag and throw her in the back of a van, alongside another body bag containing what was left of me. Maybe I should have hated her, but I felt sorry for her.

The ball was in my court and I had to lead the way. I had the map, all right. I hadn't stored it in the office files nor a safety deposit box. Don't ask me why. Maybe I wanted to savor it. Maybe I thought I could use it as bait, that I'd have to flash it around from time to time to lure certain guys I wanted to get my hands on out of hiding? I kept it well cared for and protected. It should have been proof against another burglar like Joe Tanner. But it was available. I'd meant to trap Olds with it. Now, though, Olds was the old trap-master and with his reputation for the double-cross, anyone could read the finale. Olds would have both halves of the map, with nobody to stand between him and the hoard of gold. Samantha and I would be dead.

Where I had the map was under a false bottom of my middle bureau drawer. A thin layer of matching wood, cut to the dimensions of the drawer, lies on top of the bottom, with shelf paper and clothing piled upon that. The map lay between the two bottoms. The point is, unless you're looking for it and are sensitive to depths, you won't know there's an extra layer of bottom in the middle drawer.

The map was what Newman Olds wanted to see and it was what I had to show him. If I refused, I'd be killed, but if I obeyed, I'd also be killed. The only difference was about two minutes of time. If I gave him the map, I'd live about two minutes longer than if I refused. If I gave it to him, he'd walk out of my condo two million dollars richer. I would be endowing him with two million dollars for two extra minutes of a helluva life. Nor would those two minutes be all that enjoyable. I wouldn't bribe an executioner five cents for those two minutes, yet I would offer my killer two million dollars.

It doesn't make sense, except that every tick of the clock produces one more possibility of turning the tables, of throwing the switch and derailing the train. The only thing going for me was the gun in my pocket and maybe that's what spurred me on. The trouble was, he was riding such close herd it might as well have been in the glove compartment of my car.

We went up to the bedroom where the light was bright and where Olds sniffed the atmosphere like a hound dog testing for skunks. If I'd been alone, I could have snatched my gun from my pocket and had a chance. But Samantha was between us and the muzzle of Olds' gun was boring into her back.

Then we were inside the bedroom, I by the bureau, bedraggled Samantha sinking on to the side of my bed. Olds, always in command, monitored our behaviour from the doorway, keeping his distance as a good commander should.

His eyes never left me. He was waiting, suspicious as hell. Double-crossers expect to be double-crossed. He was sure it was a stall. Newman Olds wouldn't dare believe he could have me in his clutches and the map too. Pennies don't rain from heaven in real life. So he expected me to be conning him, to have faked all this crap, and he was waiting for my desperation move when I couldn't carry the charade any further. His finger was so tight on the trigger it was white and his eyes darted from Samantha to me as if he thought we were in cahoots.

I hoped that if I made enough to-do about removing the undergarments from the drawer, stacking them on top, then removing the false bottom, I might distract him enough so that I could get a hand on my gun. The trouble was, the gun was in my right hand pocket and that's the pocket that was facing Olds. If I'd been left-handed and it was in the other pocket, I think I could have plugged him. He wouldn't have seen it coming. So much for the vagaries of fate.

Slowly I piled the contents of the drawer on the dresser top, then pried out the false bottom with my fingernails. Olds came a step closer for that. He didn't know what kind of booby trap I might spring.

I put the false bottom on top of the contents and held up the map. An eager light came into his eyes, but that was all. He didn't drop his gun and clap for joy, he didn't throw his arms up in the air and praise the Lord. He didn't do anything that would give me an opening.

He stepped a half pace closer and held his left arm out, fully extended, for the paper. I was to hold it out to him with my own arm fully extended. He didn't want to have to kill me until he'd taken a good look at what I held. If it wasn't the map, he'd want to offer me one final opportunity to make good. He was after gold as well as revenge and was going to give himself every chance.

It was the right map. He could tell it when he got it. I could tell, too, by the way his eyes lighted. Certain of its features established its credibility, but if I'd thought there was a chance his greed would throw him off guard, forget it. He was a pro and he never forgot where he was and what he was doing.

To his left, Samantha suddenly swayed. Her eyes closed, and she fell. That was the one thing nobody expected—that Samantha would faint.

She keeled over, but it was towards Newman Olds. If he didn't get out of the way, her body would strike his on its way to the floor.

He saw her and started, and jumped aside. But she wasn't fainting, she was attacking. Halfway down, her eyes opened wide and she dove for his legs. It was a last gamble and she knew it and her timing was perfect.

She caught him just below the knees and he was as much startled to discover the faint was a feint as to find himself tackled and brought down.

Olds was startled, but he didn't lose his cool. No matter what Samantha or I tried to do, he was the man with the gun and, against unarmed opponents, the gun would prevail.

But one opponent wasn't unarmed. He didn't know that as he hit the floor. He looked up at me as he brought his gun around and the look on his face said, 'Now you're gonna get it,' because he had the genuine map and my time had come and if I thought that this bitch tackling him would—

He found himself staring into the muzzle of my gun and the change of expression was something I won't forget. The look of dismay when he saw what the end of the story was really going to be would soothe a thousand nightmares.

I put three bullets in him before his gun ever moved. He was staring at me with his jaw hanging and I gave it to him in that moment before he could summon his muscles into action.

And then he was dead, stretched out on the floor with blood coming out of three holes, spreading across his upright chest, running down his neck on to the carpet. Well, the carpets were due for a cleaning anyway.

Samantha came into my arms. I was standing, spread-legged, glowering, arms hanging, gun in one hand. She was wet, cold, and thinly clad. She'd catch her death if she didn't get out of those sopping clothes. And the revealing way they clung, they weren't giving her any protection anyway.

I dropped the gun and held her tight. She held me too, and neither of us could breathe.

My hands were under her orange top against her back. Her skin was icy to my touch. Dead bodies weren't as cold as that. But she wasn't dead. She had her arms around my neck and kissed me as if it was all that kept her alive.

I had an equal and complementary reaction.

CHAPTER THIRTY-FIVE

It was a long time before Samantha and I were able to face the problem of what to do next. I brewed us a pot of coffee and we sat at the kitchen table, I in my pajama pants, she in my pajama top. Her orange lounging outfit was drying on a bathroom hanger. Newman Olds' body still lay on its back, soiling my bedroom carpet. We weren't weeping for the dead, Samantha and I. We walked around the body when we left the room, and Samantha spat on it. It wasn't ladylike, but she wasn't a lady. And I didn't blame her. I wanted to kick it, myself.

We drank coffee, and we smoked cigarettes, and I sighed and told her that I would have to call the police, that I would have to undergo a great grilling, that, while the killing was an obvious case of self defense, the police would give me a very hard time. That, however, was not Samantha's problem and the question was what to do about her.

We decided, since she had access to Olds' abode, and what clothes and possessions she had were there, that she'd better return before the servants found out the master was dead. She got back into her nearly dry lounging pajamas and I phoned for a cab and gave her some money.

We kissed and clung and I saw her off down the storm porch stairs, then locked all my doors and phoned for the police.

They were out in force in twenty minutes and it was the same ring around the rosy again. Don Lasky wasn't on the case this time—maybe he was avoiding me—but a Lieutenant named Masters was and he was nearly as bad, I knew him from my own days on the force and while we got along, we weren't that friendly. Add to that the fact that I wasn't going to reveal any more information about Olds' presence than was obvious to the detectives and the photo lab, and that meant an uneasy time.

'What was Olds doing in your apartment?'

'He was going to kill me.'

'Why?'

'That's what I'd like to know.'

Needless to say, my piece of map had been returned to its hiding place before Samantha and I went down for the coffee. Outside of the unmade bed and the body on the floor, the room was as neat and tidy as I ever keep it.

Masters sniffed for perfume and looked around the pillows and sheets for bobbie pins. 'There was a woman in here, wasn't there?'

'If I entertain a woman of an evening, it's none of your business.'

'He came here because you had his woman here with you. That's it, isn't it?'

'No it isn't. I don't need other men's women. There're enough to go around.'

'I'm going to have to impound your gun.'

'Oh no you're not. This is the third guy who's tried to kill me in a fortnight. It's only because I've got a gun that I'm still alive. Nobody touches my gun.'

'We're going to have to run ballistics tests on it.'

'Why? The bullets in him came from this gun. You don't have to prove it, I'm not denying it.'

'What other bodies caught bullets from your gun?'

'Those two punks in my office, the ones who tried to kill me and my secretary.'

'Those we didn't run a check on. How about the two guys who were killed behind the cemetery a week ago? You think those slugs came from your gun?'

'Instead of talking about it, why don't you match them with the slugs in Olds?'

'We will, Kaye, we will. And what're you going to say when we find they do match?'

'If you can match them, I'll think of something.'

'Come on, Kaye, Olds came here to kill you because you knocked off two of his men. That's the real story, isn't it?'

'Ask Olds. I can't read his mind.'

'How'd he get in here?'

'I told you. He rang the bell. When I answered the door, he stuck a gun in my face and made me let him in.'

'He had a gun on you, but you killed him? Just like that?'

'I had a gun in the pocket of my dressing gown. He didn't know it and got careless.'

'You always answer the door with a gun in your pocket?'

'At that hour of the night, I do.'

'And how come, if he was bent on killing you, he didn't open fire on you in the foyer, or when you opened the door? How come it's up in the bedroom?'

'Again, as I said before, you're got to ask him. I'm no mind reader.'

In the end, they could do nothing more than take the body away, but I knew damned well they'd be comparing the bullets in Olds with those they'd taken out of Theodore and Murray. And when they did, they'd be coming around again and I would need better answers than I had this time.

CHAPTER THIRTY-SIX

I didn't hear from Samantha over the weekend and I didn't expect to. She pulled a lemon her first try for a rich man's patronage, but that was her orientation and I guessed she was casting around for her next berth. Certainly she wouldn't be looking my way. She preferred those orange lounging pajamas to wearing the tops of mine.

So, by the time Sunday evening came around, I was relaxed and ensconced, watching television, of all things, and letting it wash over me while I geared myself for the start of a new week.

Naturally, the doorbell rang. The powers that arrange these things aren't going to let Simon Kaye get too sedentary. He might vegetate. He might get enough sleep. His body might heal all its various wounds.

I did a quick run-through as to what enemies of mine were running around loose and might wish to do to me what Olds meant to do. I couldn't think of anybody I'd harmed recently so I didn't think I needed to run upstairs for my gunbelt and holster. In fact, I had a hunch it might be Samantha announcing that whoever was executor of Olds' estate had refused to extend her camping privileges and she was on the loose again.

It wasn't Samantha; it was, instead, her sister, Veronica.

Veronica was somebody I'd forgotten about. Veronica was somebody who'd gone underground. Nobody knew what had happened to her. Nobody I knew of cared. So here she was, on my doorstep at seven thirty on a Sunday night, looking pretty and well-dressed and as appealing as she could make herself—and that was pretty appealing, if you didn't know the Veronica who resided underneath. That Veronica had sharp claws and great big teeth.

'Well, hello.' I smiled but didn't lay out the welcome mat. God only knew what she wanted. All I knew was that I wouldn't like it.

She was crisp and businesslike. 'I've come for my sister.'

My smile broadened. That was a good one. 'Your sister isn't here.'

'I happen to think differently.' She handed me a folded piece of paper.

I opened it. Written on it was the statement, 'I'm at Simon Kaye's. I need you. Samantha.' On the top was written 'Sept. 12,' today's date.

'Where'd you get this?' I asked, for it couldn't have been mailed.

'It was hand delivered to me half an hour ago.'

280

'You're kidding.'

'No, I'm not kidding. I want my sister. What have you done with her?'

'I'm not kidding either,' I said. 'She isn't here.'

'I don't believe you. I insist on looking myself.'

I pocketed the note, stepped aside and pulled the door wide. 'Be my guest.'

She stalked through the foyer, looked into the living room and around the kitchen.

'See?' I gestured, following. 'Empty living room, the television going—you interrupted my viewing. Only one set of dishes in the sink.'

'Very cute,' she said, facing me in the kitchen, holding her purse against her with both hands. 'But I know better. Where's your bedroom?'

'Up those stairs.'

She preceded me up the carpeted steps into the master bedroom. The bed was made (I may batch it, but I keep things reasonably tidy), the windows were open on to the outside woodlands and there was nice cross ventilation from the open windows of the guest room. It was cool and comfortable up there.

I stood in the doorway while she cased the room. I said, 'You can poke around in the closet, but try not to disturb my pet rattlesnake.'

She turned around and now she was tight-lipped and narrow-eyed. She still held the purse, but now it was in her left hand. In her right, she aimed a thirty-two caliber revolver at my chest. I must say I couldn't guess what her game was, but I hadn't really expected that. I slowly raised my hands to shoulder height and waited.

She motioned with the gun and the way she handled it and the situation meant that she knew her way around both guns and confrontations. 'You will sit on the bed,' she ordered, 'and put your hands on your head.' Then, to make sure I wouldn't misunderstand, she added, 'I will kill you if you try anything. If you're smart, you'll believe me.'

I was smart. I believed her implicitly. In fact, I wasn't at all sure she wouldn't kill me even if I didn't try anything. I sat down on my bed and put my hands on my head.

What she did next was very interesting. She went to my bureau and, keeping me well covered, plunked her bag on its top and pulled out the middle drawer. Then, with one hand holding the gun, she removed the contents, throwing underwear and socks on to the floor until she had it emptied.

After that, she used her fingernails to pull up the false bottom and slide her hand underneath. It was there, George Geary's half of the map and her eyes lit up. She brought it forth and let the false bottom drop in place. Yes, it was the genuine article, she could tell it was. I hadn't changed the hiding place. I hadn't tricked her.

I had my hands on my head during all this. I was obeying her orders exactly. At the same time, since she was only watching me out of the corner of her eye, I was able to unstrap my wristwatch without distracting her.

Now, just as her eyes were lighting with recognition that the paper she held was, indeed, the map, that her goal had been achieved, that her search was over, I threw the wristwatch at her.

She saw me move, but at the same time her eye caught the wristwatch coming. She might not have known what it was, but she knew some small object was flying in her direction and instinct made her flinch and shy away.

That was all I needed, for I sprang at the same time and reached her almost as soon as the watch did. I wrenched away the gun and she screamed, for I wasn't fooling and I sprained some of her fingers. That wasn't all. I threw her over my leg and snatched back the map at the same time. I was really revved up. She hit her head on the floor so hard she didn't move for a couple of seconds and when she finally looked up at me, her eyes were glazed.

'You're a beaut,' I told her. 'A real first prize.' I retrieved the watch, and yanked her to her feet by the top of her dress. The clothing ripped but I didn't really care. They say where you're angry is where you're afraid, but I wasn't afraid, I was irritated. The nerve of the bitch. Did she really think she was going to sashay into my home, and by pulling a gun on me, walk off with whatever she wanted? Her grand ideas were an insult.

I threw her on to the bed and her head hit my cabinet headboard with a loud crack. Her scalp started to bleed, but I didn't care. 'So,' I said. 'Samantha's been telling you things. All about the false bottom in my bureau drawer and what I've got in it. Where is she?'

Veronica, her dress torn, her head bleeding, massaged her injured fingers while her eyes slowly cleared. The glaze turned to a glower and she called me a dirty name.

'Is she in it with you, or was the idea of robbing me strictly your own?'

'All right,' she muttered. 'Call the police. That's what you want. Have me arrested. Call the police.'

I laughed. 'What would you do if I did?'

She held her right hand tight to her waist and rocked a little. Those fingers really ached.

I pocketed her gun and pulled out the paper she'd handed me. '"I'm at Simon Kaye's. I need you. Samantha,"' I read. 'What did you do, write that note yourself?'

'What if I did?'

'Did you really think it would buy you anything?'

'You let me in.' Tears were starting to form in the corners of her eyes. She wanted me to know how she suffered.

I put the note on the dresser and removed a slip of paper from my wallet. Veronica, lying on an elbow now, clutched her hand and watched. The slip bore Arnold Saydecker's name and address, written in a flowing hand. It was the paper Joe Tanner was carrying in his wallet when he was killed. I compared the two handwriting specimens. 'They match,' I said to Veronica.

'What does?' She was still the girl in pain and a tear started down one cheek.

I held up the slip. 'On this paper,' I said, 'you wrote out Arnold Saydecker's address for Joe Tanner and he stuck it in his wallet.'

The tear came to a halt and she just stared.

'Joe Tanner was in your pocket,' I said. 'When I chased him down your fire escape it wasn't because he climbed up to spy, but because he'd climbed out your window when I came in the door. You were entertaining him in your bedroom and to keep me from finding that out, you screamed and pretended he was the mysterious blackmailer.

'He and Luke and Leo were working for you. You had them lying in wait outside Saydecker's place to waylay Mutt Stark. That's the way it was, wasn't it, sweetheart?

Olds got Mutt to murder Saydecker and steal the map and you knew it. And Tanner was new in Olds' employ and you seduced him and used him and got him to waylay Stark and bring you the map. Only he and his hirelings didn't know Mutt and picked me up instead.'

I laughed suddenly as more pieces fitted together. 'And when they couldn't find the map on me, they took me away and held me till you could tell them what to do. And it was you who came to look at me while I was blindfolded, and you told them they had the wrong guy and to take me back where they got me.'

I paused and studied her. She wasn't watching me now, her face was turned the other way. The tears had dried and the blood had dried and her immobile face was a piece of stone.

'And you came to me. You hired me. You tied me up for a night on a phony case so Tanner could search my office and home. What did you think? That I was the one with the map after all? You learned that Mutt Stark had been killed and there was no map on him. Someone had beaten Tanner to it, hadn't he? And you didn't know who. But you thought it might have been I since I was in the area. And maybe I'd secreted the map so that just because you couldn't find it didn't mean I didn't have it.

286

'You didn't know where I fitted in, but you had to find out. You hired me to spend the night with you while Tanner ransacked my things. And when he couldn't find anything, you decided I wasn't involved and wanted no more to do with me. But I burst in on you when Tanner was there and he fled and you pretended you didn't know him.'

Another couple of puzzle pieces clicked into place. 'And Leo and Luke, those minions of Tanner's. Who sent them to my office to ambush me? Tanner was dead by then, so who was pulling their strings?

'That would be you, sweetheart. You wanted me out of the picture. Nobody else had control of them. And why did you want me dead? Let me guess. Because Newman Olds was going to haul me in and ask me a lot of questions about maps and things, and if I should let it slip that I'd been kidnapped by Joe Tanner right where Mutt Stark was supposed to pass, Mr Olds would know someone was double-crossing him. And he'd know who the double-crosser was. You were afraid of what I might say and you wanted me dead. And your guys beat Olds' hoods to my office. They didn't get to kill me, but since I didn't say anything about you to Olds, you won out anyway.

'Which reminds me. You were scared to death when Olds sent his car for you. Was that what you were afraid of—that he

287

suspected you of a double-cross?'

Veronica didn't move. She lay on her side, her eyes fixed on the farther wall.

I took her gun out of my pocket and hefted it. 'You know something, Veronica? The afternoon that Joe Tanner got killed, some woman phoned the police that she heard shooting in Tanner's house. And when the cops arrived, they found Tanner dead on the floor. They didn't find me because I'd got out in time.

'But they were supposed to find me there! That would have tied me in tight to the killing. Of course Joe Tanner wasn't killed with a .38 slug. It wasn't my gun that did the job. But that wouldn't matter too much. The cops would spend a lot of time trying to fit the murder bullets to a gun I might have had, to a gun I could have hidden.

'But what woman neighbor lived close enough to that house in the woods to go calling the cops?

'And who killed Joe Tanner? It wasn't I. I was supposed to die with him.

'The killer was someone who hid in Tanner's closet when I knocked on the door. It was someone who was with Tanner, who didn't want me to make him talk. Why? Shall we guess? Because he'd tell me who was behind it all, who'd ordered him to search my condo and my office. He'd tell me who seduced him into betraying Newman Olds and helping her get hold of Saydecker's half of the map.'

I held up the gun and studied it. 'Who,' I asked, 'would want to keep him from telling me? Who was trying to make me believe Tanner was her enemy? It's only a guess, Veronica,' I said, 'but I wonder if the .32 bullets in this gun wouldn't match the bullets in Joe Tanner's body.' I turned the gun over and back. 'That's not for me to guess at,' I said. 'Ballistics will give me the answer. Ballistics will give us all the answer.'

CHAPTER THIRTY-SEVEN

Veronica rolled slowly over and her eyes held me in a baleful glare. 'You're a bastard,' she said in less than heartwarming tones. In fact, the chill of her voice told me I was right on target.

I said, 'I don't understand you, Veronica. All these elaborate schemes, all these double-crosses and murders and the rest? For what? To get one half of a map that's worthless if you don't have the other half? Like now! You come crying to me with a phony story, just the way you did before, and you risk your life—or my life—in a desperate effort to get a worthless piece of paper. Why didn't you, when you were Newman's number one girlfriend, try to get your hands on *his* map?'

Veronica's expression changed slowly. She still held her right hand in her lap, but she wasn't thinking about the pain any more. Her eyes took on an eerie glow and she started to smile. It was a warming smile, a smile of love. 'How would you like to be rich?' she said.

I laughed. 'Don't try to tell me you've got Olds' half of the map. I know better.'

'I mean it.' She moved to the edge of the bed and stared, studying me, looking me over. 'Yes,' she said, 'you wouldn't be hard to take. You wouldn't be hard to take at all.' She smiled once more. 'You and I. I wouldn't be hard to take either. Look at me.' She smoothed her hands over her body. 'I'm not bad. I can show you more if you need convincing.'

'Not necessary,' I said. 'I got a load of you three weeks ago. I don't think you've changed much.'

I was still smiling and she didn't want that. 'I mean it, Simon. I'm talking about big money. I can make you rich, both of us rich—richer than you've ever dreamed.'

'About a million dollars apiece?'

'You know what the map is, then?'

'Four hundred pounds of buried gold.'

'Ten pound bars,' Veronica said, her eyes turning gold at the thought, her voice rising and speeding up. 'Newman kept one. They all did.' She rose and grabbed my arms. 'And they're all ours, Simon. All for you and me. Think what we can do!' Her eyes were burning, her grip like clamps, injured fingers forgotten. 'Anywhere in the world! We can go anywhere. We'll own the world. The Riviera, Acapulco, Hawaii, Monte Carlo, all the resorts of the world at our feet. And we'll be beautiful, you and I. Veronica and Simon. We're young, we're handsome, we make a good pair. We'd be the envy of them all.' She shook me. 'Think of it!'

I wasn't responding properly and she shook me again. 'Simon, I mean it. It can all come true.'

'On one half of a map?'

'I've got the other half. Don't you understand that?' She grew petulant. 'You can't be that stupid. Why the hell do you think I've been doing what I've been doing?'

'You mean trying to waylay Stark? You mean double-crossing Olds?'

'Yes, yes. Why do you think I was doing it? Because I had the other half of the map!'

'Olds had the other half.'

'But I copied it, when I was his first and best mistress! When he told me things and showed me things. I copied the map behind his back.' She shook me again. 'What did you think, Simon Kaye, that I was an idiot? Did you think I couldn't foresee a day when he'd throw me away for a younger girl? Of course I foresaw it. So I copied his half of the map. And when he threw me over for that Lavinia bitch, I kept up my contacts. I had more brains than she did. I was the one he liked to talk to even if he didn't want me physically that much any more. And when he expanded his operations and got some new people in, I got my hooks in them. I'm not a fool.'

'You mean Tanner? You get your hooks into Luke and Leo too?'

'They took their orders from Joe. They were his friends. But he knew all good things were going to come from me. And he had them trained. What I wanted, they did. That's how I rigged it for them to get the map from Mutt Stark when he was going to bring it to Newman. Only the bastards picked you up by mistake.'

'And when you told them to kill me, they hurried right down to my office like good little boys.'

'That's when you were against me.' She tightened her grip on my arms. 'You can't blame me for looking out for myself.' She let go with one hand to jab her chest. 'I've got nobody to take care of number one except number one. You can't rely on anybody in this world. That's the one thing I've learned. Do you know what Newman would have done to me if he'd found out I'd hired you and you found Joe Tanner on my fire escape? He'd've killed me, Simon. He'd have killed me dead.'

'So you killed Joe instead, to shut him up?'

'I didn't want to. But you were going to make him rat on me. You were going to make him say I was the one he was working for. I couldn't let you know that. You'd've done the same thing in my shoes. You're not against killing either, you know. You killed Newman two nights ago. You killed Luke and Leo. You killed Theodore and Murray at the cemetery. The cops don't know it, but I know it. I can add one and one.

'And you stole the map from George Geary. So what do you think you're going to do with it? It's worthless without the other half and I've got the other half. So don't you see? We pool our resources and we're both rich. And we make a good couple, you and I. You'd be easy to love. In fact, I'm in love with you right now. And I'm not bad. You haven't tried me out, but you'll see. I'll make you forget any other girl you ever knew.

'And we'll be rich. I've had to work and wait for five years for this pile of gold and you're falling into it free. But how we'll celebrate! We'll spend a lifetime celebrating!'

She was excited. She was bubbling over trying to instill me with similar enthusiasm. But I wasn't jumping. I stayed solemn and disengaged her hands. 'This map you copied—you say you copied,' I said. 'You're doing a lot of talk, but I haven't seen it yet.'

293

'Of course. I've got it hidden where it's safe. But I can get it.'

'You're sure there *is* such a map? Why should I believe you?'

She raised a hand and spoke with all the earnestness she could muster. 'I swear it to you. I swear by all that's holy. Why would I lie to you? Your half of the map wouldn't be worth anything to me if I didn't have the other half.'

'Yeah,' I said, 'I suppose you wouldn't be coming after it with a gun in your hand if it didn't have some value to you.' I turned and picked up her purse from the dresser. It had a snap catch and I popped it open.

She made a grab for it. 'Hey, what do you think you're doing? Leave my goddam purse alone!'

I pushed her away and went through it. 'You wouldn't have just happened to have brought it along—one of your copies—to match up with mine to make sure you were stealing the genuine article, would you? Well, yes, look what we have here!'

There it was, folded in her purse, the other half of the map. 'Yes,' I said. 'This looks like it. Now, if we put the two pieces together—' and I did, 'we have a complete map of where the four hundred pounds of gold are buried. Very clever.'

'Yes, yes,' she interrupted. 'You see? I told you. We're rich. We can rent a pickup and get a couple of shovels. Newman told me it's wrapped in a duffel bag. And I know where to fence it. I know what Newman was going to do with it when he got it. We can do the same thing, and be rich.' She hugged me and gave me a big kiss. She rubbed her body against me. It was time to pull out all the stops.

I marched her over and sat her back down on the bed. 'All right, let's cool it. You don't really think I'm sucker enough to fall for that 'celebrate through eternity' line, do you? I'll bet it wouldn't be two weeks before you'd have a knife stuck through my ribs.'

'Simon, I swear—'

'I wouldn't dare go to sleep at night for fear I wouldn't wake up the next day. I couldn't sip my morning coffee without wondering if you'd loaded it with arsenic. That would be one hell of a life I'd be leading, pet.'

'You can't believe that,' she said, clutching my legs, pressing her head against my stomach. 'I need you. I can't hack it alone. A woman needs a man—for love, for protection. She can't go through life alone. She has to have a man. I have to have you. You're my man.'

I disengaged her again and picked up the phone. 'With two million dollars and your looks, you wouldn't have any trouble picking up men to love and protect you. The one man you don't need is the one who knows what I know about you. Sorry, sister, but I'm not going with you.' I opened my phone number index at F.

'Who're you going to call?'

'The local FBI office to start. Also my lawyer, the local police and, as soon as I can find out who they are, the insurance company that covered the gold shipment.'

'What for?'

'I live in this town. I work in this town. And if I want to keep on living and working there comes a time when I have to pay my dues. This is one of those times. I've been running fast and loose the past three weeks, and while I've been able to get away with it, it wouldn't be for much longer. The police in particular would clip my wings. So I'm going to call in everybody who is anybody and confess my sins, explain what I've been up to and why. As you note, the police don't know yet who killed Theodore and Murray. But as soon as they match up some bullets, they're going to know. I want to tell them before they tell me.

'And if I can turn over to the proper authorities four hundred pounds of stolen gold, that ought to enable me to run fast and loose again for a long time without anyone saying anything. And since that's the way I do my job, that's going to be money in the bank.'

She looked up at my eyes and there was

fear on her face. 'And what about me?'

'They'll put you in jail. At least I hope they will, because I wouldn't want you running free and loose after I turned you in. That would be almost as uncertain an existence as teaming up with you and traveling around the world with two million dollars in my pocket.'

She knocked the phone out of my hand and came clawing for my eyes. I had to handcuff her to make my calls.

CHAPTER THIRTY-EIGHT

What else is there to say? I did tell my tale in front of a handcuffed Veronica, the local and state police, the FBI, my lawyer, and all the rest, even the mayor. The gold was recovered—I held my breath till it was found—which lent credence to my story, and I was something of a hero to the press. Even the police gave me an official pat on the back for clearing up some 'minor' points in the most mysterious investigation in the city's annals.

There were pictures on the front pages of the local journals, and on the TV news, showing the duffel bag full of ten pound gold ingots being uncovered and dug out of its hole in the ground. I'm second from the left in the row of onlookers.

Veronica went to jail for the murder of Joseph Tanner where, as of this writing, she's still awaiting trial. Our justice system being what it is, for all I know, when this book goes out of print, she may still be in jail awaiting trial.

As for what happened to Samantha, I have no idea. Though I can deduce that Samantha, after I last saw her, had enough contact with Veronica to tell her where I hid Saydecker's map, Veronica has denied any knowledge of Samantha's activities or whereabouts since throwing her out of her apartment the afternoon Samantha arrived in town.

Suffice it to say, Samantha never came near me again after running off in her half-dry orange lounging pajamas to retrieve whatever she could from Newman Olds' abode. I'm not going to speculate as to why she told Veronica where I hid the map or what she thought would result from the telling. Maybe she's found herself another millionaire, hopefully a more palatable one than Newman Olds.

★   ★   ★

Knowing Samantha, the question isn't so much, 'Did she get aboard another gravy train?' as it is, 'What kind is she on?'